DEVON'S CAFE

DEVON'S CAFE
BOOK 3

NICOLE D. MILLER

NDMILLER
PUBLISHING

ISBN: 979-8-9935184-0-4

Editing by Gwendolyn Valerius

Book cover design by Sherita Carthon

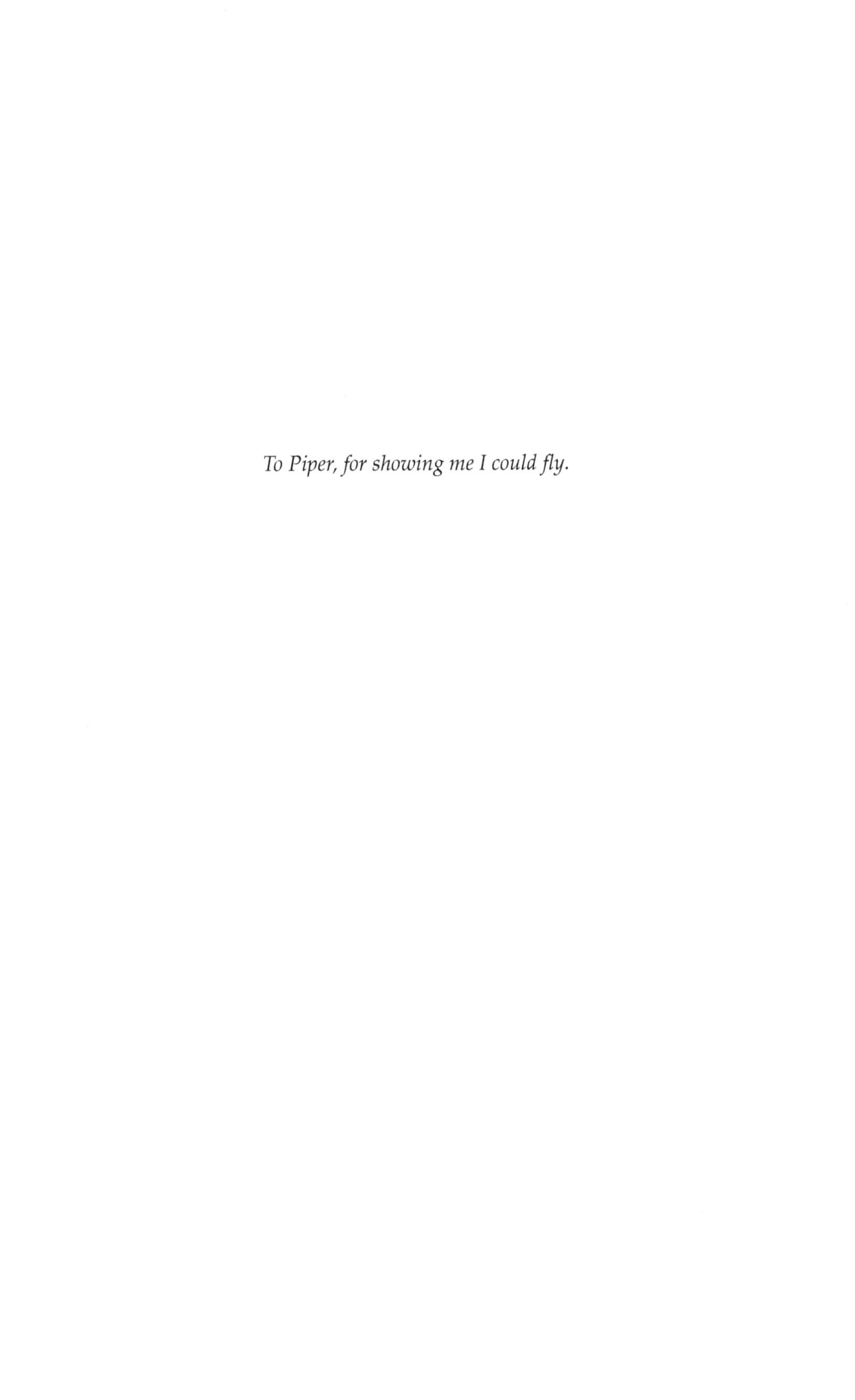

To Piper, for showing me I could fly.

CONTENTS

PREFACE

When I first started the Devon's Cafe series, I didn't even know that I was starting a series. I was sitting in a Literary Cleveland workshop for short story fiction writing. My roommate was a writer and had shared with me a short story she had written. It was the first time I realized I, too, could write a short story. Up until that point, I had only written my first two books, both nonfiction. Well, when I sat in that writing workshop, Lisa's character was born. Fast forward three years, and I picked up that story along with a few others I had written, compiled them, and put them into my very first fiction book, "Stories for the (Urban) Soul." The very first two short stories in that book were "Lisa" and "Joe." Both took place at a Black-owned cafe in Harlem belonging to a young man named Devon. When my friends and editor heard Lisa's story, they said, "You've got something here" about the characters, particularly Denise. While I was editing Urban Stories, I started writing "When Love Wins." It was coming like a flood. My very first novel, one I never thought I could write, was oozing out of me. That's when I fell in love with fiction. I was also able to view Devon's Cafe from a different lens of the young 20-something scene, whereas with Lisa and Joe, it was more of the grown and sexy vibe. But then, even as

I was in the midst of "When Love Wins," I wrote the first three chapters of Lisa's novel. I'm a stickler for finishing what I start, so I made myself stop and complete "When Love Wins" before I picked up Lisa's story again about a year later. Of course, we glimpse Devon in these short stories and novels, but he's always the side character. I knew, as the Devon's Cafe series was unfolding, I would eventually need to write the eponym's book! But when I thought of Devon, he honestly seemed rather boring. That is when I felt the Holy Spirit prompting me. "But who was Devon *before* he became the established man we see in these other books? What was his journey to becoming that man?"

Something new happened while writing Devon's story. It felt like God was writing through me. Maybe this had been happening with my other books the whole time, but suddenly I became more aware. As the novel unfolded, in many ways I felt like God was telling me the story, and then I was writing what He was showing me. Often, I was blown away by what He said was going to happen, because I never know ahead of time what I'll write. It comes as I flow.

Another thing was that I was super emotional. While I definitely cried while writing "Unfinished Business," this time it was a whole other level of feeling deeply for the characters. It was like they had become real! I was like, "God, what is happening?" I also had some supernatural activity surface during this time, which inspired me to incorporate more of those experiences into this novel. While I dabble with the charismatic and gifts of the Spirit in the other two novels, with this one, I stepped it up. God was showing me that His body needs to be open and educated about His original intent for His gifts, as many people are seeking the devil's counterfeit gifts because they lack the knowledge that God is the Author of the supernatural. I also modeled Devon's story after my own in undergrad, which was a high time of prophetic, supernatural activity for me and many of my friends.

During undergrad, I endured my first heartbreak, as detailed in my first book, "How to Overcome Heartbreak: Recovering from Misguided Love." It was wild to channel some of those old feelings of pain into this book, when I've been decades removed from them, but it reminded me of how hard it was to endure being a student, perform in my position as an RA (Resident Assistant), and grieve the loss of that relationship. God carried me through, and now He gets all the glory! I also gave Devon a lot of the messiness of my decision-making when dealing with that relationship and others. As much as I wanted to make Devon's choices ideal and tidy, God reminded me how rocky my own path has been and how much He enjoys partnering with us in our mess. He enjoys walking with us through it and patiently cleaning us up. Our transformations are never overnight, and as one character in this book said (Lena), we're always learning.

I included many hot topics in this book that are currently raging in our culture. I was honestly nervous to "go there," but I think we need to have more of these discussions in the body of Christ. I can't say I staunchly land on either side 100 percent on such divisive, polarizing issues, but my goal isn't necessarily to show *my* views; it's to show that *God is with us.*

It also stretched me to write a male protagonist I didn't always agree with, and to write other characters in this book whose views I didn't always agree with, but my goal was to capture life. There are people in this world we don't always agree with, but God sees them and loves them, too. *And* He doesn't always agree with us, but still loves us and teaches us His ways…if we're willing to learn them.

Another wild thing that happened while writing this book is that it was born out of a self-imposed writing challenge. My good friend and editor at ND Miller Publishing, Piper, said she wrote her book in 30 days. I was blown away. I had this thought that if I wrote a chapter a day, I could finish in 30 days, and so I gave myself the writing challenge. It took me three years to write my first novel (one full year of that was editing), but I completed the very first manuscript of *Devon's Cafe* in 25 days. My God! That experience really showed me how much we limit ourselves. We really need to see ourselves as supernatural beings and take the limits off. Once we do, I believe, we will be blown away by what we're actually capable of. Just as Devon says in this novel, we will truly be superheroes.

I hope you can see God with each character and that it helps your understanding of Him. I honestly believe He wrote this book, and that the overall message is one of redemption. God redeems even the messiest of circumstances. And, as Lena says, He can bring good in even the worst kinds of circumstances.

-Shalom

PROLOGUE

Vibrant oranges mingling with startling reds and warm yellows tap-danced along the thick oak trees at Morrison University. These trees had paid their dues. They'd started out as tiny seeds and took their good old time growing into the magnificent trunks and sturdy branches that dominated the campus. Devon appreciated those trees. It takes a distinctive kind of patience to sink deep roots into soil, plant one's identity into its habitat, and, after waiting decades, sprout leaves of purpose. He saw himself in those trees. Devon had been groomed for purpose since he could walk. He was on the verge of sprouting said purpose in his final year at Morrison University.

"Bro! Watch out!" Antonio's voice was a second too late because a football veering in his direction dug into Devon's side. He had been too focused on the damn trees.

"Ouch!" he cried, hunching over and rubbing the injured area.

"Dude. I tried to warn you," Antonio said. He peered at him with concern. "You good?"

"Yo. Toss the ball!" A hefty brotha with shoulder-length locks called. Devon blasted him with a scowl, still gripping his side.

"Bro. You hit my boy!" Antonio said.

"Yo. You ok?" Darion was at Devon's side, patting his shoulder.

Devon eased his way up. "Yeah. I'm cool," he mumbled. His pride was more hurt than anything.

"Look like he good. Now toss us the ball!" Locks shouted over the field of curious gazes that covered the small area Devon was standing in. These gazes were the source of his hurt pride.

Antonio swooped up the ball at Devon's feet and hiked it to the inconsiderate jock, saying, "Next time, watch where you throwing!"

The ball smoothly sailed over the field and found its owner. After Locks caught it, he went off to join the crew of burly students without a look back. His group, however, navigated to a less crowded area.

Devon sighed and straightened his spine as much as possible amidst the onlookers, dodging their eyes. Under normal circumstances, the Black Student Meet N' Greet event was one he never would have attended, given he avoided most party-style events at all cost. But since his boys had insisted they go, and he was outnumbered, he relented. Now he wondered if the football was a sign. They had barely been there ten minutes, and already there was an omen.

"Let's get some food!" Darion said excitedly as the trio scoped the layout.

The quad burst with brown bodies in shorts and hoodies, a fitting combination for the Indian summer that had taken hold of the climate. Darion, Devon, and Antonio blended in with their variations of shorts, t-shirts, and hoodies, their school colors proudly displayed. With his ensemble, Devon opted for white converses, declining Darion's offer to lend him his triple-black Nike Air Maxs.

The buzzing of conversation and excitement thronged the boys on all sides as they headed for the food trucks. Flashes of tables from student-led organizations and student-owned businesses were stationed on each side with clusters of interested attendees. Hip-Hop clouded the atmosphere as they approached the food. Finally, Devon could make out the DJ jammin' with headphones. Folks began line dancing right in front of his setup.

"Dawg. I'ma need a hot dog foreal. But, man, ain't no liquor at this party?" Antonio said as they stood behind three females giggling and talking loudly over the music. There were only two food trucks, one with hamburgers and hot dogs, and the other serving tacos. Since the food was free and it wasn't campus food, Devon wasn't about to complain.

"It's way too many underage students here," Devon replied to his friend. "The school would be under fire if they had alcohol on campus."

"Shooot. Then we gon' have to find the afterparty foreal foreal," Antonio said.

"Oh. I'm *all* the way with that!" Darion agreed.

"Y'all comin' to the after party?" One of the girls in front of them turned around, and Devon's tongue became glued to the roof of his mouth. He was speechless. His eyes zoomed in, mesmerized. Sun radiated off rich cocoa skin that paid homage to the ancestors. Large doe-like eyes peeked mysteriously at him beneath thick, full lashes. Her mouth sat taunting him, daring him to respond. And oh, how he wanted to! Devon tried, but nothing would come out.

"Oh, you know we there!" Antonio said. "Where it's at tho?"

The vocal one half-smiled, and even though she addressed his friend, she only had eyes for Devon.

"It's at the 'Roof Top'. You know, the club off Nelson Road."

"Bet!" Antonio said. The other girls introduced themselves.

"I'm Kimberly," said the small one.

"I'm Sheila," the cinnamon-skinned, curvy one said. She had slid in front of Kimberly, who was standing nearest to Antonio, when she spoke.

Devon waited almost breathless with anticipation. His heartbeat sped up. The rowdy chatter staining the atmosphere died. He tried not to stare, tried not to look like he was pining for her words.

"And you are?" Finally, he had found his voice! Devon swallowed nervously after he had spoken, aware that everyone was looking at him. One of her girls, Kimberly, he remembered, even giggled.

"Jasmine. My name is Jasmine," she finally spoke, putting him out of his misery.

Devon smiled. "I'm Devon," he said, and held out his hand.

ONE
WHEELS FALL OFF

THE BROODING SKY DRAPED THE AFTERNOON BETTER THAN A BLACKOUT curtain, but that would do nothing to affect Devon's mood. It was the weekend. He had completed his last exam for Econ, and the countdown was on for spring break. Pretty soon, Jasmine would be clad in a skimpy bikini, baking in Cancun next to him. He would then slather sunblock on every single inch of her winding chocolate curves. Life didn't get any better than that. Devon's mind rushed ahead to the pending vacation. Freedom with his boys, a break from the rigorous rhythm of school, and best of all, time alone with Jasmine.

"Um…earth to Devon. Did you hear what I said?"

"Huh?" Devon ripped his gaze from a menacing cumulus cloud drifting by. A storm was coming.

"I said, I think it's gon rain. We should probably bounce." Slight annoyance gripped Jasmine's tone as she jumped to her feet and dusted off her plump bottom.

Devon's head pivoted back to the sky, and, deciding she was right, he followed his girlfriend's lead.

They had spread out an old blanket of his, decorated it with sandwiches, chips, and those little chocolate chip cookies Devon's favorite dining hall served. The picnic was Jasmine's idea to celebrate him acing his last exam, even though he wouldn't get his results back for another week. Yet Jasmine was insistent, so confident that he was going to, once again, "kill it." She wanted to celebrate in advance. Devon never could deny those doe-like eyes. They were the first thing that had drawn him to her. Well, one of the first. Aside from her looks, Jasmine was also one of the most driven women Devon knew, and so certain about her future. That was a quality he loved.

"Babe, Sheila said the party is gon be *lit*. I can't *wait* to rock my hot pink dress. Remember to wear the lime shirt I bought you…"

Jasmine's rambling painted the atmosphere while Devon stuffed the remains of their picnic into his fists before trailing her across the quad. She was talking about the spring break fling. It was a last-minute party before break, held by one of the major Greek fraternities on campus. That meant any and everybody would be there. The party was a silent, glow-in-the-dark event where multiple DJs played different music stations, and attendees' headphone settings dictated the genre of music they heard. Devon wasn't the party-goer Jasmine was, but he had promised her he'd go since she had attended his chess tournament last month. The girl hated chess, often complaining that there were no balls flying or dudes fighting, which happened in any sport she was able to sit through. In these moments, Devon laughed Jasmine off, explaining that the purpose of chess was to develop critical thinking skills. Jasmine was adamant that if she wanted to develop her critical thinking, she would read a book or do her Calculus homework. Not watch a sport.

They were so different, yet being with Jasmine had been a huge boost to both Devon's self-esteem and social status. So many dudes were on her, but she wanted *him*.

For nearly five months, they had been going strong, a fact that still wowed Devon. The classic closet introvert, before dating Jasmine, he had never been to as many parties on Morrison University's campus. It seemed like he had sufficiently made up for the lack of partying his last two semesters in grad school. Additionally, Jasmine was in a sorority, president of a women's rights group, and ran the Black student on-campus organization. It was hard to keep up with her sometimes, because Devon's own schedule, obtaining his MBA in Entrepreneurship, being an active member of the chess club, a TA for Business Mgmt. 202, and helping to run his parents' restaurant back home, ate up his time. But Jasmine had him hooked, and Devon just couldn't seem to say no to her. His little brother Darion was quick to point it out, frequently taunting him that he was whipped. Darion said that Jasmine had so much masculine energy, she pulled dudes like men typically pulled women. He even coined her "J.T.," opting to use her initials, which sounded more masculine than her actual name. It didn't help that Devon's 20-year-old little brother was his roommate and had an eye-witness account of the kryptonite of Jasmine Thomas.

Yet, Jasmine's strong personality didn't bother Devon one bit. In fact, he felt it complemented his quiet, easy-going style. Jasmine was the very thing he needed, but with that discovery came a lot of questions. For almost five grueling years, Devon had been tunnel-visioned on his air-tight plan to graduate with his MBA at Morrison. Right after that, he would return home to Brooklyn Hts. to run his family's restaurant, Jack & Jill. Now that Jasmine was in the picture, Devon had a lot to think about. He couldn't see himself breaking things off after graduation. *But how will I make it all work*? Uncertainty straddled his shoulders, weighing them even more than the blanket and dishes in his grasp. As the grassy knoll passed by along with a gust of wind, Devon frowned. The only thing that was becoming certain was that Jasmine was in his future.

A drop of rain burst onto his forearm, abruptly snatching him from his musings. The couple speedily walked, but as they reached his dorm, the coils in Devon's stomach tightened again. Did he really want to break up with Jasmine when he graduated? Jasmine was a free spirit, and Devon simply couldn't see her doing the long-distance thing. Shooing the question away, he clutched the entrance door, holding it open.

When Jasmine sauntered inside, it was hard not to miss the immediate attention her hips grabbed from the room. As she sashayed to the right of the parlor, past a few students at study tables, a kid previously engulfed in Organic Chemistry transformed into a rabid dog. He was practically salivating at the mouth. Devon traipsed behind, breezing past the row of windows that held a wide ledge that students sometimes perched on. A few stragglers sat there, and one guy's eyes became entranced as the couple passed by. Within seconds of them nearing the steps, the men plopped at small study tables, eased their eyes over their textbooks. One dude's gaze was so stark that the girl across from him cleared her throat and cut him an ugly, mean mug. Quickly, he ducked his head back behind his book, but the message had been sent; Jasmine was in the room.

Standing at the foot of the stairs, Devon chuckled to himself. His girlfriend always had that effect, but he wasn't bothered as so many men could be. If anything, he felt even more special that she had chosen *him*.

"Girl, this party is 'bout to be cray-zee," Jasmine chirped into her phone, oblivious to the happy home she had just broken up. She was probably talking to Sheila.

Devon continued enduring the hefty climb up the three flights, strangling the blanket in his arms. A few Tupperware bowls wobbled beneath his chin, and he steadied himself. Once again, his earlier questions about their relationship after graduation piqued.

You still got two and a half months. Just chill, Devon tried to comfort himself, then focused on not falling down the stairs. When they successfully made it to the top, he reached for his dorm key.

"Yo, son. Wuz good!" His Day One, Antonio's gangly frame headed towards them, draped in a loose jersey and baggy shorts, his arm clutching a basketball.

"I just stopped by yo room and was hittin' you up, but you ain't answering yo phone. Now I see why." Antonio's gaze dropped to Jasmine. It then engaged in a tug of war with her figure wrapped in skinny jeans and a fitted white T. Almost painfully, he dragged his eyes back to Devon.

"Y'all comin' tonight?" he asked.

Devon smiled. Antonio had been his boy since undergrad, and whenever he felt up to being social, he was always his preferred buddy.

"You know it. You wanted to hoop?" Devon eyed the ball in his arm.

"I did, 'til I saw it started coming down." Antonio whipped his head in the direction of the window just as a clap of thunder sounded. "Sup, Jas," he offered a distracted Jasmine. She was still gabbing on her phone while leaning against the railing, but gave him a silent nod.

Devon chuckled, then said, "Yeah. We had to wrap up our picnic a little early." One of the bowls started slipping when he gripped his key, and Antonio swooped to his side.

"Let me help you out," he said, grabbing a few of the bowls from Devon.

Steadying his balance, Devon muttered, "Thanks." Jasmine remained unaware.

As they ambled down the long corridor, the booming sounds of Hip-Hop and Pop blended with students' voices, serenaded the hall from open doors. A hodgepodge of other tunes snuggled the trio when they approached Devon's dorm room. Students who had completed their midterms were happily bumping music in anticipation of the upcoming break. The atmosphere was in sharp contrast to the uber-studious environment that hugged the first floor.

"So, how was the picnic? Mad tho I didn't get an invite. Wuz up with that?" Antonio joked after they entered Devon's room and could hear each other. His amber-hued face scrunched into a look of hurt.

"You ain't a good enough student!" Jasmine piped up while sliding past Devon and into the room. She had finally ended her call with Sheila. After kicking off her heels, she stuffed her cell into her jeans, fell onto Devon's bed, and propped up her feet. "We was celebrating, and you ain't got nothing to celebrate," she finished smugly.

"Ouch. It's like that, Jas?" Antonio grabbed his chest as if she'd physically assaulted him.

Jasmine cheesed, her countenance shining like the sun peaking over the horizon. The expression stole Devon's heart. Eagerly, he dumped the items from his hands onto his desk and got comfortable behind her on the twin bed. Jasmine slid backward in between his legs, and Devon couldn't have been happier.

"You know you only here cuz yo dad is friends with the Dean," Jasmine shot back, while falling into Devon's chest. His beige T-shirt was smooshed by her bed of kinky coils, while a magnificent scent of some type of curl pudding smothered his nose. It was like his favorite dessert mixed with Christmas.

"Dag. Just cuz my dad work here don't mean I got it easy." Antonio had slammed on top of Darion's bed onto his side when he clapped back. Propping one elbow against the cover, he casually draped the other over his basketball. "Shoot. If I had it like that, I would be on the Dean's list like y'all nerds every semester."

Devon laughed. "Son, first off, I ain't been on the Dean's list since junior year, and second, if you applied half yo energy to completing a major that you do for your dating life, you would be on it too."

Antonio smacked his teeth, his eyes narrowing. "Look. Everybody ain't lucky in love like you, my man. And ain't everybody got a girl as fine as Jasmine to be tied down to. I mean, half these chicks is on some dumb stuff anyway. They want a six-figure brotha with a six pack to treat 'em to a six-star meal. But they ain't tryna *wait* for a brotha to get a degree and a six-figure salary. And they *definitely* ain't tryna treat a brotha to some six-star sex."

"Umm. *My girls* ain't on that. You sound like you been listening to that stupid podcast…" Jasmine said, and Antonio's eyes darted to her.

"Yo. Michael Davis is the *truth*. These broads ain't on nothing but gettin' theirs, so we need to be on getting ours."

Devon shook his head, already knowing where this was going. Michael Davis was the new influencer everyone was flocking to for relationship advice. Mostly guys followed him, but some women too. His polarizing views and comments seemed to have the die-hard feminists up in arms. Devon's girlfriend was one of them. When Jasmine's body tensed up, Devon tried to calm her by stroking her arms.

"And what exactly does that mean?" Jasmine said. When she sat up a little, she slipped out of Devon's grip.

So much for calming her down, he thought.

"Look, y'all. Let's just chill on all that. We finally done with midterms. We got the party tonight. Then we got Cancun," Devon interrupted, trying to defuse the situation. "Y'all killin' the vibe. We should be celebrating." He pulled Jasmine back down to lay on his chest.

She breathed out a short, "Fine," and Antonio huffed out, "Yeah, 'aight," but the peace was bound to be short-lived. Devon's best friend and his girlfriend were always head-to-head on one issue or another. If it wasn't politics, it was gender wars. If it wasn't money, it was school. If it wasn't for him, the two would never be in the same room together, let alone go on a whole trip out of the country. Yet that's exactly what they would be doing. In just two short days, their flights were leaving for one full week, and Devon couldn't wait.

The trip was initially for the guys. Darion was the one who suggested it, and Antonio was immediately down. Then, just a month after they bought their flight tickets, Devon started dating Jasmine. He simply couldn't see being away from her that long. She, of course, wasn't about to be the only girl on an all-guys trip, so she invited her two friends, Sheila and Kimberly. Sheila had a thing for Antonio, which he was well aware of, so when Devon pitched the new plans, he eagerly agreed. Darion was a little disappointed that Kimberly wasn't as thick as Jasmine and Sheila, but said he would make it work.

Devon had never been to Cancun. Though his parents made a pretty good living, they chose to invest their hard-earned funds into their children's education and comfortable lifestyle. That left little for traveling. Every spring break, Devon was back in Fort Greene, Brooklyn, being put to work at Jack & Jill. Since Darion and Devon both worked at college for extra spending cash, they set aside their pay to make the trip happen.

At first, Devon was hesitant because his parents usually relied on him to be home during breaks to assist with the family business. But Darion was adamant. He had insisted they go as it was their last turn up before Devon graduated, and he was slaving away at Jack & Jill. He even poked out his lower lip the way he used to when they were little.

There was just something about the way that Darion had said, "slaving," that caused knots to mount Devon's stomach. So he caved.

The boys booked a fancy three-bedroom ocean-view beach house listed on Airbnb. They got a great deal, and it worked out that the girls didn't mind sharing a room. Antonio insisted he wasn't rooming with Darion and that he would be posted in the upstairs bonus room. He didn't care that it was open to anyone who passed by; it had a queen-size bed. In his typical brash style, Antonio boasted that the girls could take turns sharing his bed, or better yet, sleep with him at the same time.

As Devon pondered the upcoming trip, a lump formed in his throat. Would his people get along? He didn't want to waste his time being the referee between Jasmine and Antonio. He wanted to have fun. He wanted to make memories. It was too soon that he wouldn't have this moment right here anymore. After all, he had spent almost five whole years on Morrison University's campus. His MBA program had allowed him to complete an advanced degree faster than a normal graduate school curriculum in that time frame. Devon's attending college wasn't necessarily for him to learn business operations and ownership, though. His parents, the Woods, had been grooming him for entrepreneurship for as long as he could remember. He had also been helping with their restaurant as soon as he was of age. There was no question in the Woods' minds that Devon was taking over the family business. Getting his degree was just a formality. Something for him to fall back on, as his dad would say. Just in case life didn't go as planned.

Yet everything seemed to be going as planned. Academics was always smooth sailing for Devon, and making A's was never the issue. What wasn't a part of the plan was his sudden romance. Devon's heart pinged every time he thought about leaving his girlfriend after gradua-tion. His strong emotions weren't because Jasmine was his first girl-friend, but there was a real possibility they *were* because she was his first love.

"Bruh, get off my bed!" Darion barged into the room, jerking Devon from his musings. While scowling at Antonio, Darion tossed his shoes to the side and whipped off his soaked, ivy green apron. The intimate space seemed to shrink with another body in the room, and the tension that Darion had brought with him filled its capacity. The brothers had barely squeezed in two twin beds, two desks, a stacked TV, microwave, and a mini fridge near the one window facing the east side of campus. Even though the small dorm room was a challenge, one perk was that Devon could room with his brother.

"Man, you act like you *been* here. You just got here," Antonio sat up and said. "Hello to you too!"

"I mean, you laid yo nasty, sweaty self all on my comforter. That's my mom's *good* comforter."

"Yo, I ain't sweaty. I ain't even play!" Antonio sniffed his underarms and raised them for show. "See. No sweat stains."

"Dang, D. You drenched. You had to walk all the way here from Tyson?" Jasmine asked. She was referring to the dining hall on the other side of campus where Darion worked.

"Yeah. I wish I had known it was gon rain," Darion huffed. "I woulda grabbed my raincoat or at least caught the bus. But it started when I was already on my way home." He cocked his head at Devon and said, "Bro. Why you let yo man lay all on my bed like that?"

Devon rolled his eyes. "Look. You wasn't here, and he needed a place to chill. What, you want him cuddled up with me and Jas?"

Instead of answering, Darion started stripping. "I gotta get out these wet clothes. Y'all still going tonight?"

"Yeah, but I need to get to Sheila's cuz I'm changing over there. Babe, can you get me an Uber? Oh, and pull out your lime shirt for tonight so you don't forget." Jasmine peered at Devon with her doe eyes, and he melted.

"I got you."

"I got you," Darion mocked, now shirtless and wiping his face with a towel.

"Well, I'm a let y'all get y'all selves together for tonight." Antonio jumped to his feet, still gripping his basketball. "Hit me when y'all leave."

"Bet," Devon said. Ignoring his brother, he pulled out his phone to order a rideshare for Jasmine. Since Sheila lived off campus, Jasmine had to either take a ride-share or the bus to get to her house in this rain.

"Yo. Tell Sheila I'ma be lookin' for her tonight," Antonio said with a cocky smile.

"Boy, she is not on you. But 'aight," Jasmine said, clearly trying to cover for her girl.

"Puh. She be liking my posts *too* much. I know that girl checkin' for me."

"See, that's the problem. Brothas think sistas supposed to be checking for *them*!"

And just like that, another round of gender wars emerged.

Devon sighed, catching eyes with Darion, who tried stifling a grin. To interrupt the spew of nonsense bubbling out of Antonio's mouth, Devon said, "Babe, the rideshare is on its way. Let me walk you down."

"I'ma head wit' you since I ain't tryna see Darion's only fans. Brotha 'bout to be butt naked in a sec!" Antonio said. He was right. Darion was down to his briefs and barely wearing those.

"Look. Y'all in *my* room," Darion proclaimed, but he went to grab a robe and a shower caddy from the tiny closet.

"Later, D," Jasmine said, as they all headed out.

When the trio reached the dorm entrance, most of the crowd had cleared, leaving just a few students talking near the 70-inch flat-screen. Devon grabbed Jasmine's hands, pulling her to face him.

"Baby, call me when you make it."

"Will do," Antonio replied behind him in a fake female voice, and laughed.

Devon threw him a look.

"Ok. And don't forget the lime shirt!" Jasmine said, before pecking him on the lips and leaving for her ride. Devon hard-stared after her, then felt his friend's presence next to him.

Antonio said, "Man. I know you love to watch that girl walk away!" Devon hit him over the head with the back of his hand.

"What Jasmine and I have is so much deeper than yo shallow brain could ever comprehend."

"Yeah, yeah. One of these days, you gon get hip to Michael Davis. But until then, you go right ahead and keep on bein' a simp. I'll see you later. And make sure you wear that lime shirt!" Antonio called back.

Devon watched his friend jog in the rain and hop into a blue Ford Focus through the water-stained, slender windows by the front door. It was just like Antonio, the biggest player Devon knew, to call *him* a simp. His boy had run through more women in the three years Devon had known him than Devon had in his whole life. It was obvious it was due to his own insecurities. Antonio wasn't the best-looking guy, with a large, splotchy birthmark on his chin that didn't help. Nor was he the smartest. But he had this amazing charisma that seemed to draw people. Devon felt he could be great in politics if he'd buckle down and stop switching his major. Yet whenever the subject came up, Antonio brushed him off, saying he had plenty of time. Still, Devon wasn't so sure. Even though Antonio was only a year younger than him, he hadn't accumulated nearly the amount of credits he needed to complete his undergrad degree. For that reason alone, Devon put little weight on Antonio's advice on relationships and life. In the world of guiding others, his boy's credibility was shot. Regardless, Antonio was still his boy and was there whenever he needed him. Devon just hoped his good example would one day rub off on him. Until then, he'd ride with Antonio until the wheels fell off.

TWO

AS LONG AS WE'RE TOGETHER

It was after 8 PM when Devon stood in front of his bedroom mirror, assessing his image. He had paired the lime green button-down Jasmine bought him with a pair of dark blue khakis and all-white Vans. Normally, he wasn't too obsessed with his appearance, but being with Jasmine had made him more self-aware. Devon's natural attractiveness had often worked in his favor. Typically, what he wore wasn't something he had to put much stock in as far as dating was concerned. Lucky for him, he'd inherited his mom's smooth, even nut-brown skin tone and his dad's height, nearing 5 feet 11. Often, Devon could get away with saying 'six feet' because, who would really know the difference? He kept his hair in a short fade, which complemented his face nicely. Full lips and almond-shaped eyes sat in near-perfect symmetry with his semi-wide nose that alluded to the Maasai warriors in his African bloodline. A fact known only to Devon because his mother, the most pristine historian he had ever encountered, had inherited a remarkably detailed family tree album that traced their ancestry even to slavery days. The royal bloodline of Kings and Queens of the African diaspora flowed confidently throughout each of their family members' achievements. They now seemed to be beckoning Devon as he wrapped up his collegiate career.

But what were the ancestors saying?

Spirituality was never Devon's strong suit. Sure, his family went to church on the quintessential holidays like Easter and Mother's Day, and he knew most of the Bible stories from Sunday school. But to think about there being a divine plan for his life that led to a huge epiphany of purpose was an entirely different notion. Yet those thoughts seemed to be seeping in lately, and Devon really wasn't sure what to do with them.

What *was* his purpose? Running Jack & Jill had always been top on the list, but now it felt like Jasmine was coming in a strong second.

"Maybe I'll talk to Pops," Devon murmured. *Get some guidance on how to do both.*

Darion, who stood a few feet away, jamming to a song by his favorite mumble rapper, stopped mumbling to look at him.

"Talk to Pops about what?" His brother peered over with a curious expression while primping his nappy haircut .

"You heard that over this loud ass music?" Devon looked at him with a doubtful face in the mirror instead of turning his head to look behind. The truth was the music wasn't that loud, but it was the first thing he could think of to deflect from his embarrassment.

"You over there talking to yourself is weird, bro. I'm definitely gon here *that*! You know what Mom would say."

"Yeah yeah. It's ok to talk to yourself as long as you aren't answering yourself." Devon repeated the mantra in a voice that mimicked their mother's, and the brothers shared a laugh.

"I'm just thinking about the future, that's all," he replied.

"Bet. Well, the future is looking nice. You 'bout to graduate, inherit the family biz, so I don't have to, and put a fat ring on J.T.!" Darion grinned and began throwing on his shoes before spraying on cologne.

"How you know I'm thinking 'bout *marrying* her? We ain't even been together six months," Devon replied, trying to sound surprised.

His brother blinked. "Dev. I been yo Day One since I was born. I *know* you. You locked in, and you gon lock *that* in."

Devon tried to smother a grin by running a hand over his face. "I ain't gone lie," he responded, "I would love for us to have something more. But Jasmine still has a year left, and she's bent on living in L.A.

She wants to do cinematography. How is that gon look with me managing Jack & Jill?" It felt good to finally voice his thoughts out loud, and he let out a deep breath.

"Y'all will figure it out," Darion was quick to say. "I can tell she's on you, too. I mean, you ain't *all that* and look at you pullin' her!" His brother laughed, and Devon reached for the wet towel Darion had used earlier to whip it at him.

"Hey! Don't mess up my drip. You 'bout to get me wet!" Darion jumped backward, trying to dodge the flying towel coming at him. Though he successfully avoided it, he banged his knee on the desk.

Devon laughed. "That's what you get! Besides, you look just like me, so if I'm ugly, so are you!"

His statement was at least half true, as the brothers were a dead-on resemblance to each other. The three-and-a-half-year age difference was barely noticeable now, and Darion loved to remind Devon of it. For years, Darion was the little pip squeak at Devon's hip. Then, somewhere around 16, he shot up and filled out in the areas that mattered. Even still, his personality was more outgoing than Devon's. As a result, Darion's walk carried more swag. Regardless of their differences, they were two peas in a pod, and Darion was right about being Devon's Day One. Devon often saw them running Jack & Jill together, but Darion had other dreams. He wanted to be an engineer and was looking to Devon to receive the torch for their parents' legacy. It was still too early to see what their little sister Debra would decide. As the oldest, Devon was expected to shoulder more responsibility, so he hadn't even included Debra in the equation.

Devon stopped messing with Darion to search his phone and checked his messages. His eyes bugged at one from Jasmine:

Baby, where are you?

He had also missed her call.

Whoops.

"D, we're running late. I'm a hit up Antonio and let him know we rolling out," Devon said to Darion while texting Jasmine the same information.

"Bet," Darion said, and slipped on his Yeezy 350s. Since it was a glow-in-the-dark situation, he wore a loud yellow polo with stone-washed skinny jeans.

It was still raining, and the party was at a club off-campus, so the bothers caught a rideshare. The view of the school swiftly diminished behind them as they road to their destination. When it wasn't raining, Morrison University was a vibrant landscape of fresh greenery, colorful spring foliage, and tall cathedral-like buildings. Accentuated with pops of navy and mustard, the school colors, the atmosphere was simultaneously welcoming and comforting. Tucked inside a small town near Syracuse, New York, it had the luxury of being its own community hub but held fast access to the larger city vibes Devon always seemed to crave. Those city vibes zoomed by as he sat back in the rideshare, soaking in the fleeting moments of freedom. There was always a million and one things to do between schoolwork, being a TA, and of course, Jasmine. Now, finally, he was on top of things and could just chill.

This is probably exactly what I need to stop trippin' about my future, Devon thought, bouncing his head to the latest hit from Wizkid. Both Devon and Darion loved Afro beats, and their heads bobbed in sync in the small SUV.

"Oh, y'all like dat, huh?" the driver said in a thick Jamaican accent. His bulky locks draped his head while examining them in the rearview mirror. When the boys nodded, he turned up the volume. Devon let his earlier doubts melt into the eclectic mix of West African rhythms. Maybe he didn't know *what* the ancestors were saying, but whatever it was, it sounded good. His brother belted out the lyrics like he'd written them himself, and Devon joined in. The driver did too, and the three were still vibing when the coal-brick building, resembling an office, masked their view. A multitude of windows ran up and down the exterior, allowing easy access for anyone needing to peer outside. It was the only one on the street that was active on the inside and stood out even more with an all-white entrance door. Flashes of colors from moving bodies sprinkled the bottom floor of windows, and a line snaked out the door all the way down the block. Since the first two floors were lively and the rest of the building seemed dead, Devon figured the frat must have only rented those floors.

"Dag. What y'all doin'? It's mad people here, but ain't no music. Is anything foreal goin' on inside?" the driver asked, confused.

Darion laughed. "It's a silent party, so you can't hear the music."

"So y'all havin' a party…without music? Y'all kids are crazy." The driver made a face. He had to be well into his 30s and obviously didn't have a clue what a silent party was.

"No, sir. Everybody has on headphones, so you can't hear it outside."

"Ok. But that sounds even more weird than not having music at all!"

The driver shook his head, and Darion gave up trying to make sense of it. He gave him a five-star rating on the app for the good vibes.

As they escaped the vehicle, Devon received a text from Jasmine.

"Jas said they not letting no more dudes in, but she waiting at the door for us, so just go to the front," he told his brother.

"Puh. Figures. Where's Antonio?"

"She said he in there already," Devon shared. They marched to the front past the angry onlookers, mostly men. As a slew of neon colors draped their walk, Devon kept his gaze straight so he wouldn't feel bad about cutting.

At the entrance, Jasmine beamed, causing Devon's insides to crumble. "Baby!" she cried. Beside her was a man who looked like he could bench press a whole freshman. His hardened expression softened some as he looked from Jasmine to the boys and realized they were with her.

"Jas, you know we cuttin' off the fellas," he said in a gruff voice. Jasmine immediately hit him with her signature smile and batted her lashes.

"Bruce, this my dude. You gon make me turn up without my man?" She placed a hot-pink nailed hand on her hot pink waist and waited. Devon tried to suppress a lopsided grin. Her openly taking possession of him like that made him feel like a state chess champion.

Bruce peered back at the two and gave them a quick nod. "You owe me," he muttered, and Jasmine stroked his arm. It was just long enough to insinuate that she would pay him back, but not too long to insinuate it would be in an X-rated way.

Still, when Devon brushed past the door keeper, he fought a tinge of jealousy. Yeah, Jasmine could flirt, but this time it was in his favor. Should he really be trippin'? As he wrestled with the question, his girlfriend grabbed his hand and pulled him forward.

"We're in the corner!" Her heavy, long twists fell to the right when she nodded, extinguishing Devon's concerns.

I can trust her, he thought, then let his Vans trail her inside the dimly lit room. They bumped around a few shadows until finding their way to a circular table where headphones lay stacked. A few feet over, three different DJs were bangin' on their MacBook Airs and DJ controllers. Darion and Devon grabbed two sets of headphones, then followed Jasmine to the corner where hers were. Antonio was perched there with an arm slung around Sheila. Both were looking a bit under the influence. When Antonio's gaze lifted, he stumbled to his feet and gave Devon their special handshake: two slaps, one dap, and one fist bump. Both grinned silently since everyone had on headphones. Devon turned his to the station Jasmine was listening to. To his surprise, it was Afrobeats. He let her drag him to the floor, and they found their groove. Her dark brown skin glistened in contrast to the hot-pink, tight-fitted dress she wore. Devon couldn't fight the arousal when she turned and pressed her butt between his legs.

Whew! This girl is fire, he thought, and let her hips guide him. It was then that Devon decided Jasmine could flirt with whoever she wanted because at the end of the night, she was all his.

After a few more Afrobeats tunes, the couple switched their station to Hip-Hop. A grin exploded from Devon as a Migos throwback blared through his ears. Immediately, he searched for his boy. Antonio was already on it and had ditched the chocolate chick with the large chest he was dancing with.

Devon turned to Jasmine. "Yo!" He mouthed over the song. "I gotta get it in real quick!" She looked at him, confused as he pointed to his friend, making his way eagerly through the mass of dancers. In seconds, Antonio and Devon began waving their hands like fanatics in each other's faces, shouting all the lyrics to one of their favorite jams.

Jasmine stood by laughing, but Devon didn't care. This was his joint! There had been too many times when "Bando" would play while he and Antonio would be working out at the school rec or riding in an Uber. Like clockwork, their eyes would widen, and their lips would flow in sync, not missing a beat.

"Man, you fried!" Antonio said after the song changed.

Devon held out his fist for a dap. "Bruh, we still got it!" he said, and it felt like old times. Like nothing in the world could ever change their bond.

A few songs later, different fraternities and sororities took turns strolling. The crowd formed a circle just for them, stepping back and giving them space. Two of the three DJs stopped playing, and everyone switched their stations to the only active one. When Beyoncé started belting a classic, Jasmine and her chapter hit the floor. It was a sight to see everyone in perfect synchronization, and Devon's eyes never left Jasmine. His girl had the crowd eating out of the palm of her hand, and he had taken the biggest bite.

The evening wore on, and Devon was in need of refreshments. Both he and Jasmine had been on the floor for a good hour.

"Baby, I'm hungry," Jasmine whispered next to Devon when they sat at the long table Antonio had claimed for their crew.

Devon looked at his girl. "You read my mind."

"Aye, y'all getting food?" Antonio said on his other side. They had taken off their headphones and could now hear each other. It was a sight watching the crowd dance to music that only played in their ears. The room echoed with footsteps and movement, but no music.

Devon nodded to his friend, and Antonio added, "Bring me back some of that red stuff."

Swiftly, Devon and Jasmine left to make their way to the second floor. The hallway was illuminated in blue, the frat colors of the Titans who were throwing the party. A few couples made out near closed doorways as Devon and Jasmine passed by.

"I gotta pee real quick," Jasmine said, then pointed to the sign that read 'food.' "Can you grab my plate for me so I don't have to wait?"

"Babe, I don't know what they got. And I gotta get Antonio's drink." Devon's gaze followed her finger. Signs hung on the walls indicating which direction to take for each option. The food and the bathrooms were on opposite sides of the building.

Jasmine pouted, crossing her arms. "Baby. You know what I like. I ain't picky." She batted her eyes.

Devon melted. "I got chu." After watching her saunter to the women's restroom in the opposite direction of the food, he turned the corner, and was met with another line. Dag. Not only was he gon have to try to carry all this stuff, but he was gon have to wait too. Minutes ticked by. A text came through from Jasmine:

> I'm in line at the bathroom.

She included a sad face emoji.
Devon texted back.

> It's one for the food too.

He included a shake my head emoji.

They did that for a few minutes until Devon didn't hear anything else. When his phone vibrated again, his eyes scanned eagerly in anticipation, expecting his girl. His face fell.

Darion:

> Bro. You getting food? Can you bring me some water?

Devon shook his head and texted back.

> No. I ain't got enough hands!

Darion:

> Dude. I see how it is.

Dang. Now he was gon have to get a drink for his brother!

Devon started a text, **"Bring yo ass up here and get yo drink,"** but he deleted the message. He felt bad. How was he gon put Antonio before his brother? They were both his brothers. He would get the damn drinks.

When Devon reached the front, three card tables scattered with finger foods sat in a row. Chicken strips, chips, pizza, and cookies donned the plastic blue tablecloth. Another table held water bottles and cans of pop, and still another had a large bowl of suspicious red punch.

That must be the punch Antonio wants, Devon figured.

A few guys standing next to him grabbed plates and napkins.

"Aye. You wit' Jas, right?" one of them asked.

Devon felt a surge of pride. "Yep. That's my girl."

"Dope. You wanna come hang with us after the party? We thinking about riding to MLK Park."

Devon hesitated. The guys were probably offering to get high since that was usually what people did there. "Aye, I appreciate the offer, but me and Jas got plans. Another time," he said, not wanting to seem lame. Devon could count the number of times on one hand that he had gotten high.

"Bet." The guy gave him dap before loading his plate.

Devon tried not to smile too widely as he loaded his. Jasmine was his instant popularity card. Folks he had never seen before in his life were constantly talking to him. Probably because she was always posting their pictures on social media. As he tossed some chips on top of the pizza on his plates his phone vibrated in his pocket. Carefully, Devon set down his food to read the message.

Jasmine:

> Baby, I'm out the bathroom. I'm in the photo booth getting pics for social media.

Devon smiled. Of course she was. Another text.

Jasmine:

> It's in the room next to the bathroom.

Devon huffed a sigh. Now he was gon have to lug these plates to the photo room and hopefully not spill the drinks. He had to forego getting a drink of his own. He just didn't have enough hands!

Ok.

That was all Devon sent. The short distance to the photo room felt longer as he balanced two plates and three drinks, but he chose to focus on taking it one step at a time. A few couples side-stepped him, while making his way down the hall, but other than one near collision, he was unharmed.

This girl owes me, Devon thought, turning into the room with a large white sign that read "photos" in blue. It was there that he nearly dropped his food. Jasmine was hugged up in the arms of Bruce, the bouncer. Spotting him, she stepped away and pointed to the photo machine.

"Babe. You just in time. I was just taking a pic with Bruce, since, you know, I told him I would, since, uh, he let you in." Her eyes were wide like a deer caught in headlights.

Devon looked from Jasmine to the big dude who had been at the front door.

"Yo. You not mad is you, homey?" the guy said in a taunting tone. "I mean, I *was* nice enough to let y'all in," he added. He looked Devon up and down. Devon bit the inside of his jaw to keep himself calm.

"Why would I be mad? It's just a picture." He kept his voice monotone.

Jasmine hurried to his side. "Thank you, baby." She grabbed a plate and one of the drinks. "I'm ready to smash."

Bruce laughed. "Yeah. Yo girl ready to smash."

Catching the double meaning, Devon's fist flexed beneath the plate he was holding.

Don't do it, he told himself and took a few breaths. He wanted to smash the plate in the brotha's face.

"Let's go," Devon commanded, and Jasmine scurried after him out of the room.

As soon as they made it into the hall, she said in a low voice, "Baby, it was just a picture."

"Yeah. I know," Devon said as they fell into step. "I know." He repeated it more to himself than to Jasmine, though annoyance at the whole scene still clawed his mind. His girl in some other dude's arms was never a good look. Jasmine stopped Devon in the hallway and peered up at him.

"I'm here with *you*," she said in a clear, loving voice. Then she planted a firm kiss on his lips that sent chills running from Devon's upper torso to beneath his belt line.

He swallowed down his tension. "Yeah. I know," Devon said again, this time more softly.

Jasmine's eyes glistened with care in the dim lighting, and once again, Devon chastised himself.

She's with me. I'm trippin'. He shook off his insecurities, put his free arm around his girlfriend, and they walked together hip to hip down the stairs to join their friends.

——————

As they lay in bed, Devon held Jasmine's body, stroking a hand over her back. The warmth from shared sweat glued them together, creating an indescribable sensation of oneness. It was well after midnight. An hour prior, they had made it back to Devon's dorm. That's where all of the night's activities culminated in his girlfriend showing him just how well she could work her hips. The dance floor simply could not handle all of Jasmine's moves.

Darion had taken one for the team and stayed the night on Antonio's hardwood floor. That was the brothers' arrangement when Devon and Jasmine needed alone time since she also had a roommate. Devon tried not to take advantage of his brother's generosity too much, though. Plus, his and Jasmine's schedules were always so crazy. It was a fight to get in their time. When they did, it just made Devon fall harder. Jasmine was the whole package, and his brother was right; he *had* been thinking about marriage. He just wasn't sure if she had.

"What are you thinking?" Jasmine murmured against his left peck.

Devon wasn't nearly as muscular as Bruce the bouncer, but his chest was pretty filled out. He was more like Michael B. Jordan in "Just

Mercy" and less like Michael B. Jordan in "Creed," even without consistently hitting the gym. Turning Jasmine's question over in his mind, Devon waited a beat before answering. Was it safe to be 100 percent honest?

"How much you mean to me," he settled on.

"Aww. Baby. You're always so sweet." Jasmine lifted her head and rested her chin on him. "I wish this could last forever."

The statement was everything Devon had wanted to hear. Yet she had said it wistfully, as if it couldn't last forever. That left his nerves dancing.

"Well, maybe it could," he suggested cautiously.

Jasmine laid her head back down, and her hair caressed his face. When she didn't say anything in return Devon worried that he had been too forward.

"Yeah. Maybe," she finally said, but that was it.

Devon wasn't sure what he expected. He *was* further along in his life than she was. Jasmine still had to complete another year of college. Marriage was a big deal, but even though they hadn't said, "I love you," Devon couldn't deny how strong his feelings were. He had never felt this way about anyone. Before Jasmine, Devon's plans were rock-solid. He would graduate, move back to Brooklyn Hts., take over Jack & Jill, and run the family business. Now that she was here, he felt ready to re-arrange his plans. For a rule-follower like Devon, that was like an earthquake hitting New York City. It was just something that never happened.

"Do you ever think God has a plan for our lives?" Devon asked suddenly.

This time, Jasmine's head jolted up. She squinted at him. "What? What made you ask *that*?"

"It's just—something I been thinking about lately. Like, I've always thought about my parents' plans for me—about my plans and even my brother's. But I've never thought, like, if *God* had a plan."

Devon knew he was throwing a lot out there. This was definitely unknown territory, as he and Jasmine had never discussed God. They'd gone to church together a handful of times, but Devon couldn't think of a single conversation where they'd discussed God outside of that.

Shouldn't you talk to the woman you're going to marry about Me?

The thought had sprung out of nowhere. It was so surprising that Devon said, "Huh?" out loud.

Jasmine looked at him. "I didn't say anything," she said.

"No. Uh. I know. Umm. Sorry," he stuttered.

That was wild. Was that *God* who had spoken to him? Or was he trippin'? There was *no way* that the Creator of the universe would talk to Devon about something so minor.

"Sure, I think we're here for a reason," Jasmine answered nonchalantly. "I think the universe, or *God*, or whatever, has us here and we just need to follow our hearts to figure out the reason."

It wasn't necessarily the answer that Devon had an issue with. It was more so the *way* she had said it. As if this higher being was somehow *around* and didn't really care *what* they did with their lives. Well, that was Jasmine. She was the kind who had a made-up mind about what was going to happen, and really no one, not even God Himself, was going to make her change it. On the one hand, it was one of the things that attracted Devon so much to her: her self-assuredness. Right now, though, it felt like her flippancy with a concern that was nibbling at him (his future) was a little unsettling.

"But, baby," Jasmine murmured, "as long as we're together, I think everything's gonna work out." A landslide of love flooded Devon's insides. But then doubt attacked him again. How could she be so sure? How did she *really* know things would be 100 between them?

Jasmine started licking Devon's lips with her tongue and teasing them with her teeth. All kinds of sensations rushed his libido before subsequently burying all of his doubts.

She's right. As long as we're together, that's really what matters, Devon thought, enjoying every single act.

As Jasmine stroked and rubbed and licked, Devon gave into the urge, sat her on top of him, eased her thighs open, and made her straddle him. The thin white cotton sheets slid down her mid back and swaddled her hips, as they geared up for round two.

THREE
AIN'T GOIN' NOWHERE

"NAME THREE INDICATORS THAT DEMONSTRATE A BUSINESS IS SUFFERING, and the measurements that can be put into place to boost revenue."

Devon scanned the intimate group with expectancy. He was leading a special study session to prepare students for their midterm that afternoon.

Kevin, a freckle-faced young man who always wore a blazer to class, raised his hand. Devon nodded to him. "When your sales revenue diminishes, when your number of clients drops, and…" Kevin paused with a sneaky look on his face. "When your social media following dives."

Devon chuckled along with the other five students. Only a few dedicated souls were up early enough to catch the last-ditch effort of preparation, and that always stood out to Devon. If you were willing to go the extra mile in the classroom, you were usually willing to do so in your business. He would be sure to note the names of attendees to Professor Marx, who taught Business Mgt. 202. The students wouldn't be given extra credit, but it would be interesting to see how they tested. Even how they fared in the future in the business world.

"Kevin, I know you're being facetious," Devon responded, "but that last statement is still an indicator that maybe you're not reaching your target market. *And* the social media numbers could possibly reflect sales. But please give the *correct* answer you know Professor Marx is gonna accept on the test."

Kevin smiled and said, "When your inventory isn't moving as fast as shown in prior quarterly or annual reports."

"Yep. That's good," Devon affirmed, strolling around the circle of chairs they'd formed.

This class was one of Devon's favorites during undergrad, so when Professor Marx offered the TA position, he eagerly accepted. Even better, Devon found that he enjoyed teaching. Though he didn't feel he was supposed to be an actual teacher. It was more like he enjoyed training others as a leader. It was that training part that offered him the opportunity to witness others transform before his very eyes throughout the semester. Also, maybe because he was still so close to the students' ages, in some ways, their transformation mirrored his own.

Devon turned his attention to another student. "Monica, what are solutions to these specific challenges?"

Monica hesitated before speaking, her mahogany brown face tensing up some. "Umm, well… you could look into creating partnerships with other businesses in your industry."

Devon nodded his encouragement. "That's good. What else?"

"Maybe do a focus group and see if there are certain products that customers aren't interested in anymore? Maybe beef up R&D to find more relevant products?"

Her full manicured brow rose in question, and Devon nodded for her to keep going.

"Possibly consider a rebrand to recapture a new audience?"

Devon clapped both hands while leaning forward in his chair.

"Yes. Those are all great suggestions!"

The other students took notes as Devon stood to cover additional items Marx was sure to test them on. They continued their dialogue for another hour until Devon announced, "Alright, y'all. I'm kicking you out. You're ready. Besides, Professor Clark needs her classroom, and I need to get breakfast since y'all had me up too early to eat."

The students chuckled as they dragged the chairs back to their original tables. When they were done, they trailed out of the room one by one, thanking Devon as they went. The students seemed more alert and prepared for their exam. That made Devon feel even better about prying himself from Jasmine's arms that morning.

Monica was still gathering her things, so Devon walked over to her.

"Hey. You're doing great, Monica. You should be more confident in what you know."

"You think so?" She brightened, and her large brown eyes fluttered with pleasure. "I just never know, being one of the few Black women in here. Sometimes it just feels like a lot of pressure." She looked up at him, both pink lips sagging into a perfect pout.

Devon's heart went out to her, and without thinking, he laid a hand on her shoulder to squeeze it. "Yo, I got you. But just know you're *supposed* to be here. And you're the one to show them just how amazing Black women can be."

Monica's lips spread into a smile, but then, she did something that caught him off guard. She grabbed Devon into a hug. "Thanks. I really needed to hear that," she murmured into his chest. Monica was a good foot shorter, and her long black locks scratched against his chin.

Feeling a little uncomfortable but not wanting her to feel rejected, Devon allowed the sign of affection. After a few seconds, she released him and continued shoving the rest of her books into her bag. Devon was just about to turn to leave when she said, "I know you mentioned you were hungry. You interested in breakfast? I don't have anything until this exam." She looked up at him expectantly, and Devon kicked himself for even being found in this position. There was no one else around and no witnesses to how this was going to play out.

"Aww, my bad. I don't go out with students. Plus, I have a girlfriend." Devon decided to answer honestly. He wasn't sure whether there was a policy against TAs and students, or even whether what she was suggesting fell under the category of "going out," but he figured it would help soften the blow to use those words.

Monica's face fell a little, but she lifted her chin in an effort to shield her embarrassment. "Oh. Yeah. I understand. I was just thinking… since we were both hungry…" She let the statement die and hurried to throw her book bag over her shoulder. "But no worries. Uh, thanks again."

Before Devon could eke out another sentence, she fled the room.

Shoot. I wish I hadn't touched her. That's what misled her. Devon scolded himself while gripping the back of his fade. He had never been in a situation like that before and really wasn't sure he had handled it correctly.

Maybe I'll talk to Marx to get his feedback, he decided before leaving the room. He still had to drop off the key to Professor Clark, another one of Devon's favorite professors. She had agreed to let him use her room for their study session since Marx taught a morning class a few rooms down. Still a little disconcerted by Monica's forwardness, Devon mulled over the situation as he walked. The hallway became a distant blur of students and chatter against the clamor of his inner thoughts.

Did I let her down easy enough?

Yet his worry ceased when he arrived at Clark's empty office. Devon was surprised, as Clark had said she would be there all day grading. Since she was MIA, he decided to just leave the key on her desk.

Maybe she went to the bathroom, he thought, heading for the stairwell. Trotting down quickly, he dialed Jasmine.

"Baby, you still at my spot?"

"Hey, love. Yep. You kept me up all night, so I'm draggin'," she murmured into the phone.

"Oh, I kept *you* up? If I remember correctly, *you* was the initiator of both rounds two *and* three." Devon grinned at the memory. "I would love to take credit, but that was all you, baby."

Jasmine's giggle was music to his ears.

"You want me to pick up breakfast?" he asked.

Immediately, she started listing items that would require him to go all the way across campus to the only dining hall that offered them.

"You gon eat all that?" Devon asked with a frown, while dodging a girl on a bike.

"Sorry!" the girl called back after nearly running him over. Midterms made people psycho sometimes.

"Yep. Like I said, you wore me out. I need to rebuild my stamina. Plus, I have a long day ahead. There's my chapter meeting, then Sheila and Kimberly want to go shopping for the trip. I'ma need some protein for real."

"Ok. Be there soon." Devon shook his head and hung up. As he speed-walked to Franklin Hall, the only place he could get a freshly made omelet, it dawned on him that he should check in with his brother. It was nearly 10:30 am, and there was no telling when Darion would return home.

"Sup," Darion answered.

"Yo, D. You at Antonio's?"

"Naw, we out at Brunch & Bros. Kimberly and Sheila wit' us."

"Oh, word? Ok. I'ma text you when Jasmine leaves."

Devon breathed a relieved sigh at the sight of Franklin Hall. *Just a few more steps.*

"Bet. You know we got the call with Mom and Dad at 3 pm. They not gon let us leave the country without it," Darion reminded him.

"Right. Thanks. I'll hit you later." While making his way inside the dining hall, Devon hurried off the phone. He wasn't the only one in the mood for a freshly-made omelet. Everybody and their momma seemed to be there. Avoiding a flock of girls giggling on their way out, he posted behind the long food line. It seemed he was always in somebody's food line for Jasmine. Devon flipped open his phone to check his social media. Jasmine had already posted the pictures they took last night on her page. Seeing how good they looked, he smiled. *That dress was fire!* he thought, zeroing in on her figure and pinching the image to make it larger. After what seemed like eternity, he was up.

"What you want?" A short, round girl asked. The dingy white apron plagued with food stains, stretched around her waist and clung for dear life.

"Yeah. Can I get two orders of peppers, onions, cheese..." Devon said over the glass divider, then paused to peek at the notes he'd taken on his phone. "Olives, bacon, spinach..." he proceeded. The server made a face and huffed a sigh of impatience. He shrugged.

"My girlfriend's hungry."

The server threw his items into a bowl and passed the order—Chipotle-style—to the next server, who started on the eggs.

"Well, if it isn't the boyfriend."

The statement rushed Devon's ears from behind, tugging his neck around in its direction.

Devon's stomach dropped. "Yo, wuz up," he greeted the bouncer from last night.

Dude was just as big and muscular in the daylight, but this time he was with two other big dudes. One was light, and the other was as dark as him with a deep, long scar indenting his right cheek. The brotha looked like he had been in a fist fight or two. They were all wearing matching Greek apparel, so it was obvious they were in the same fraternity.

"Sup, my guy. So, how long you been with Jas?" Bruce asked, as if Devon had initiated a full-blown conversation.

"You ordering?" The girl from behind the station said it with enough annoyance to catch Bruce's attention. He spit out his order before laser-focusing his gaze on Devon again, but Devon, ignoring his question, had stepped forward a few feet in the moving line.

"Bro. You hear me?" Bruce said, his tone more forceful.

Devon fought annoyance. *Who this dude think he is?*

"Yeah, what's it to you?" Devon asked, barely looking back at him.

"Oh. Jas got them boxers in a bunch, I see." Bruce and his entourage laughed.

Devon hesitated. He didn't really want beef, especially when he was outnumbered.

"Look. I ain't buggin'. You cool with Jas, you cool with me," he said to diffuse the situation.

The big dude slapped a hand on Devon's back. Devon tried not to flinch and instead turned around to make full eye contact. Bruce needed to know that he was no punk.

"Aye, partna. We good. I was just giving you a hard time. Jas be running through 'em, that's all. I was just wondering how long *you* been able to last," Bruce said, shrugging both meaty shoulders with a look of feigned innocence.

Devon tried not to let the man's statement ruffle him, though anger did splinter his heart. It was known that Jasmine wasn't the settling-down type, and that was something he tried not to think too much about. Now it was being thrown in his face with blatant disrespect.

This fool got some nerve.

"Your omelet's done," the blond kid in front of him said, and Devon turned to the server handing him two large white to-go boxes.

"Aye, can you add two pancakes?" Devon asked the server. Swiftly, she threw two pancakes into one of the boxes from a hot pan. Devon grabbed the boxes, too lost in his own thoughts to thank her. His irritation was growing by the moment. To save his rep, he had to respond.

"Yo," he said, glancing over his shoulder and adding a little more base to his tone. "*I'm* with her now, and that's what it is."

"Yeah, that's what they all say." The cackling behind him bristled the little hairs on Devon's neck.

I just need to get my food and bounce.

When Devon paid for his food, he turned to leave, but Bruce stepped in front of him. He was holding his phone out, and Devon couldn't help but see the picture of his girl in Bruce's arms. It must have been the one he had walked in on them taking from the party.

This asshole.

"Yo girl lookin' good in my arms, right?" Bruce said with a huge smile.

Without a thought, Devon shoved the phone out of his face, and it clattered on the ground. Both of Bruce's friends stepped up as if they were ready for a fight. Devon tensed up.

I can take 'em, he told himself, even though there was no way on earth that he would win. Still, he had to try. Quickly, he weighed his options. He could throw the food into the air as a diversion and start swinging.

Instead of Bruce getting angry, though, surprisingly, he laughed. Bending over, he swiped up the phone by his feet and held out his arms in front of his friends, a sign for them to stand down.

Stares from nearby students burned into him, but Devon kept his gaze locked on Bruce's.

"Jas like water, homey," Bruce said with that same cocky smile. "You can't hold on to her, but you can try." He suddenly turned to get his order, and though Devon was pissed as all get-out, relief shot through him. He took the out, pivoted on his heels, and dashed to the exit.

Damn. He must be jealous as hell, going out of his way to come at me like that, Devon thought once again in the cool spring air. The grassy green campus became background music to the bouncer's words playing on repeat in his mind. Devon didn't realize he was practically stomping across the field until a couple holding hands and coming his way looked at him strangely. *Alright. I need to chill.* As he slowed his pace, he shook off Bruce's words. The brotha was obviously some type of scorned ex-lover or thirsty wannabe. If so, then why were his words causing such angst? Figure eight knots straddled Devon's gut. His forehead lay in a steady crease. His heart pumped from more than just the brisk walk. Shaking the thoughts from his head, he peered up at his dorm. A quick glance at his phone told him he'd made a 20-minute trip in less than 15.

Dag, I was rolling out!

At the door, while clutching both boxes in one arm, he flashed his phone to the dorm's scanner. Just as he stepped inside, a gust of wind rattled his unzipped jacket, nearly sending the food to the ground. Thankfully, he caught the breakfast in the nick of time. *That was close!* The last thing he needed was to disappoint Jasmine with no breakfast. Devon stopped and swallowed deeply. The whole event had flustered him in addition to his interaction with Bruce.

Dude was definitely on one, Devon decided in disgust. He let out a long sigh and stood in place to gather himself. *But I got the girl. I can't let this fake fan get in my head.* He then perked up when he thought about Jasmine laid up in his room. *Who cares about that hater when Jasmine is freaking waiting in my bed. All this brotha got is a damn picture.*

Swiftly and feeling more at ease, Devon made his way through the first floor. The dorm was still for late morning. Most students had probably either already gone home for break or were currently taking their last exam. *Just one more day and we out!* he thought, scaling the stairs like an Olympian mountain climber. Devon became giddy again at the prospect of their pending vacation.

The crew's flight left at 8 am the next day, which meant they had to be there by 6 am, which meant no late night tonight. He'd have to remind Darion, the night owl, that they could *not* miss their flight. Devon especially needed rest, given he barely got any last night.

"Finally!" Jasmine cried, still snug in his bed and looking at her phone when he opened the door. Devon inhaled sharply. His girlfriend was wrapped beneath his sheet, and, from what he could glimpse, wore his lime green shirt from the party. Her cocoa skin shone in the morning light, and her tousled hair hung wildly around her face; evidence of last night's events. Devon wondered briefly if they could get it in again before his brother came home.

"You better be glad it's me and not Darion," he said, shutting the door behind him. Placing the food boxes on his desk, he kicked a few pairs of Yeezys out of the way. His brother always had some shoes lying around, and Devon almost broke his neck one too many times.

"Look. Y'all about the same height, weight, everything. I wouldn't be mad…" Jasmine made a joking expression that, under normal circumstances, wouldn't have bothered Devon. Now, after the run-in with Bruce, it made him a little uncomfortable.

"You been checking for my baby brother?" He tried to ask the question lightly, but even *he* couldn't deny the edge in his voice.

Jasmine slanted her head to the side, shooting him a funny look. "What chu' mean by that?"

To relieve her of any misinterpretation, Devon floated towards her with one of the food boxes.

"Nothing. I'm just tired. I ain't get to rest like you," he teased, opening the box and kneeling in front of her on one knee. Pleasure invaded him as her eyes widened at the spread. "Voila, my queen."

"Thank you, baby!" she squealed. "I'm *starving*." Jasmine snatched the box and plasticware and crossed both legs to get comfortable. Devon plopped across from her on the bed and did the same.

"Oh. Wait. I have something for you!" Suddenly, Jasmine set aside her plate, went to the microwave, and pushed a button. The light and buzzing sounded, and Devon furrowed his brows.

"Babe. You running the microwave with nothin' in it?" He cocked his head from confusion. All of their food was spread out on the bed.

Jasmine tucked in her lips to hide her smile, then, when the machine beeped, pulled out a large plastic to-go cup with "Java's" stamped in cursive. Devon's eyes nearly burst from his face. "For you, baby," she said, handing him the steaming liquid. She smiled proudly.

Devon took the mug in awe and held it as if it were a prize. "You got me coffee? From Java's?" When he sipped the fresh brew his heart soared.

"Yep. I had it delivered," Jasmine said. "I knew you didn't have time this morning to make some from your Keurig." Devon set the cup near his foot and pulled her to him. "And I know you *hate* the dining hall's…"

"Baby. You are the best! I lo-" Devon stopped himself. It wasn't time. "I *love* that you did that for me."

Jasmine slipped from his grip and flopped back down to pick up her plate. "Babe. It's the least I could do. You went all the way across campus to get me this damn omelet. Besides, I know how you are about your coffee." It was true. Devon was borderline a coffee fanatic and a coffee snob. He only drank campus coffee under dire circumstances. Java's Café was his favorite off-campus café, but he was barely able to make it there except during his chess practices. It never occurred to him to just have a cup delivered via a food delivery app. Not only was his girl gorgeous, but she was also a genius! Devon kissed her on the cheek as she chewed, and Jasmine giggled.

Carefully, Devon picked up his cup, closed his eyes, and drank slowly, savoring every sip.

The couple went quiet as they got their fill. Jasmine was the first to break the silence. "So, how was the study group? The kiddos appreciate you sharing your brilliance?"

"Yeah. They did good. I'm sure they'll all do well on the test. Most of them are pretty good students in general…"

Devon's voice dwindled when he thought about his encounter with Monica after the session. He had almost forgotten about it.

"This one girl did catch me off guard, though," he started, wondering how to word it. He didn't want Jasmine tweakin' on the girl. She couldn't have been more than 19, since it was a class filled mostly with sophomores.

"What chu' mean, caught you off guard?" Jasmine asked, stuffing in another mouthful.

"I guess she got the wrong impression cuz she kind of asked me out after class," Devon shared sheepishly.

Jasmine stopped chewing, and deep lines settled into her forehead. "What chu' mean *got the wrong impression*? What did you *do*?"

"I didn't do anything," Devon hurried to answer. "I was just trying to encourage her. I kinda squeezed her shoulder, and she hugged me. Then asked me to go to breakfast." The words tumbled out of his mouth faster than he could snatch them back. Concerned she would flip, he studied Jasmine.

"Hmph. Now you *know* you gotta be careful, Devon. These chicks is thirsty. You a young, fine TA and these young girls gon be crushing on you," she said while wiping crumbs from her mouth with his shirt sleeve. She looked so cute, his heart skipped a beat. Devon grabbed her hand.

"Babe. You ain't got nothing to worry about. You know all I want is you," he replied in a husky tone. A small smile crept along Jasmine's lips, and he stroked her fingers. "If anything, *I'm* the one that needs to be worried," he said.

"And what does that mean?" Jasmine asked, picking up her fork and going in again.

Man, this girl can eat! Devon marveled at her appetite.

"I mean, I ran into yo boy Bruce at the dining hall."

Jasmine looked at him blankly.

"Bruce. The bouncer from last night?"

"Oh. The Titan? Yeah. What of it?" Jasmine shrugged a careless shoulder and took another bite.

"He seems to think I'm just another victim in your trail of lovers." Devon examined her face closely to see any signs of a reaction, but Jasmine only smirked. "He threw that pic y'all took last night in my face too."

A guilty expression stained her face. "Baby. You know I did that for you to pay him back for letting you into the party. For us." Jasmine dropped her fork and ran her hand over his, her eyes pleading.

"I know. I'm just sayin'…" A mixture of emotions tussled Devon.

You didn't have to look so boo'd up with him in the damn picture. He swallowed his thoughts with more coffee.

"Bruce been tryna get with me since freshman year," Jasmine added. "He'll say anything to somebody I'm dating to make them insecure." When Devon didn't respond, she said, "Look, I don't have the best record with long-term relationships like you do." Fidgeting with her fork again, she dropped her eyes before peering back up. "But I also haven't clicked with someone as much as I've clicked with you. I mean, you have your head on straight, Devon, and know what you want. Just like I do. That's a first for me."

This was probably the most serious Jasmine had ever sounded. Most things with Jasmine were adventurous and fun and sexy. She was always moving and shaking and looking for the next thing. Like with her intentionality in taking on so many leadership roles, or her active social life, never missing a party. Even with her history of short flings with men. Yet now it seemed she was simmering down with him. Putting down roots with him. Devon couldn't ignore the excitement bubbling in his stomach. It was exactly what he needed to hear her say. She was in this with him.

'F' Bruce, he thought.

Without waiting another second, Devon removed the food boxes spread open between them and grabbed Jasmine's hand, causing her to drop the fork.

"Thank you for saying that. I've been wondering where you were with things." He stroked her hand and pulled her into his arms. She kissed his cheek and snuggled inside the crevice of his neck.

"I ain't going nowhere," she whispered.

Devon knew it was true. And he knew that he wasn't going anywhere either.

FOUR
WHAT MATTERS MOST

THAT EVENING, DEVON DID THE THING HE HAD BEEN THINKING ABOUT doing for a while now. He typed engagement ring into the search engine. The options were endless—princess cut, round cut, yellow gold band, white gold band, platinum... *But what would Jasmine want?* And did she want a big wedding or a small wedding?

"Definitely a big one," he murmured to himself as his eyes studied all the different rings. The navy-blue comforter bunched around him while Devon squinted at the screen with only the phone's light as his companion. As an extra precaution he kept his back to Darion. The last thing he needed was his brother catching him in the act. Especially since Devon had been giving him such a hard time about going to bed early. But he couldn't help himself. As much as he had promised that he would be asleep by 8 pm, even making Darion turn off the lights at that time, it was now after 9:30 pm. Even though marriage was a huge step, and he didn't have all the details figured out, Devon was determined to make it work. He would find a way to fulfill his obligations to his parents *and* become a husband. *I got this*, Devon told himself, his eyes studying all of the rings. After Jasmine confirmed to him how she felt in his bed that morning, he was more certain than ever. Now was the time to take this next step. They would have to wait until she finished school, of course, but that was perfect because it gave Devon time to get established and build a cushion. Looking into his parents' eyes earlier that day on their video chat reiterated how much they loved him. Though they had their hearts set on Devon taking over Jack & Jill, at the end of the day, they wanted what was best for him. Once they met Jasmine, they would know that she was the best.

Jasmine was like the sunrise at the end of a long, dark, dreary winter. She brought life and warmth to every room, and Devon couldn't picture a day without seeing her beautiful, smiling face. Maybe he was out of his mind, but even his own brother had called it, and Darion knew him better than anyone. Finally, after another half hour of searching, Devon made himself shut off his phone. As his eyes adjusted to the darkness, they landed on both sets of packed bags side by side near the door. Darion's snores softly coddled the background. Indeed, they were ready. Devon just needed to wind down and stop thinking about this soon-to-be-proposal! Finally, he shut his eyes and drifted off to sleep.

DEVON PEERED out the window while standing in the middle of the bedroom of an old home. Large pieces of the ceiling dangled from above, and patches of the floor lifted beneath his feet. Yes, the home was definitely in bad shape. By the state of the inside, he could only imagine what the outside looked like. *I wonder who lives here?* Devon thought. As he stared outside, fluffy white clouds suddenly turned a dark, menacing mass that huddled together. To his surprise, they began charging towards him. Fear gripped him as lightning flashed in the sky, bringing with it a downpour. It was like no other storm he had ever seen.

"There's no way this house is gon make it through this storm," Devon whispered. Just as he uttered the words, the house began to shake. Claps of thunder echoed louder than applause after a home run in a baseball stadium. All around the room, items fell from their posts and shattered. When the desk slid and flipped over onto its back, he immediately grabbed the ledge of the windowsill. When a chair was knocked onto its side, he fell into a squat to sturdy his stance. The bed snapped in two, and each part slid against the door, barricading him in. Speedily, Devon whipped his other arm behind him on the window frame to keep from falling. Finally, when a mirror hanging nearby shattered into shards of glass, he searched around for cover. There was nowhere to go. His eyes zeroed in on a closet in the room—*my bedroom* —he realized. He made a dash for it, slamming the door behind him. Curling onto the floor, he ducked his face between his arms and knees. The closet door burst open from the storm but Devon was too afraid to get up and close it. The storm lasted for a long time, and he even wondered if it was more than one because it would stop and then, moments later, begin again. Yet even though the whole house rocked, miraculously, Devon didn't roll to the side or get tossed like the furniture. Instead, he remained pinned to the same spot. Eventually, the storm ceased, and he bravely peered outside the closet.

The image took his breath away. The sun shone a bright, beaming light through the window, illuminating a brand-new room. It was bathed in peace. The falling ceiling was now perfectly intact, and the walls were painted in a fresh turquoise, jubilant with hope and possibility. The floors gleamed, newly laid with a different substance entirely. They seemed to sparkle like 24 karat gold. Even the furniture had been replaced with stylish, modern pieces. In place of the broken bed sat a magnificent king-size, trimmed in shining mahogany, ready for its royal guest. Staring around in awe, Devon was unable to comprehend what he was seeing.

"I make all things new," a strong voice said, filling the room.

Devon startled awake, clutching his covers at his sides, perspiration dampening his forehead. As he peered into the darkness, the same message ricocheted in his rapidly beating heart:

"I make all things new," it said again.

Devon wondered what it meant.

———

"I feel sooo bad for Sheila, baby! She is so salty that she can't come," Jasmine said for the umpteenth time with a pout. The group stood in the airport decked out in sweats with only a few minutes until boarding. Unfortunately, Sheila wasn't with them. She had been nauseous since the night before, Jasmine explained. After shopping, she started feeling ill and headed home early to get some rest. "That's when her symptoms started," Jasmine informed.

"Dag. You think it was that hash, egg, and cheese sandwich she had at Brunch & Bro's?" Darion volunteered. "I was looking at that thing like, is it safe?"

The others all nodded with matching sullen looks.

Devon felt bad for Sheila, and maybe even for Antonio, since that was supposed to be his vacation bae, but he was also super pumped about his plan to discuss marriage with Jasmine. All morning he had rehearsed the conversation over and over and finally felt ready to propose.

"Bruh, you good?" Devon asked Antonio, referring to Sheila's absence.

Antonio smiled. "Ah fa sho." He bowed his head closer to Devon's and said in a low tone, "I already hit that man, so I'ma be on the prowl for some new ass."

Devon just shook his head. *Why am I not surprised.* He glanced at Jasmine, huddled in conversation with Kimberly. Now that things were lopsided, he wondered how their trip would play out.

The line began to move as their sections were called. Devon, Darion, and Antonio were originally supposed to sit together because they bought their flight tickets at the same time. Once the girls were added, Darion agreed to give up his seat to Jasmine so she could sit with Devon. They planned to keep that arrangement, except now Antonio and Darion would both be with Kimberly. She didn't seem to mind since the boys were going above and beyond to gain her attention. Each boy was cracking jokes and trying to one-up the other with stories from his childhood. Devon just rolled his eyes at their shenanigans.

"You see those two?" Jasmine murmured to Devon once they were seated on the plane. She nodded toward some seats a few rows ahead, where their friends were.

"Yeah, and I didn't even think Darion liked Kimberly all like that,"

Devon admitted. He laced his fingers between Jasmine's on their shared armrest beneath a light blue blanket.

"You know the male ego couldn't care less about being attracted when it comes to winning," Jasmine said frankly.

Even though Devon wanted to refute her statements and defend his brother, and possibly the male species, he couldn't.

"What podcasts you been listening to, Ms. Thomas?" he joked instead. "I know it ain't Michael Davis."

"Naw. He woulda said, 'The woman is there to bring division and contention between brothers and only plots to divert and distract men from the real purpose of their assignment of earthly conquest'." She had said it in a fake male voice and Devon laughed.

"Is he that bad?"

"That brotha is the most toxic example of toxic masculinity I've ever seen," she huffed. "I mean, it's one thing to be pro Black and pro men, but another to be anti-white and anti-woman." She had snatched her hand back and folded her arms when she spoke, causing the blanket covering them to slip.

"Well, what about the Black Girl Magic Movement. Or, more historically, the Feminist Movement? There's always negative extremes in any movement. Does that mean we need to throw the whole baby out with the bath water?" Devon said.

Jasmine rolled her eyes. "If there was a baby with this water, then no. But ain't no baby. Just injured, hurt men spitting injured jargon."

"Ohhh, jargon. Maybe you should switch your major to English, babe," Devon said to lighten the conversation. He took back her hand and re-braided their fingers together. There was no way Michael Davis was about to break up this relationship.

"Nah. You know I'm gonna be the dopest Black female filmmaker there ever was." Jasmine lifted her chin and smirked, softening some, but still strong on her Black feminist stance.

She looked so cute, Devon couldn't resist sneaking a quick peck on her lips, happy to have the row to themselves.

As he nestled by the window, Jasmine rested her face on his shoulder from the middle seat. It was their first trip together and

Devon's first trip to Cancun. There were so many firsts, and excitement, once again, grabbed his insides.

"Let's take a pic," Jasmine said, and before Devon could respond, she held her phone up for a selfie. After showing it to him, she hurried to post it before she lost service. They both looked a little tired but giddy in the photo, donning their matching school hoodies.

After the flight attendants went over their spiel about safety measures and made sure they were buckled in, Devon leaned back for the four-hour flight. It would be early in the day when they landed, so he figured he should get some rest. Suddenly, the plane began shaking from turbulence, and Devon remembered his dream. A weird feeling planted roots in the pit of his stomach, and he squeezed Jasmine's fingers.

"Babe, you ok? It's just a little turbulence," she said. She lifted her head to look at him.

"Yeah, umm, my bad." Devon loosened his grip with a nervous chuckle. Within a few minutes, the plane found its rhythm again, and the ride smoothed out.

It was just a dream, Devon told himself. For the life of him, he couldn't figure out why he didn't believe that it was.

———

"Yoooo!! This is DOPE!" Darion exclaimed when he opened the door to the beach house with Devon seconds behind. The inside view was just as impressive as the outside ocean waves. A wide-open layout with light tan hardwood floors, high ceilings, and sunlight streaming in through glass doors to the deck met them upon entry. The rest of the group barged in after the brothers, eager to explore. To the left was the kitchen, all stainless steels and marble countertops. Stocked with every appliance imaginable, the owners had spared no expense. Devon took special note of the top-tier Keurig coffee maker. He breathed a sigh of relief that he wouldn't have to succumb to the instant stuff he had packed.

"Damnnn. They got it fully *loaded!*" Antonio raved. He was shouting from the walk-in pantry, so Devon hurried to his side. The space was wall-to-wall with all types of treats, including several bottles of white *and* dark liquor.

"Nice!" Devon said.

"We 'bout to get *lit*!" Antonio shrieked with glee.

The others dove deeper into the space, and Devon grabbed the suitcases near Jasmine. The couple passed a wine cooler built into the front of the sink that held beer and more wine, before trailing Kimberly onto the second floor.

"I got this room!" Kimberly called. Since her roommate was sick, she'd have the luxury of a queen-size bed all to herself. She was only five feet tall, so the extra space was like a Barbie dream house. Darion shouted from the first floor that he was claiming the only bedroom downstairs. Antonio bounded up to the bonus room on the second floor, whizzing by Devon and Jasmine.

"Man, y'all bout to see it *all* cuz I sleep in the nude!" he announced, throwing his head back and laughing like a madman. Both his hands strangled the rafters.

Devon and Jasmine kept moving past the bonus room until they reached a bedroom tucked into the furthest part of the house. This one held the only king bed with grey and white decor along with splashes of yellow and turquoise accents. The pearl-white walls perfectly complemented the pop of color, balancing the room's mood. Little candles with an "ocean" scent were scattered throughout, and a glossy wide-screen TV was mounted on the wall across from the bed. It also held a private bathroom off to the side, an added luxury. They'd barely have to leave the room if they didn't want to.

Jasmine turned and looked at Devon with a stealthy expression. "You thinking what I'm thinking?"

"That I'm hiding out at night so I don't see Antonio butt naked?"

Jasmine tossed her head back and laughed. Then she slipped off her Cool Grey 11's and hopped onto the bed. Devon grinned and did the same.

"We on vacation!!!" They both screamed, jumping up and down.

Darion appeared in the doorway and folded his arms, "Y'all are some straight fools!" he chided, then pulled out his phone to record them.

"We need to do shots!" Antonio shouted, and everybody hurried to the kitchen. He already had a huge bottle of Hennessy in his grip.

"I found the glasses!" Darion announced, pulling several out of a nearby cabinet.

"Yo, son. Take it easy. I promised Mom and Dad I would look after you." Technically, he was the only one under the legal drinking age, and Devon didn't want him to overindulge.

"Dev, don't do me like that. We turnin' up! Now, where's the music?" Darion asked. Kimberly whipped out a speaker from one of her bags. "Yes! I knew you was the dependable type," Darion chirped, winking at her.

Devon just shook his head.

"Kimberly, to you, for making this whole trip unforgettable." Antonio jumped in and handed Kimberly the first shot glass filled with brown liquor. She beamed, her short lashes fluttering.

My boys are fried, Devon thought, watching the two fight for Kimberly's attention. The girl was clearly soaking it all up.

Jasmine made eye contact with Devon, and her humorous expression confirmed what he suspected. It wasn't that Kimberly was ugly; it was just that Jasmine's body always seemed like it deserved a round of applause. Then, Sheila's always looked like it belonged on a poster. Kimberly was more of a quiet soul, and that spirit got lost in the rowdiness of their generation. In some ways, Devon felt like he could relate to her. Even in more ways than he related to Jasmine, since they were so different.

The party started that afternoon around 2 pm, with the music being amped up and shots being taken until someone suggested they grab food and hit the beach. High on adrenaline and liquor, Devon moseyed up the stairs to change. His mind finally felt at ease; the weight of academia and his pending future had sailed away into an exhilarating bliss. While in the bathroom, he was enjoying his momentary solitude, but just as he was sliding on his trunks, Jasmine popped in.

"Babe, I'm not done!" Bent over with his trunks only halfway up, he laughed. Then his jaw fell. As Jasmine twirled in a two-piece that looked more like a half-piece, a whistle escaped Devon's lips. Her curves popped ferociously in a bright orange number that squeezed all the right places.

"Wait 'til you see what I brought for tonight." She winked seductively, then shut the door in his face.

Devon hurried to pull up his trunks.

Damn. This girl gon give me a heart attack. He chuckled, but then thought, *At least I'll die happy.*

Once changed, Devon caught a glimpse in the mirror. His reflection was glowing. Toasted almond skin drew tautly over an almost four-pack thrusting against his abdomen. Wide broad shoulders exuded strength and solidity. Youth pulsed through every pore, smoothing his skin like a newborn's. He looked *happy.*

You doing it, boy, he said to himself.

It was rare for Devon to appreciate his own physique. That was more of his brother's style. Once again, Jasmine was rubbing off on him. Her confidence, her charisma, her charm, were becoming his. While thinking about her, Devon pulled out his cell phone and took another look at the picture of the ring he had selected. It was perfect. Earlier, when they were figuring out their plans, he found a moment alone with Kimberly to tell her he needed Jasmine's ring size. Her eyes had widened with excitement when he showed her the picture. Kimberly promised to help with the engagement and wished him luck. That was all he needed. If Devon ordered the ring tonight, it could be delivered by the time they were back at school. He was so certain about this next step that he decided to use half of his savings for it. His entrepreneurial instincts had kicked into high gear, and that risk-taking element of his nature was in full throttle. Yet this was no risk. There was no doubt Jasmine was the one. His only regret was that he wouldn't have the ring with his proposal. Still, in the end, that didn't matter. Devon would have the woman he was going to marry in his arms, and that's what mattered the most.

FIVE
YOU WIT' IT I'M WIT' IT

THREE DAYS IN A FABULOUS BEACH HOUSE OVERLOOKING WHITE, SANDY beaches and the crystal-clear waves of the Caribbean Sea was anybody's dream come true. Especially a group of young adults with no supervision and ample resources to enjoy every excursion. The crew went jet skiing, parasailing, and, yes, swam with the dolphins. Devon's eyes stretched beneath his goggles as the mammoth, sleek creatures sailed by. He'd reached out a hand, and, to his stark amazement, was able to touch one! It was like experiencing creation on a whole other level. His heart was full. The evenings were complete with dancing and playing games. Spades was a definite contender as Antonio was the king, but he borderline resembled a Nazi when it came to anyone reneging.

"Bruh, it's a game," Devon told him one too many times. His friend's eyes remained wild when he slapped a card on the table that he believed would win.

"Yo, son. To *you*, it's a game. To me and mine, it's *war!*"

Very rarely did they watch TV or do anything they could do at home, other than Spades, but even that was way more fun since there were so many of them. If anything, the beach became their best friend. Devon could already see his nut-brown skin turn a muddy brown, and

Jasmine was rocking a more espresso look herself. It took his breath away when he noticed it in pictures.

She looks like a goddess, he thought.

At some point, it became obvious Kimberly had chosen Darion. Devon passed by one night and caught them boo'd up on the bright yellow couch in the living room.

"Ok, D," Devon said, giving him props. "I see you."

Darion looked up and half-smiled with his arm around Kimberly. "I do what I can," he replied in his normal cocky manner.

Antonio didn't seem too perturbed by his loss. He popped out his vape and came home that night with twins. They were heard carousing on the deck and eventually in the bonus room 'til well after 3 am. Devon had to give it to Antonio; he was never down and out. It was one of the things he loved about him. No matter what life brought, his boy stayed with a positive outlook. His grades were trash, "I'll switch my major," was the response. His girl dumped him, "They like buses, another one comin'," he chirped. Even when he got hit with the loss of his favorite uncle, and Devon took the trip with him to Cleveland for the funeral, Antonio demonstrated unparalleled leadership. He handled the arrangements and was the shoulder for his father and aunt to lean on. "They not gon be able to do it, man," he had said to Devon, his voice cracking. That's what had really won Devon over. He suspected that Antonio's constant boasting and bragging were really covering a softer side of him, one he protected fiercely. Since he had chosen to let Devon in on that side, Devon counted it an honor and treasured their friendship all the more. It was for that reason that Devon decided to have both Antonio and Darion be his best men. Though Antonio would understand him choosing Darion, Devon wanted him to know that blood wasn't always thicker than water. There was room for both.

Devon's musings came to a halt when Jasmine slid a hand onto his shoulder and squeezed it. During his reverie, he was lounging in the chair, mindlessly staring at social media. He peered up, then smiled, "Sit down," and motioned for her to sit on his lap.

"No, sir. I gotta help Darion cook, remember?" Jasmine gave him a brief kiss before her hips swayed towards the kitchen. Devon allowed his eyes to linger longer than necessary.

"Y'all wanna do the bonfire tonight?" Kimberly suggested, scrolling through her phone. They had been talking about using the bonfire beneath the deck that was set up with large rocks and an ample supply of firewood, but hadn't made any moves. The owners of the home were definitely getting a five-star rating for their stellar setup and A-1 instructions on the local food stores, activities, and nearest shopping plaza.

Everyone agreed it was time for the bonfire. That's when Devon knew it was also time for his special question. Kimberly had come through with the ring size and the ring was due to be shipped next Wednesday, as Devon suspected.

Anticipating the evening ahead, gnats nibbled Devon's insides. Nervously, he watched Jasmine cook with Darion in the kitchen. The two were voted the best cooks of the house and each night, prepared a scrumptious meal for the group.

Devon caught Kimberly's eye, seated near him on the couch. "I'm doing it tonight," he whispered.

Her brown eyes widened in a mixture of pleasure and surprise. "You got this," she whispered back.

Antonio, rooted by the patio doors, glanced up from his phone. "What y'all talking about?"

"You'll see," Devon said. He wanted it to be a surprise. He could just imagine how tripped out everyone would be. His gaze drifted back to Jasmine. She looked sexy in a domestic sort of way, barefoot in an apron tied over jean shorts and a white midriff top. Devon wanted to give her some type of heads-up, though, figuring they would take pictures after the proposal. He was sure to get an earful if she didn't look her best. When they returned to their room to get dressed for dinner, he made sure to suggest her outfit.

"Baby, you should wear that yellow dress you brought with you."

"I was thinking about that dress," Jasmine murmured. "I guess I'll take that as a sign."

Standing near their bed, she turned to him and locked both arms around his neck. Devon snuck a kiss and then stared into her doe eyes.

He forced a lump down his throat and swatted away the hesitation snowballing in his gut. Finally, he whispered, "You know I love you, right?"

There. He had said it. It was the first time, but the words flowed because they had been brewing in his heart like a bag of Expresso roast, for a while.

Jasmine lowered her gaze and nodded quietly. Devon lifted her chin.

"It's ok if you not ready to say it back. I know how you feel." To reaffirm his words, he stroked her lower back.

"I do—I do *love* you. I just…" she trailed, her voice catching.

"You just what, baby?" Jasmine teased her bottom lip with her top teeth, dancing a little in her bare feet. After her hesitancy, he added, "You can tell me anything."

"Sometimes you just feel too good to be true," she whispered, her eyes still stuck to the floor.

Devon squeezed her by the waist, making his forehead kiss hers. "I feel the same way," he said softly.

They stood like that for a while, in each other's arms, until a hard knock interrupted them.

"Y'all comin' or what?" His brother yelled on the other side. "We tryna' eat!"

Devon sighed. *This boy know how to ruin a moment.*

"Yeah, we comin'!" he answered before releasing Jasmine and leaving the room so she could get dressed. Devon had landed on a button-down, short-sleeved, white-collar shirt over a white T, with dark blue khaki shorts and white sneakers. His favorite cologne was the final touch.

At the dinner table, his friends were already seated but stopped their chatter to look at him.

"Where yo other half?" Darion was the first to ask. Right when the words left his mouth, the door from their bedroom opened.

Devon, now at the bottom of the steps, turned to look up at her. Everyone fell into a hush until Antonio whistled.

"Dammnnn, Jas, you tryna kill 'em huh?"

Jasmine emerged wearing a see-through yellow material that

draped over her dark brown skin like satin. Every time she stepped in her white open-toe heels, a near-hip-high slit on the side revealed a plump thigh, teasing her onlookers. The dress was strapless, the tops of her cleavage bare and bouncing with joy.

Devon's heart nearly stopped. *Straight goddess,* he thought. He reached for her hand like a knight to a queen. When taking his hand, Jasmine batted her thick black lashes, uncharacteristically shy in the moment. Her hair was swooped up in a bundle of tiny ringlet curls still damp from her shower. As she stood near him, the whiff of something delectable called to Devon like the sirens in Greek mythology. He was under her spell.

"Y'all were waiting for me?" she asked, sounding oblivious to all the attention.

"Woman, if you don't sit yo ass down so we can eat," Antonio said. This seemed to snap everyone out of their trance. Soon they were passing plates and stuffing their faces. The dinner was filled with light chit chat, and someone suggested they go skydiving tomorrow.

"*That* ain't happenin'." Darion shut that all the way down. "I'm coming home with *all* my pieces intact!"

"Yeah, I'm scared of heights," Kimberly cosigned timidly.

"I wish Sheila was here," Jasmine said, not for the first time. "She would definitely be down. I talked to her earlier, and she's still super sick. But she's hoping to be good enough to catch a flight in a day or two. She said she'll keep us posted."

The group nodded, and the conversation shifted back to what they wanted to do the next day. As he thought about the proposal, Devon's stomach flip-flopped. It was now or never. What better way to get engaged than on a tropical beach with his dearest friends? Peering around the table, he realized these *were* his dearest. Jasmine's dearest were now his dearest. Suddenly, he wanted to make sure his people knew how important they were to him and include them in this moment. Devon cleared his throat.

"Y'all, excuse me."

Four gazes landed on him.

"Let's toast," he said, holding up a stemless glass of white wine. Everyone lifted their glasses in obedience.

"What we toasting to, bro?" Darion asked.

Devon smiled. "To life. May it keep topping this moment."

"Here, here!" Antonio cheered, banging his fist on the glass table as everyone clinked glasses.

Dinner was followed by more wine and cocktails while Antonio passed the vape to anyone brave enough to take a hit. When the group was feeling toasty, they drifted out to the already stoked bonfire Darion had started.

"Guess the Boy Scouts Mom made us join paid off, huh?" Devon teased, slapping a hand on Darion's back.

It was a perfect evening, not too warm, and the fire was soothing. Devon grabbed Jasmine's hand and led her to one of the white wooden chairs available.

"You look amazing," he whispered in her ear before planting her down on top of him.

"Thank you," she said and kissed him lightly. She then turned to Kimberly, who was seated to their right, to get the tea on her and Darion.

Devon waited for everyone to get comfortable and for the chatter to simmer. When Antonio was good and high, and his brother was leaning back in his chair with his hands loosely grasping Kimberly's, he told Jasmine to slide over so he could stand.

"D, can you turn the music down?"

Ella Mai crooned from Kimberly's Bluetooth and, though she was a dope singer, Devon didn't want that to be the focus. After his brother complied, he cleared his throat and turned to Jasmine.

"Jas, can you stand for a sec?"

Looking at him curiously, Jasmine rose to her feet, smoothing her dress in the process. Her feet were now bare, and her hot pink toes sparkled in the dark evening. Devon walked over to her, barefoot as well, and grabbed one of her hands before kneeling on the sand.

"Aww, shoot!" someone whispered, but Devon couldn't tell who it was.

"My whole life, I had a plan," he started, looking up at Jasmine. He paused to swallow the lump in his throat. The moon and stars shone brightly, the waves sang like a heavenly choir, and the flickers from the bonfire clapped eagerly. It seemed all of creation was rejoicing at this moment.

"But until we met, the romantic part of my life was a mystery. I knew I would be an entrepreneur. I knew I would go to college. I hoped that one day I would get married. Then, after meeting you at the 'Black Student Meet N' Greet', that hope became definitive."

Devon ignored the chuckles and stayed focused. He stared into Jasmine's eyes with intentionality and clarity. He wanted her to know how sure he was of this request. He'd never been more sure of anything in his life. As their gazes met, he saw the tears. He saw the fear, too. To calm her, he stroked her hand, forcing his own sense of peace into her skin. He hoped to rub away any doubt.

"As long as we're together, remember?" Devon stated, and Jasmine nodded quickly, though her hand started to tremble.

"I don't want to take my next steps in life without you taking them with me, Jasmine Thomas. Will you marry me?"

The night grew quieter as Devon waited, breathless, staring at his love. Time stood still. Only the ocean spoke. Until finally, Jasmine did too.

Tears slid down her face as her head bobbed up and down, before she whispered, "Yes. Yes, I will."

Immediately, Devon was on his feet, holding her in his arms, rocking and squeezing from joy. Distant cheers rang in his ears, and after a moment, hands were patting his back.

"You did it!" Darion said, beaming as they embraced.

"Congratulations!" Kimberly gushed, and he hugged her too.

Darion found a bottle of champagne and popped it open.

"Baby, I don't wanna be tacky but..." Jasmine looked at Devon bashfully.

He laughed, pulling her to him. "The ring is comin' next week."

"Ok." She giggled with relief.

"I gotta tell Sheila!" Jasmine then half-screamed, waving her hand in the air. "Where's my phone?"

While Kimberly helped her grope for it in the semi-darkness, Devon's eyes searched until he found his friend off to the side. Instead of being met with Antonio's trademark grin, however, his boy only stared. Devon frowned. Then, casually, Antonio lifted his chin in acknowledgment before puffing from his vape. Still, the same somber expression remained in his eyes.

An uncomfortable sensation swarmed Devon's midsection. *Hmm. What's up with that?* he wondered. Before he could speak out, Jasmine had Sheila on video chat and shoved the phone in his face.

"Girl, I'm engaged!" she screeched, jumping up and down.

Sheila went on a rant about not being there. "Devon, how could you propose and not tell me?! Oohhh, you gon get it when we get back to school!"

"Aww, sis, I really wanted to surprise Jas, and I know you're her bestie. I knew you would leak it. My bad tho, foreal!"

"Ugh. You ain't right. You owe me, Devon. I'm the whole reason y'all met! If it wasn't for me, she wouldn't have been in the food line for hamburgers at the Meet N' Greet. The girl wanted tacos." Sheila wouldn't let him off so easily.

Devon said, "I know. You right. You right. Jas has told me a million times you were the one who wanted a hamburger. That's why y'all was right in front of us when we went to get food. Look. I'm a shout you out on social media when we post the engagement. I'ma give you mad props. I promise!"

"Well, I *guess* that'll work. Make sure you let 'em know. My girl is engaged because of *me!*"

Devon and Jasmine both laughed before ending the call and hurrying inside to take pictures. Darion was the photographer as Devon and Jasmine posed in the living room, then at the top of the stairs, then in front of the glass doors by the patio.

"Baby, I'm so glad you told me to wear this dress!" Jasmine squealed in between one of their shots.

Devon smirked, "Your man knows you," and leaned in for a kiss.

"Got it!" Darion yelled.

Devon laughed. He couldn't have been happier than at that moment. Except, when he and Jasmine went downstairs to take pictures with everyone, the disconcerting feeling from earlier reemerged.

"Smile on three!" Darion called, holding his arm out for a group selfie. When Devon examined the photo, he noticed that Antonio seemed to barely hold a smile. His eyes were so low that a crowbar could pry them open.

"Now another one with different poses!" Darion commanded. Everyone held out arms and did silly faces, but Antonio only gave a lazy grin. He was standing slightly distant from the group as well. Devon sighed inwardly but tried to keep his outward expression joyful.

He's probably just high, he told himself, shrugging it off. *I'll talk to him tomorrow.*

After all the commotion, Devon glanced down at Jasmine in his arms, bouncing around in his lap and commenting on all of the posts. They were cuddled in the larger stuffed chair in the dining room, which he had invited her to sit in earlier. *Finally,* he thought. He leaned back and stroked her arm. While lying on her side with her phone in her hand, she had her legs tucked beneath her. Devon had never seen her so happy. He didn't think he could be happier in his entire life if he tried.

———

It was after 11 am when Jasmine and Devon woke up. She'd kept him up all night, *thanking* him for the proposal.

"Shoot. If I would have known you was gon thank me like that, I would have proposed a long time ago!" he teased.

As they lay sprawled on the silky-smooth sheets of the king-sized bed, Devon *felt* like a King. The morning sun was shining through sheer grey curtains, as a smile sat on his lips. He looked at Jasmine, naked and unashamed. She was extraordinary. Any artist would agree that she was a masterpiece. Every curve seemed to flow seamlessly into a new curve, like a never-ending stream. Devon hadn't thought that his love for her could grow, but his heart was bursting just at the thought of becoming man and wife. *I'm engaged*! From this day forward, the vision of Jasmine Thomas would shimmer before him for the rest of his life. The impact of this revelation, coupled with being so close to her, bombarded him. Spooning her, he grabbed her waist beneath the sheet and pulled her closer, but she flipped over to face him and stuck her phone in his face.

"Babe, we got like 600 likes on this one post," Jasmine exclaimed.

"Why I need to look at that when I got the real thing?" Devon murmured, pinning her arm down to bite her neck. He had other ideas. She laughed lightly.

"Right. I know you better know what you got!"

"Oh, I do." He felt aroused again, but a loud knock at the door disturbed his probing tongue.

"Y'all love birds want breakfast?" Darion called.

Knowing this was a one-time offer, Devon hurriedly answered, "Yes!"

"Guess that's our cue," Jasmine said and flung away the sheets. She stood in her glory, walked straight to the bathroom, then turned back around.

"You comin'?" Her eyes dared him as she tilted her head with a hand on one hip.

Accepting the dare, Devon cheesed. "Yep."

After the couple showered, they dressed—Devon in a dark green Ralph Polo T and khaki shorts and Jasmine in an oversized jean t-shirt dress—then made their way down to breakfast.

"Morning!" Kimberly greeted them when they appeared. Everyone was dressed for the day, inhaling the eggs, toast, and grits that Darion had whipped up. Well, almost everyone.

"Where's Antonio?" Devon asked his brother, hitting the Keurig to start his coffee. His gaze flew to the bonus room, but he couldn't see much from his vantage point.

Darion shrugged. "I guess he still out cuz he ain't respond when I called him for breakfast."

"Alright. I'll save him a plate."

As they ate, the girls discussed their plans to explore the shopping plaza. The only history buff in the group, Darion, was bent on taking a tour to see the Mayan ruins. He'd basically be on his own.

"Spend the afternoon looking at old mountains and artifacts?" Kimberly said, her face scrunched up.

"Ugh, right. *After* a two-hour bus trip *just* to get there?" Jasmine added, looking unconvinced.

"Y'all don't know what y'all missin'!" Darion belted, grits flying from his mouth.

Normally, Devon would have tagged along with his brother for support, but he felt this nagging need to connect with Antonio. "I think I'ma chill here for a little, maybe hit the beach," he said, then took a hefty sip of his coffee. *Thank God for Keurigs.*

"You sure, babe? I can hit the beach with you if you want," Jasmine offered, rubbing his thigh beneath the table.

"Naw, it's cool. I'ma hang with Antonio for a bit."

With that, the crew began to disperse. Jasmine kissed Devon lovingly on the lips. "I'll text when we're on our way back."

Anxiety gripped him immediately at the thought of letting her out of his sight. Devon had to remind himself she was a grown woman, fully capable of navigating a foreign country. Plus, she had Kimberly. Before Darion left, the same apprehensions surfaced. Devon had been responsible for this boy for as long as he could remember.

"Be safe, D."

Darion laughed. "Bruh, I already texted you the info for the tour. I'm 'bout to catch my rideshare, and I'll be back in a few hours. *Chill!*"

In the wake of his friends leaving, Devon decided to hang out on the deck and check emails while enjoying his second cup of coffee. He was still waiting for some of his grades to come in, but his eyes lit up when he saw that he had, in fact, aced his Econ exam.

She was right, he thought, flashing back to Jasmine's statement about him always doing well.

Then his eyes fell on an email from Professor Marx.

Devon, please let me know when you're available for a chat. There's an important matter we need to discuss in person as soon as you're back on campus. Talk to you soon. -Marx

Hmm, maybe he wants to run his classroom prep for next month by me, Devon wondered. He typed a quick response, then sat pondering what the discussion could possibly be in reference to. He came up empty. Moments later, while checking more emails, Devon was still brooding over the mysterious request from Marx when a presence behind him caused his back to stiffen.

"Sup," Antonio greeted. Shirtless with several tattoos etched on his chest and upper arm, he leaned against the open patio, smoking from his vape. He looked tired, and even, a little sad.

Devon's heart squeezed. "Sup, man. Late night?" Removing his laptop from the chair next to him, he indicated for Antonio to sit.

"Yeah, I guess." Antonio took another hit of his vape while falling back into the white patio chair.

Devon waited a beat, then glanced over. "You got something you wanna say?" he asked flat out. It was one thing for Antonio to be surprised by the engagement, but quite another to not even acknowledge it.

"Naw, man. I'm just chillin'." Antonio shrugged, staring out at the ocean.

"You just chillin'? You ain't said a thing to me since I proposed to Jas."

"Bruh, I ain't *seen* you."

"You seen me last night. You didn't even say congratulations." Devon couldn't smother the hurt in his voice.

Antonio shook a leg, then took another hit of his vape. "I'm worried, ok. I'm worried for you," he finally said.

Devon turned his body to face his friend. "Worried about what?"

For the first time, Antonio looked him in the eyes. "Jas isn't who you think she is," he said darkly.

"Bruh. You been with me for three years. You been my dawg, second to my brother. I'm 'bout to make you my best man, and you comin' for my girl?"

Antonio huffed a sigh and slouched further in his chair. "I just don't want to see you get hurt."

For the first time that morning, he sounded more concerned for Devon than himself. It was clear that he was being sincere. His eyes seemed more alert than they had in days as he searched Devon's face with a pleading expression.

Devon softened. "Look. I appreciate the concern. I really do. But Jasmine loves me. And I love her." He paused. "Bro. I'm getting *married!*" Devon couldn't hold back his smile. "You know what that means? It means my whole life is about to change!"

Antonio nodded, but concern still stained his expression. "I know. And I'm happy you happy," was all he said.

They sat for a moment until he added, "You deadass? You 'bout to make me your best man?" His voice was laced with shock. "What about Darion?"

"I'm a have y'all *both* be my best men," Devon explained. "I'ma have two. Just like on *Martin*." Devon figured mentioning Antonio's favorite throwback TV show would bring a smile to his face.

"Wow. That's crazy, man. But you know Cole wasn't in the wedding episode. Martin ended up choosing Tommie."

Devon laughed. "Yeah. You right. But in real life, he would have chosen both."

That won him all the way over, and Antonio grinned. "Hey, if you wit it, I'm wit it," he added.

"I love you like a brother, man." Devon stood and held out his arms.

Antonio wasn't the touchy-feely type and just looked at him.

Devon switched it up. He stuck out his hand for their handshake, and Antonio smiled while giving him two slaps, one dap, and one fist bump.

"I love you too, man," he said when they were done.

Finally, the angst settled in Devon's stomach, but just when he was about to sit back down, his phone rang.

"Aye. Let me get this. It's my parents. I saved you a plate in the kitchen," Devon shared, already picking up the line.

As Antonio left, the picture on Devon's phone from the video call formed. He hit the accept button, and his mother's image popped in. The corners of her mouth sagged, and her eyes were red, like she had been crying. She blinked away newly formed tears while biting her lower lip.

Devon's heartbeat sped up.

"Ma, what's wrong?"

"It's your dad. He's hurt. I need you to come home."

SIX
EVERYTHING'S GOING
TO BE ALRIGHT

After his brother returned from the Mayan Ruins, Devon filled him in. "Dad broke his leg and was rushed to the hospital. They have him bandaged and stable, but he fell off a ladder trying to install some new windows at Jack & Jill."

"*What*? Why he always tryna do that stuff himself?" was Darion's immediate response. "He should have called Uncle James."

"Right. That's what I said," Devon replied while throwing clothes into his suitcase. "But you know him and Uncle James be beefin' sometimes. I guess this is one of them times." He shrugged, then zipped his suitcase on top of the king-size bed.

"I'm coming' wit' you," Darion said.

"No. It's cool. Dad's ok. They just need me to run Jack & Jill for a few days. He'll be on his feet in no time. Well, maybe not fully, but you know, Dad. He ain't 'bout to be out of work for too long." Devon sealed his gym bag and started looking for his hairbrush.

Jasmine offered to come too. "So I can meet my new in-laws!" she bubbled.

That was a whole other topic that Devon wasn't ready to tackle. He needed to at least give his parents a heads-up about the engagement before dropping a whole daughter-in-law into their laps.

Devon turned to her eager eyes. "Baby, I appreciate that. But I need to just handle business first, and then we can plan a proper meeting with them." He balled up both of her hands and kissed her knuckles. She nodded glumly in response.

The next morning, bright and early, Devon was on a plane headed home. Once again, he had a window seat, but now he was sharing the row with two strangers. A little girl was half asleep in between him and a woman who stroked her hair with a protective hand. He assumed she was her mother. Heartstrings pulled at him.

That could be our daughter someday.

The thought made Devon smile and snuggled with him beneath the blanket he was using to fight off the draft in the airplane cabin.

It seemed that the flight home was faster than getting there, not just because the landing was at JFK instead of Morrison, but because traveling home always seemed to be faster than arriving at a destination.

Turbulence hit again upon landing, which jerked Devon awake from his awkward nap. He banged his head slightly against the window.

"Ouch."

While rubbing his head, he heard, "It's ok. We're landing now." The little girl who was previously asleep when he had dozed off had spoken.

Devon peered down at her beautiful brown face. *Comforted by a five-year-old.* He laughed to himself.

Her mother said, "Honey, he knows," while patting the child's shoulder. She caught eyes with Devon and mouthed, "Sorry."

But Devon was smitten and said, "You're right. We are landing now, and everything's going to be alright."

Just after the words left his mouth, a strange sensation swirled in his gut. The statement seemed to carry weight, as if Devon was talking about more than just the flight.

Hmm. Maybe I'm just trippin' because Dad's injured, he thought, and pushed away the odd experience.

As soon as Devon got service again, the texts rolled through.

Jasmine:

Baby, let me know when you make it.

Darion:

Bruh, you there yet?

Mom:

Honey, we're outside circling the lot. Just call
when you're ready.

When he reached baggage claim and swooped his luggage, before Devon could even dial, his mom's name flashed on his phone screen.

"Ma, I was just about to call you," Devon said, a little irritated. "I'ma be out in a sec."

"Ok. We're at Lot A. We can't get any closer." Mrs. Woods sounded stressed and apologetic.

"Alright. I'm comin'." Devon hung up, his irritation melting into a smile. For some reason, his mother was adamant that she would meet him at the airport in a rideshare, a completely unnecessary act.

Maybe she needs to see me, he thought, but the thought made him uneasy.

Devon's parents had been the most solid foundation of Devon's entire existence. It was hard to picture his mother as anything but a steeled, strong-armed, GOAT. Married thirty years and still in love, the Woods were a shining example of true commitment, partnership, and loyalty. They set a high bar for what Devon's own marital partnership should look like. Though Mrs. Woods was extremely intelligent, having practiced medicine at The Brooklyn Hospital Center for nearly 20 years as a pediatrician, in a sense, she laid down her career for his father's. She was the main breadwinner for much of Devon and Darion's childhood, funding the family as their father struggled to launch a sustainable business. It was one idea after another until finally they founded a soul food restaurant that did rather well for several years in Harlem. That is, until gentrification reared its ugly head and drove their customers out of the city. This, in turn, affected their revenue.

That's when they switched to Fort Greene and opened Jack & Jill. The area was still tainted by the new wave of middle-class white residents, but not as many. Plus, everyone loved breakfast. Additionally, the Woods ensured the menu included traditional Western options, not just an ethnic niche, as the previous restaurant had. Changing their business model had ensured success.

Growing up, Devon loved watching his parents' team effort, but as he got older, he became privy to the behind-the-scenes sacrifices. As far as he was concerned, his mom was a straight "G." Mrs. Woods believed in his father in a way that Devon desired for his one-day wife to believe in him. Enough to sacrifice her days and nights working while he invested her hard-earned money into one dream after another. Devon understood that his mother believed in his father because she perceived that the long-term goal would reap a generational inheritance that would surpass their own lives. Hence, the family business *had* to continue. His parents had sacrificed too much for it not to. Guilt stained Devon's heart as he walked swiftly. He had to find a way to stay. New York was famous for being a hub for artists and creatives. *Maybe Jas will be open to staying in NYC, at least for a little while.* It would be a bona fide miracle for Jasmine to change her mind, yet Devon wholeheartedly felt that she believed in him the same way that his mom believed in his dad.

Gripping his luggage tighter, he thought, *She would do it for me.*

While maneuvering the airport crowd, a vision of his fiancée floated in Devon's mind, and a new sense of purpose embraced his heart. He was engaged! That meant he wasn't just living his life for *his* dream; he now had someone else's dream to live for. It would be the same for Jasmine. They would work as a team to figure it out, just like his parents had. As Devon's legs pumped through the swarm of travelers, the noisy environment was like a sweet melody to his ears. The muscle memory of his body effortlessly took hold as his long strides matched the other travelers in perfect rhythm. It was undeniable that NYC was home. Devon was made to hustle and bustle. He was made to be on the grind. Even though Morrison University was in the same state, the vibe was different. The city was the city, and Devon had been born and bred for it.

When his canvas sneakers kissed the damp, dirty pavement and he inhaled the smoke and smog, Devon's lungs seemed to rejoice. *Home!* Though he tried to make it back during breaks and even certain weekends when he was needed at the restaurant, homesickness never seemed to be at bay.

While trekking to Lot A as the cabs and people sped by, and enjoying the feel of the NYC pavement beneath him, a nagging thought crept into the corner of Devon's mind.

L.A. isn't New York.

His previous concern about the future flared up again, but Devon didn't have time to unpack the thought. Just a few feet ahead, his mom's slender brown shape was hanging outside the back of a black Toyota Camry. Waving frantically, he could hear her over the boisterous racket, shouting.

"Devon!"

A humorous smile split Devon's lips. Leave it to his mother to announce his arrival to the world. As if at all humanly possible, he sped up his pace.

"Baby, you made it!"

Carla Woods, draped in a long grey cardigan over a pearl shirt, was no longer hanging out the window but had flung the back door open and stood with arms outstretched. The driver, a young Asian man, swiftly grabbed Devon's bags and started loading them into his vehicle.

"Hey, Momma." Devon sank into his mother's arms and leaned into her small frame. It wasn't until that moment that he realized how much he had missed her. Devon had always been closer to his mother and Darion to his dad, and Debra was no doubt babied by both. She was a "surprise" and the only girl, so by the time she came around, she was pretty much treated like an only child. At least, that's how the boys felt. Still, no one harbored any sibling jealousy in the way that other siblings did because the Woods seemed to have a harmonious balance in their household. Everyone knew their place, and even the additional intimacy the children individually experienced with their parents wasn't an indication of more love; it was more so a reflection of their roles.

Everyone knew that, though Devon was more sensitive and emotionally intelligent like his mother, he had inherited his keen business savvy from his father. And though Darion's personality was rowdy and outgoing, like their father's, his calculated mind, bent towards engineering, was a reflection of their mother's medical astuteness. All of the Woods kids were attractive and intelligent, but they were good-looking and intelligent in their own way. That meant there was never competition because everyone had something different to bring to the table. Devon sometimes did feel closer to Darion because they were closer in age, and he was a miniature replica of himself. Regardless of that similarity, Darion didn't shrink in any way that Devon sometimes did. Instead, he flaunted every aspect of himself, confident in any environment, even at just 20 years of age. It was a quality Devon admired but would never admit to his little brother.

Standing outside the cool morning air, Devon peered into his mother's grey-brown eyes that only his sister had the luxury of inheriting.

"I missed you," he said honestly, and tears moistened her eyes.

"Thank you for coming. Get in," she said, releasing him and hopping inside before pulling him in along with her.

The ride to Brooklyn Heights was filled with Mrs. Woods updating Devon on his father's progress. Theodore, aka "Teddy," Woods, was currently holed up in their bedroom with a cast on his leg and working feverishly on his laptop.

"I tried hiding it, but somehow he got his big behind out of the bed and searched it out, so I gave up." His mother shrugged her delicate shoulders when referring to the laptop. "You know that man is not about to sit around for no six weeks like the doctors are saying." She shook her sleek strands of hair, perfectly coiffed into an elegant French roll.

Devon agreed. "I know. I figure he'll be at the restaurant some kind of way by next week. Why was he trying to replace the windows himself anyways?" He made a face.

"You know your dad is frugal, and he is not about to hire anybody to do a job he could do on his own. And of course, he and Uncle James aren't speaking right now, so *that* was out of the question..." She swatted the air in defeat.

"What about Reggie? He couldn't have helped?" Reggie was Devon's father's cousin and cooked for the restaurant. Sometimes he did odd jobs when his dad needed him to.

"Reggie was on vacation when your dad was trying to get it done, and I guess he couldn't wait for the man to fly back from Florida," Mrs. Woods huffed, then let out a sigh. "I'm just glad he's ok." She paused while nibbling on her lower lip. "He gave me a scare."

Devon reached over and gripped his mother's hand. She smiled, wiping away a tear with the other.

"But you're here now. So everything's going to be alright," she said, and when she did, it jarred him. Because that was the second time that message had come within an hour, and Devon was starting to believe it actually meant something.

––––––––

ONCE THEY ARRIVED at the four-bedroom, posh, red brick brownstone, Devon didn't waste any time racing up the stairs to his father.

"Pops, you tryna leave me the restaurant a little early, ain't you?" He stood shadowing his parents' doorway.

"I'm sorry you had to come all this way, son," Mr. Woods responded with his cast-clothed leg propped high on several fluffy pillows. When shifting his body toward the door a little too quickly, he grimaced. "I know you were enjoying yourself," he added, rubbing his back.

"Yeah yeah. Now you know you concocted this whole situation because I'm your favorite son and you wanted me home wit' you," Devon quipped. He carefully wrapped both arms around the burly figure and inhaled the familiar scent before grabbing a pillow and placing it behind him.

"Uh, thanks," his father muttered. He was not the type to be fussed over, and even a pillow made him feel incompetent.

"Dad, you *need* to rest so you can fully recover. You can't expect to just jump back into things. I can't stay for more than a few days, which means Uncle James is gon have to fill in. You know he's the only one who can adequately help Mom with the business." Devon repeated the script he had been rehearsing in his mind on the plane.

"Yeah yeah. I know. But you tell that knucklehead the next time he feels the need to try to tell *me* what to do with *my* money, it's gon be some problems."

Devon didn't even respond. There was no point. If anything, he was more concerned about his father's health and making sure Jack & Jill stayed afloat during his recovery.

"I'm gonna check in with Mom downstairs. I'll be back to discuss what needs to be done at the restaurant," he said.

His father nodded, put his reading glasses back on, and pecked like a hen on his laptop.

Devon shook his head internally, while hopping down the stairs. He found his mother in the reading room. The room was somberly bathed in red velvet decor and plush, oversized black furniture, accented by a dark wood desk catacorner to the east wall, where his mother sat. A huge oil painting of a piece called "Beautiful Woman of Color" loomed several feet above her head. As she did the rest of the house, Mrs. Woods had the room perfectly to her liking. It was stacked with some of the greatest Black literature of all time. From Langston Hughes to W.E.B. Du Bois, to Alice Walker, stories of their ancestors' voyages from Africa to a fight for freedom and Black excellence inspired each shelf they graced. While observing her hunched over the desk, memories of his mother reading to him and his siblings during summer break flashed before Devon's eyes.

Quietly, he walked inside, his hands stuffed deep in his pants. "Ma?" Devon wasn't sure what she was reading, but whatever it was, it had her so engrossed that she didn't even look up. "Ma?" he tried again, a little louder this time, shuffling forward.

"Huh?" His mother turned her neck. "Oh, hey, honey. You talk to your dad?"

Devon drew closer and flopped on one of the love seats that faced her. "Yeah. And he's definitely gonna try to go back to work in a few days." As he sank backward into the cushion, his eyes hit the ceiling in exasperation. "I'll open the restaurant back up tomorrow and reach out to Uncle James to see when he can come in. Dad is just gon have to suck up his pride and eat some humble pie."

"You know your father. Humility isn't one of his strong suits," Mrs. Woods murmured. Her face turned sympathetic. "I'm sorry this ruined your trip, honey. I so appreciate you sacrificing for us," she added and offered him a soft smile.

Devon sat up straighter. "I appreciate you saying that. Umm. There *is* something I need to tell you about concerning the trip..." Devon bent over his knees while wrestling his phone in both hands. He had a few missed texts that he hadn't responded to yet, even though he had told everyone he arrived safely. Jasmine would be expecting a call soon.

It's now or never.

Taking a deep breath and letting out a sigh, he rushed out, "Umm. I got engaged on the trip."

Devon's mother, a very poised and classy woman, actually let her jaw drop open. She stared at him.

"What? Engaged? *WHY?*"

Well, that wasn't the response I was hoping for, he thought, and decided to charge ahead. "You know I've been seeing someone. Jasmine. And I know things have kind of, umm, moved pretty fast. But things moved fast with you and Dad. And, Mom, when you know, you know. And I know," he finished, trying to sound as certain as he felt.

"But, honey, there is *no rush* in getting to know someone. You are both *very* young, and you have your *whole lives* ahead of you. And me and your father, well, that was a different time..."

His mother's voice was throttled with fear and angst. Her eyes seemed to be about to pop out of her head. Devon paused, considering her words. His mouth tightened. His mother was probably one of his favorite people on the planet, but ultimately, the woman he loved would be his life partner. Nothing was getting in the way of that.

"Ma, I respect how you feel. But I'm not asking your permission. I'm telling you my decision."

Mrs. Woods's thinning grey eyebrows shot to the ceiling. This was probably the first time Devon had ever talked to her so sternly. He made sure to be respectful, but he was a grown man on all accounts, fully capable of making life decisions. Wasn't the goal of parents to get their kids capable of making wise, responsible choices? Wasn't that what his parents had hammered home to him growing up? Hadn't he demonstrated maturity in forfeiting half of his vacation out of the country with his friends to help his parents with *their* business? Isn't that same decision-making skill applicable to his decision with his love life? All of these concerns raced through Devon as he and his mother sat in silence for what seemed like an eternity.

Mrs. Woods's expression remained neutral, but her eyes revealed that she was pondering a million things on the inside. Devon waited. He didn't know what he really wanted because, in the end, as he stated, he wasn't looking for approval.

But still, it would be nice, he thought, checking his phone again. Yep. He had a missed call from Jasmine.

"I'm sorry that I reacted that way," came his mother's soft voice. "I know you're a wise young man, and I only want what's best for you. I'd love to meet her and discuss this further with your father."

Devon was both surprised and relieved by her sudden reasonable response.

"Sounds good." He went to hug her before she changed her mind.

"I love you so much," she said into his shoulder.

"I know," Devon whispered. When he released her, he finally caught a glimpse of what had had her so engaged when he had first entered the room. To his surprise, it wasn't Morrison, or Butler, or Douglass. It was the Holy Bible.

Devon stepped back, still clutching her by the elbow. "Ma? Since when do you read the Bible? I mean, outside of church in the middle of the day?" he added, not wanting to be rude.

His mother's face softened as she turned to look at the open book on the desk next to a notebook filled with writing.

"Well, I have Bible study tonight," Mrs. Woods declared proudly. "So, I'm preparing for that. We're studying the book of Job."

Bible study? Devon wondered to himself. *Since when does my mother go to Bible study?*

And then, something even more profound happened. She looked

up at him, intrigue dancing in her eyes. "Would you like to come?" she asked, in a voice that sounded both inviting and brimming with love.

A stirring emerged in Devon's gut at the question. He recognized it from what he had felt earlier on the plane, and even after his dream of the storm hitting the house. Then suddenly, it seemed very clear that, yes, he *should* go to Bible study. Not just because one of his favorite people in the world wanted him to go, but because it felt like God Himself was inviting him.

SEVEN
NEVER BE THE SAME

"OH NO. HE'S COME TO TORMENT US AGAIN," DEBRA ANNOUNCED DRYLY from Devon's bedroom doorway. Still fitted in her school uniform, she swooned against the frame, draping a hand over her forehead and flitting her eyes to the ceiling.

Devon peered up from his bed, where he had been drooling over his friends' social media posts. They were having a blast.

"What? You still live here? I thought you would have moved out by now," he shot back.

Debra smirked and crossed both slender arms, still clasping her phone in her left hand.

"You of all people should have moved out by now. But welcome home anyway," she said with fake disdain.

Debra was at that age that every parent dreaded. Plus, she was the typical wealthy teenager that anyone would expect, given her upbringing during their parents' most lucrative years. With both Woods bringing in a substantial amount of cash, even with their mother being retired the last two years, *and* being the only girl, *and* the baby of the family, what else could Debra be but spoiled? At least, when Devon was coming up, he remembered their father as a stay-at-home dad and their mom struggling to pay the bills on her own. That was before they got the brownstone. His added responsibility of being trained to run the restaurant aided in Devon's natural bent towards gratitude. Even some of those early-year-struggles spilled over into Darion's childhood. On the contrary, his kid sister was eight years Devon's junior and had no recollection of the five of them cluttering a two-bedroom when she was just a baby. All Debra had were their stories and a few scattered pictures in the family album. Whenever someone flashed back to the "old days," she shot a quick eye roll and heaved a sigh.

Easing inside and copping a seat in Devon's desk chair, Debra asked, "You talk to Dad?" The chair's wheels rolled a little under her weight.

"Yeah. He seems to be ok," Devon replied. "I'm gonna need you at the restaurant, though, to help this week. What's your schedule?" He got straight to business and, just as he suspected, experienced push-back from his sister. Her forehead furrowed as she flipped her long bundle of Brazilian tresses over one shoulder. Taking her time, she thoughtfully scraped through a handful with long, pointy nails.

"I have study group all week for this big exam on Friday for government class. Before we go on break," she added.

Devon clicked his tongue. "Sounds weak to me. You gon be studying *all night every night* during our work hours?" He pierced her with an "I'm not buying it" look.

Debra sighed. "I'll be free after four," she grumbled. Then her face brightened. "Tell me about Cancun," she squealed. "I can't believe you left!"

That's when his sister's real motive for coming into his room revealed itself. She was practically salivating.

Devon half-smiled. He moved over so she could sit on his bed and scroll through his phone at the pictures he hadn't posted. As much as Debra tried to act like she didn't care anything about her big brothers' social lives, Devon knew his sister stalked their social media with her fake account.

"Wow! I can't wait to go. I was already talking to Amy about it.

Maybe next year, Mom will loosen the reins and let me travel for spring break. *Everyone* at school does. But Mom is always tweakin' about money." Debra rolled her eyes.

That's when Devon's annoyance surfaced. "Yeah, well, *maybe* if you got a *job* or even helped out at Jack & Jill more, you would be able to travel with *your* money. Darion and I used *our own money* for this trip, you know," he pointed out.

She scoffed. "That's what parents are for. I mean, what else do they have to spend their money on but us?" Debra's face oozed skepticism.

Devon smacked his teeth in amazement. "You really believe that don't you?"

His sister continued swiping through pictures on his phone as if she hadn't heard a thing. "I *knew* you got engaged! I can't believe you didn't tell me!" Shaking with excitement, she sat up and waved the phone in the air. "I looooove her. She is *gorgeous*!"

Devon couldn't help but crack a grin as Debra started raving about being a bridesmaid, the dress she wanted to wear, and the colors she hoped they picked. Then, abruptly, she stopped to look at him. "Did you tell Mom and Dad?"

"I told Mom."

Her thick microbladed brows raised halfway before her grey-brown eyes bloomed admiration. "What did she say?" she barely whispered.

Devon half-shrugged, still lying on his stomach atop the comforter. "What can she say? I'm grown. But she did say she wants to meet her."

Debra looked at him like he had just been crowned King of Zamunda. "Wow. I mean, I guess you're right. Well, I can't *wait* to meet her. I always wanted a sister!" Debra enthused.

Devon said, "You'll love her. She's definitely a headstrong, don't-hold-back type. Y'all will for sure get along." He chuckled.

Then his little sister did something that shocked him. Gazing at him shyly, she said, "I'm gonna miss you."

Her tone was so honest that, at first, Devon didn't know how to react.

"Aww, short stuff," he said, using her childhood nickname, which she had outgrown by the time she was 10. "Well, we not getting married for a while cuz she has to finish school, and I'll be here after graduation. So, you can't get rid of me that fast."

This seemed to satisfy her fleeting moment of vulnerability, and Debra started commenting on every picture in his phone. "I looove her dress! It's giving Halle Bailey vibes all day. I think we may even be the same size." She tilted her head, peering at the screen more closely and using her fingers to enlarge the image. "OhmyGod. I want her shoes!" she shrieked. "Yasss queen! You better do that. *Period!*"

Devon laughed. "You coming to Bible study tonight?" he threw out, not really thinking that she was, but figuring it was worth the ask.

Debra stopped her rant and looked up from his phone. "Never again. Mom's Bible study is *super weird*," she revealed in a hushed tone.

Devon looked surprised. "What chu' mean, weird? Isn't it at St. Augustine's?" He was referring to their childhood church, which he had visited a few Easters ago when he made it home for Easter.

"Uhh. No. Mom is doing this *different* church, where I can't remember the name," she rolled her eyes to the ceiling, "but all I know is sometimes they speak in this other language and lay hands on people. And they fall to the floor." A cryptic expression hovered over Debra's face. "I think Mom may be into some type of cult stuff," she added, her eyes wide.

Devon snorted. "Mom is one of the most sensible people on the planet. There's *no way* she would get caught up in a cult."

Debra shrugged. "All I know is she's been going like crazy. Sometimes they don't get out 'til super late. She be there every Sunday, and now Tuesdays for Bible study. And I always hear her on the phone with her new church friends."

"What did Dad say about it?" Devon asked.

Debra lifted a brow. "As far as I know, he hasn't been, so he don't really have an opinion. He just said Mom is probably going through a phase because her sister died last year, and to just let her mourn the way she needs to. He thinks it makes her feel closer to Aunt Janette."

Devon's phone vibrated in his sister's hand, and the screen changed.

She stared down, then looked up at him with giddy eyes. "Ohhhh, it's your *fiancée*!" she howled and handed him the phone.

Devon laughed, tickled. He figured Debra would be excited about the proposal, but he didn't think she would necessarily show it.

"Hey, baby," he answered the video chat and was immediately taken by Jasmine's beautiful face shading the screen.

"Hey, baby!" Debra sang out, standing behind the phone before pivoting to leave. She laughed on her way out, her pleated black tennis skirt swaying the whole way.

"Who was that?" Jasmine asked, hearing Debra's voice but not making out the words.

"My 15-year-old sister. What? You think I got a new girl already?" Devon teased.

"I know you not that crazy," Jasmine said. "How's everything? You never called me back from earlier."

"I know. My bad. I've just been tryna get settled and figure out what needs to happen tomorrow. Dad is good, he's just out of commission for a little while. My sister is a trip and ain't tryna help nobody. My mom is more behind the scenes at the restaurant, handling payroll and admin. But they need an actual operations manager. That's what my dad does. He's boots on the ground. So now, it's about to be me."

"That's my baby. Putting boots on the ground!" Jasmine smiled proudly, then grew mushy. "I miss you already." She poked out her bottom lip. "And Sheila is still feeling gross, so, looks like she's not coming either."

"These few days will pass before you know it," Devon said. His heart squeezed at her expression. "And then, guess what?"

"What?"

"You'll have me for the rest of your life."

Jasmine grinned. "Yes! But we'll have to figure out all the deets when you come back. You know I need to finish school..." Her voice trailed.

Devon nodded. "Of course. I'm gon use that time to save up and get us a spot and make sure we're good financially."

"And you know I wanna go to L.A.," she said, her eyes stern with more than a hint of determination in her voice.

Devon's stomach flip-flopped. He nodded quietly. "We'll talk about everything, baby. As long as we're together, remember?"

Jasmine's smile brightened the screen again. "Yep."

"Yo! You comin' or what?"

Antonio's voice disrupted the conversation, and a flash of his figure hit the corner of the screen when he entered the room.

"You go ahead and have fun," Devon said. "Send me some pics!"

Jasmine agreed. "Talk to you soon."

Before he could utter, "I love you," she hung up. Devon shrugged it off. He knew how Jasmine could be. She was such an in-the-moment-type person that, of course, she was fully immersed in being there. It said a lot that she had called him twice.

She loves me, he assured himself. *She's gonna be my wife!*

That was what Devon decided to focus on; even as he couldn't help himself, he started looking at his friend's posts on social media again. In every picture and video, they were all sun-kissed and cheesing. In one of the videos, Antonio was filming the girls splashing in the ocean waves. Jas looked amazing in her polka dot turquoise bikini, and Antonio echoed Devon's thoughts in the footage.

"Damn girl!" he bellowed behind the lens. "You tryna *murder* somebody out here!" He flipped the phone and faced the camera, then bit his finger and waved it, indicating how hot he thought Jasmine looked. When Antonio turned the phone back around, it caught Jasmine bending over and shimmying, her cleavage spilling out over her top. That was when Devon had to get off.

"Now you know yo boy is a flirt. And you know Jasmine is a flirt," Devon muttered to himself. "That's just how they get down." Still, he couldn't shake the discomfort creeping into his chest.

Maybe there needed to be some new boundaries now that they were engaged.

I'll talk to Jas about it next week at school, Devon promised himself before getting ready to visit his mother's spooky church for Bible study.

———

North Star Ministry appeared normal enough. The church was a cathedral-style building with moderate updates on the inside. Stationed in the center of Bed-Stuy, it was shouldered by a homeless shelter and a soup kitchen.

Well, I guess they helping the community, Devon figured.

A long hallway met him and his mother upon entering the sturdy wooden double doors. Mrs. Woods led the way. As they traipsed down a few different corridors, she seemed elated that he was there. It was for that reason alone that Devon was glad he came. He couldn't help but notice the bounce in her step and how she knew almost everyone they passed by.

"Hi, Mrs. Woods," visitor after visitor greeted as they approached what Devon assumed was the room where the Bible study was being held. It wasn't a large room, but more of a medium-sized one with 20 chairs in a circle. By the time they had arrived, about half were filled.

"Son, can you hold that open?" an older voice croaked from behind, and Devon turned to an elderly woman hunched over a cane. She was accompanied by a younger version of herself.

Devon swiftly shuffled to the side, holding the door open.

"Of course. After you!" He smiled and waved the ladies inside.

"That one of the sons you told us about, Carla?" The woman said to his mother as she passed Devon by.

His mother gave a gracious smile. "Yes, Mrs. Smith. That's Devon. My oldest."

"Now you done raised him right! If only my Tina would get her somebody like that! I don't know why she keep datin' all these triflin' brothas," she said, her eyes falling on the woman behind her. Devon assumed that was Tina by the embarrassed look on her face. He offered her a sympathetic smile.

More folks spilled in as Devon followed his mother's suit and grabbed some refreshments at the long table against the back wall.

"You Carla's son?" someone asked as Devon reached for the spoon to eke out more hummus.

"Yes, ma'am," he replied to a middle-aged woman in a suit.

"Nice to meet you! So glad you could join us," she said, then swiped a handful of chips from the bowl.

Warmth rushed Devon. If, in fact, this was a cult, these folks were definitely making him want to join. He couldn't remember ever attending a church where the attendees were this friendly.

By the time the chatter died and the leader began the discussion, it was nearing 6 pm. Devon sat back, munching on veggies, figuring he would play it lowkey. He hadn't even brought a Bible and assumed that he would share his mother's.

"Hey, everybody!" A light brown woman with freckles and a cute short haircut started the conversation. She couldn't have been more than a few years older than Devon and he was surprised. He expected there to be only older people in attendance. He especially didn't expect a younger person to be leading the study. However, by the way she carried on it was clear that she was comfortable taking charge.

"I see we have some new faces so, before we get started, let's get some introductions. I'm Lena Williams, and I'll be hosting our talk tonight on the book of Job." Lena stopped and called on a few others to introduce themselves until they got to Devon. He cleared his throat.

"Hey, y'all. I'm here visiting from college and came because my mom asked me to," he said simply. Warm smiles and head nods sailed his way, as well as a few, "Welcome, Devon!"

Once again, Lena took the lead. "Most of you know my dad pastors this church. We usually take turns assigning teachers to each topic. I chose this topic because of a really hard season I had to walk through that made me feel like Job. You know how he lost everything and was tried and tested to the utmost until he found God in a deeper way? I've definitely been there. How many have felt like Job or gone through a Job season in here?"

Many agreed, with "Mmhmms," and palms waving in the air.

Devon didn't know who Job was, but he seriously doubted that someone so young could have gone through hard enough things like someone in the Bible.

"Now, I know we often idolize characters in the Bible, but these were real people going through real things. We may even go through a different set of circumstances that make us feel the same way they did," Lena said. She seemed to be answering the very question Devon had just wondered about.

"Preach!" someone shouted.

"Mmhmm, that's true," another person agreed.

Clearly, this was a vocal bunch. Devon tightened his lips so he wouldn't laugh. But when he snuck a peek at his mother, a look of intensity sat on her face. That's when he realized how important this was to her. He vowed then that he would open his heart to the discussion for her sake.

Don't do it for her, do it for Me.

Devon's eyes widened. There was that voice again. Once again, he had a distinct impression that God was talking to him. Devon glanced around to see if anyone else was experiencing it, but all eyes were on Lena.

"Now, we're starting chapter 32, and this is where Elihu, the youngest of the group, basically rebukes Job and his friends…"

Lena dove into the reading, and Devon followed along in his mother's Bible. He was surprised to see that she had a newer version, not the King James version she would take to her old church. This newer version seemed to be doing the trick because Devon's comprehension of the story felt somehow enhanced. Every word seemed to make sense, and he wondered at how he had never been interested enough to read this book of the Bible before. Or any book for that matter.

"So, what can we learn from this passage?" Lena asked, after reading through the chapter.

To Devon's surprise, his mother was the first to respond.

Raising her hand, she said, "That no matter your age, you can have wisdom."

Lena's face lit up. "Yes, Mrs. Woods. We did read in the chapters prior that even though Job's friends were older, like him, it took Elihu, who's described as being the youngest, to speak the real."

Devon felt a rush of pride at his mother's insightful answer. She was already a very esteemed woman, with a PhD, being a business owner, and mothering three children, but there seemed to be this humility about her in this setting. Finally, he could put his finger on it. His mother seemed almost *childlike.* A look of wonder sparkled in her eyes. The corners of her thin lips tilted upward, hinting that a smile could burst at any minute. She seemed *at peace.*

If this is her mourning, then God is really comforting her, Devon observed.

The rest of the conversation was just as informative. Lena continued her easy-going style of asking open-ended questions, allowing people to chime in. It felt like everyone mattered, and what each had to share was valued. Some even opened up about very hard things they had gone through. Lena vulnerably talked about a season where she had a miscarriage, found out that her husband was cheating, went through a divorce, and lost her best friend.

Devon's eyes nearly burst out of his head. *Oh my God! That's why she said Job season*, he thought, now understanding more about what that meant. He felt bad that he had misjudged her.

At the end of the study, Lena announced, "Now, those in need of prayer, we will end our discussion, and you can stay for prayer. Those who need to leave, we understand and will hopefully see you at the bake-off on Friday!"

The crowd murmured amongst themselves, as chairs screeched and some stood to leave. Others stayed and lingered to chat. Devon looked at his mother, who was in deep conversation with the older woman, Mrs. Smith. Suddenly, a yearning rose in him, and he thought about his fast-approaching graduation date. He was confident about his decision to propose, but still wondered how things would play out with Jasmine wanting to go to L.A.

I guess it can't hurt to ask for prayer about it, Devon thought.

Part of him felt weird for wanting prayer about something so trivial. Others had talked about loss and death and different types of trauma, not their next steps after graduation. Just when Devon was about to talk himself out of it, his eyes happened to look up and lock with Lena's. She was standing to the left of the snack table with three other ministers. She was the only one who didn't have anyone to pray with. She beckoned for him to come. It was as if his feet had a mind of their own, because, without a thought, Devon walked the short distance and towered over her.

Unsure of what to do next, he said, "Hi," in a sheepish tone.

Lena's smile was so disarming that Devon felt like he could tell her anything. "Taking the first step is often the hardest, Devon." Devon nodded, still plagued with uncertainty.

"So, what brings you here? I mean, I know your mom brought you, but was there any other reason you came?" Lena asked.

Devon licked his lips. "Well, at first it was for her. But then I actually…" he stopped, embarrassment tightening his throat.

"Go on," Lena's tone gently prodded.

"I actually think *God* spoke to me. Like in the Bible study. I think He said He wanted me here. For *Him*."

Lena's smile grew. "Wow. That's wonderful, Devon. I think you're right. God did speak to you." She paused and dropped her eyes to the floor. Her mouth started moving quietly before she lifted her gaze back at him. "God loves talking to us, Devon. And He talks to all of us in a lot of different ways."

Devon was intrigued. Lena seemed to be so in tune. Maybe she had the answers to his inner questions. "Umm. I just. I just don't think I've ever heard of God talking to people directly like this. And it just. It keeps *happening*," he revealed. "About stuff—stuff I didn't even think He cared about."

"Oh, God cares about everything. Scripture says even the very hairs on our heads."

"Wow. I guess, I never realized…" Devon swallowed and fiddled with his hands in front of him. He sensed he was on the brink of something. He just didn't know what it was. "I've been wondering about graduation and my plans," he offered, finally feeling like maybe these things *were* important to God.

Lena nodded thoughtfully. "Give me your hands, and we'll pray."

When Devon let his hands fall into Lena's, it was like a magnet pulled down his head, because as soon as he closed his eyes, his head bowed. A force like nothing he had ever experienced before erupted within him. Goosebumps swarmed up his arms, a wild sensation flooded him from head to foot, and his ears rang with a rushing, wind-like sound.

Distantly, he heard Lena's words: "Son. You have heard Me by the hearing of the ears but now you are about to see Me face-to-Face. I have called you for such a time as this. Your desires will be My desires.

Your thoughts will be My thoughts. You are called to do My work." The room disappeared. Euphoria squeezed him like an infant swaddled by its mother. It was as if Devon was drowning in love. God was here!

Then, hands were on his back, and a foreign language exploded from his lips. It was coming from behind. It was coming from beside him. There was no question that after this moment, Devon would never be the same.

EIGHT
ALL THINGS NEW

"Momma?" Devon lay on the floor for some time, soaking in the wake of an encounter with the Most High. The black and white tiles blurred his vision as he rolled to his side in pure bliss.

What just happened? he thought, in utter awe. And then, his mother, rolling over also, emerged into view. This was the most unkept version of her that Devon had ever witnessed. Her pearls were strewn across her blouse. Her Manolo Blahnik black heels were scattered near both stocking-clad feet. Her hair had escaped from its smoothly coiffed French roll. Yet, when they caught eyes, she had the biggest smile Devon had ever seen.

After Lena prayed with Devon and spoke the message God had for him, the spiritual gift of tongues began to flow. That ushered in a wave of praise into the room. A presence so powerful and stronger than anything Devon had ever felt engulfed him. For the first time in his life, he had no doubt, he was feeling the very presence of God. Tongues, he learned from Lena, was one of the spiritual signs of someone receiving the Holy Spirit. It seemed God had given him His Holy Spirit!

"Baby," his mother breathed as she placed one arm on the floor and pushed herself to a sitting position across from him. "God is so *good!"* she confessed, then closed her eyes while lifting her chin to the sky.

Others were rolling around, murmuring and echoing her sentiments. Devon also lifted himself up, though it was a struggle. Not because he felt weak, but because he didn't want this experience to ever end.

"Devon." A hand softly touched his shoulder as he sat. He peered up at Lena.

"God is going to do some amazing things through you," she said with certainty. The intensity of her gaze caused Devon's heart to flutter.

God wanted *him*? Out of all of the billions of people on the planet, God wanted to use *him*? Devon felt so humbled. So honored. So *inept*.

"But, I'm just a college student," he mumbled.

"And David was just a shepherd boy. And Jesus was just a carpenter," Lena said. She gave him a sweet smile. "You can't even imagine what He has in store."

Devon exhaled a deep breath. He may not have been able to imagine, but what he did know for sure was that he had never experienced anything like this in his life.

"He's been calling you for a while," Lena added. "It's time." And with that, she drifted over to the other bodies, slowly rising to their feet.

Time? Devon wondered. *Time for what?*

Time to know who you are, came the voice he was starting to grow accustomed to.

"Oh my Lord. Look at the time!" Mrs. Woods said. "We gotta go. Your dad's gonna *kill* me." She hurried to her feet, still staring at her watch. "Now, where is my purse?"

Devon heard her rummaging from behind him near the chairs they were seated at, and couldn't help himself. He laughed.

His mother glanced behind her shoulder. "Oh, you think this is funny?" she said, but then she started laughing too. There was so much joy in the room that the few stragglers who remained joined in. Devon gave up trying to get up. He fell on his back and clutched his gut because he was laughing so hard.

I don't think I've ever felt this much joy! he thought in amazement.

That was when Devon first discovered the joy of the Lord.

———

THE WOODS MOTHER-AND-SON duo caught the C-train back to Brooklyn Hts. after tearing themselves from the floor of North Star Ministry. It was a quiet commute with only a handful of passengers due to the late hour. It was after 11:30 pm. Internal questions bombarded Devon, competing with the subway rattling and the graffiti-stained walls zipping by.

What did God have for him? What did He mean by *'learn who he was'*?

Instead of voicing his thoughts, Devon covertly eyed his mother next to him. They had always been close, but somehow the experience they had just shared knit them even closer.

"Mom?" he said after a while.

His mother peered at him. Her eyes were smiling, but her exterior exuded the same put-together, quiet demeanor she always wore. One would never suspect she was just rolling around on a dusty, cold, hard floor.

"How long have you been hiding this?" Devon asked.

His mother chuckled. "Oh, baby. I've always had a relationship with God. But *this*?" She paused and sighed, gripping her beige bucket Coach purse. "I've been experiencing *this* for about a year now."

"And, why didn't you tell us? Why didn't you tell Dad?"

Mrs. Woods glanced out the window briefly before meeting Devon's gaze again. She shrugged. "Your dad wouldn't understand. But I believe in time, he'll come around."

Devon said, "But, what about us? What about me?" Suddenly, he felt left out of this very important part of his mother's life.

"Would you have believed me if I tried?" she replied simply.

Devon was quiet, weighing her response. "I don't know," he murmured honestly. "It *is* hard to believe," he admitted.

"Yes. But very biblical. The gifts of the Spirit are described in the Bible, and they're still here today. But the churches I was raised in and the ones I took you guys to didn't believe in them. Plus, I knew you would have to experience it for yourself. So I prayed and waited. For all of you. I know each one will come to Him in their own time. But I'm glad you were first." She winked, then leaned over and tilted her head on Devon's shoulder while laying a hand on his wrist. Warmth and love hugged Devon before settling into the seat with him for the entire ride home.

By the time they walked inside the elegant brownstone, it was nearing midnight. The sleepy street flickered with streetlamps to a beat that no one could hear. Soft shadows loomed, the late evening complementing the quiet mood of mother and son as they entered their home. While the two crept up the stairs to their individual bedrooms, only the moon beaming through the windows served as their guide. Devon hadn't thought to check his phone until stripping and hiding under the covers. Exhaustion weighed his body. He had an early morning opening the restaurant. Finally buried beneath the fluffy cotton comforter in his boxers, he slid open his phone. Three missed texts from his brother glowed on the screen.

> Hey. How's Dad doing?

At 8:03 pm.

> Why you not answering your phone?

At 10:08 pm.

> You better call me back.

At 10:43pm.
Devon felt bad and hurriedly responded.

> My bad. Was at Bible study with mom.
> Everything is good here. Hit you up tomorrow.

He sent the message immediately. As Devon continued scrolling and responding to various messages, one from Uncle James who said,

"Yes, I'll meet you at Jack & Jill's tomorrow to help," and even one from his sister who asked, **"How spooky was the spooky Bible study?"** Devon realized that there was nothing from Jasmine.

Maybe she tried to call.

Swiping from his text messages to his missed calls screen, disappointment stroked him. The only thing he had was the missed call from his brother. No missed calls from his girlfriend.

Quickly, he flipped open his social media account and went to Jasmine's page. There were no new posts after their engagement announcement. He scrolled to his brother's, whose latest one was of himself visiting the Mayan ruins from two days ago. A sinking feeling met Devon. He decided to visit Antonio's Snapchat. The latest video his friend shared showed the four of them on a boat, drinking and laughing. They were all smooshed together, with the girls in the middle and the guys on the ends. Devon could tell there were others on the boat, which is probably why they were bunched together like that. What bothered him most, though, was that, not only was Jasmine practically sitting on top of Antonio, but her hand rested on his thigh as they joked around in the video. Antonio's eyes were so low that Devon doubted he could see much of anything.

He's definitely high.

Then Jasmine winked at the camera and blew a kiss. She seemed pretty intoxicated herself with a liquor glass squeezed between her thighs and a small umbrella sprouting from it.

Devon shut off the phone. Yeah, *we definitely gotta talk about some serious boundaries,* he thought.

He set his mind on going to sleep, but he tossed and turned as frustration from not being with his friends wrestled his thoughts. It was hard to nod off. Then Devon remembered all that he had just experienced at North Star. He never could have imagined that the supernatural was real! Other than demons and vampires and stuff he witnessed in Halloween movies, he didn't know there were supernatural gifts. Especially ones that existed for God. Now his heart and mind seemed more enhanced to a Being greater than anything he had ever been aware of. This voice that he kept hearing in his heart had a name—

Jesus Christ. A small smile stretched Devon's lips before he finally dozed off.

God was real!

———

DRAGGING himself out of bed the next morning was brutal. With only a few solid hours of sleep under his belt, Devon wondered how he would get through the day. Then, suddenly, the evening's events charged his mind. He was flooded with joy.

When he hopped into the shower stall, the water felt like it was giving him the best massage he had ever had in his life. When he toweled himself off and glanced out his bedroom window, the traffic noises of the city resembled a heavenly orchestra. Instead of the sky appearing dreary and semi-gloomy as it probably did to the rest of the world, to Devon, it hinted at a day of adventure. Everywhere he looked and everything he did that morning felt like it was for the first time. It was like life was brand new.

I make all things new.

The remark resurfaced from Devon's dream, and his mouth gaped.

I need to figure out what this means, he decided. After getting dressed, he hunched over his bed and popped open his phone. When he typed the mysterious sentence, "I make all things new," into the search engine, he almost fell on the floor with what it showed.

REVELATIONS 21:5

> *And he who was seated on the throne said, "Behold, I am*
> *making all things new." Also, he said, "Write this down,*
> *for these words are trustworthy and true."*

Who knew this was a passage of scripture?! Devon thought. He sat astounded.

Wow. I really do *hear God.*

Then he realized, *That means my dream was from God. I wonder what it means?*

When Devon was ready to go, he peeked inside his parents' bedroom. His poor father was propped at an angle by pillows against the headboard, the TV remote glued to his hand. Mr. Woods's large leg cast still sat atop more pillows. Even with Devon's presence, his eyes stayed stuck to the news on the television.

"Dad. I'm 'bout to head to Jack & Jill's," Devon informed, peering from the doorway.

"Ok, son. Let me know if you need anything. Remember, Reggie should be in by 10 am, but Martha is covering until he gets in. And Brian is coming in to deliver inventory and should be restocking the toilet paper. And if you need to, you can just call me on my cell." His dad started rolling out a list.

Devon nodded. "I got you, Pops. It's all good. Talk to you later!" Before his father could mention another thing, Devon skirted out. After bounding the spiral staircase, he shot past his mother, appearing from the kitchen.

"You want breakfast, baby?" she called, as Devon leaped across the foyer.

"No ma'am. Running late. I'll grab something at work. See you later!"

"Not even a good cup of French press?" That's when Devon noticed the to-go cup in her hand. She knew exactly what she was doing.

"You're amazing!" he pivoted on his heels and grabbed the cup before dashing back to the front door. His mother was a doctoral student of his heart. Suddenly, Devon stopped with his hand on the knob. "I love you!" he shouted with a boyish grin. When she smiled back, it was like they shared a secret.

"Love you too!"

Eager to catch the A train, Devon semi-jogged to the nearest station through the hodgepodge of morning commuters in the brisk air. He was rushing because his uncle was a stickler for time. That was just one of the ways he and Devon's father were similar.

Uncle James was the spitting image of his brother, only a shade or two darker. Over six feet tall, over 250 lbs., and over caring about others' opinions if it meant they disagreed with him. That was the real reason that Devon's dad and uncle clashed so much. They both liked to be right. Even still, when there was an emergency or someone was in a clutch, the other one was there. For that reason, his uncle could be counted on to assist with Jack & Jill.

When Devon arrived at the restaurant at 7:02 am, James was loitering outside the front door, smoking a Newport and talking on his cell phone. Devon tried to catch his breath while traipsing up to the small grey building with a white awning protruding over the entrance. He had already finished his coffee and silently thanked his mother for her consideration.

"Uncle James. Thanks for coming!" Devon huffed, ambling up to the door.

His uncle nodded, but his focus remained on whoever was on the other end of the phone line. Instead of responding, James opened an arm for Devon to fall into. Devon tried not to inhale the puff of cigarette smoke that clogged his nostrils when they embraced.

"Yeah. Yeah. I'm at my brother's restaurant, so I'll call you back," James said in a raspy tone once they had entered inside. Stuffing his phone in his back pocket, he looked at his nephew.

"How you been, Devon? How's school?"

Devon started taking down the chairs from the tables, which had been flipped over by whoever had closed last.

"It's been good. Definitely looking forward to being done." His uncle began assisting him with preparing everything for their customers while they chatted.

"I'm glad you asked me to help. I know your dad can't be happy he's laid up like that," James mentioned when they were done setting up. "You said you wanted me to finish with those windows? I see he only got one installed when he fell."

Devon nodded. "Yeah. Let's take a look in the storage and his office and find his tools." As Devon suspected, the remaining windows, ladder, and tools were inside the restaurant's huge storage space in the back.

While his uncle got started on his job, Devon began reviewing paperwork and checking emails. Teddy Woods kept great records, but it was always tedious sifting through his stacks of papers because he was old school and made copies of everything.

Around 7:30 am, Martha, the cook, came in to start the food. 15 minutes later, Shelly, one of the newer associates, showed up to work the register. Two servers trailed her from behind. Then, right at 8:00 am, Devon flipped over the sign in the front to read "open."

The morning flew by as Devon processed paperwork, answered calls, responded to emails, and directed employees. Being in that space was bittersweet. Devon had been the go-to guy for his parents for as long as he could remember when it came to helping with their business. Especially whenever it was all hands on deck. That meant he could perform managerial duties in his sleep. That was the sweet part. Everything was familiar, and, in a sense, comfortable. The staff was friendly and even though Devon was at least ten years younger, they listened to him. The bitter part was the recurring constriction in his gut whenever he thought about doing this particular job with no end in sight. Sitting behind his father's desk, looking at his father's computer, working his father's business, felt somehow *wrong*. Yes, Devon could do it, *but did he want to*? Where was the passion? Where was the excitement of having something of his own? Something to build from scratch and start from the ground up. Ahh, *that's* what it was.

Jack & Jill didn't belong to him.

But it will *be mine,* Devon tried to convince himself. His face screwed up at the numbers on the Excel spreadsheet comparing last month's inventory count to this month's. "I would inherit it," he murmured, clicking on the "total" column. Yeah, he would…when his father was too old to work. Even then, his dad would always be hanging over his shoulder, watching from afar. The truth stared at Devon from the computer screen. He wouldn't truly have Jack & Jill, all on his own, for years. Maybe even decades. The numbers before him danced, and he rubbed his eyes to take another look. For some reason, the math wasn't mathing. No matter how many times Devon double-checked his figures, they weren't adding up. And it wasn't just with the inventory numbers; it was with his future.

That inner voice started speaking again. *"I have something else,"* was the impression on his heart.

Fear straddled Devon's being. What did God have? Devon had been walking the straight and narrow since he had learned to walk. Firstborns are the dependable ones. They're the leaders. They're the ones everyone calls to grab the hose when the house is on fire. Darion could go off and do his own thing, and no one blinked an eye. Debra wasn't even a reliable option for after-school help. Devon couldn't remember any type of leeway given to *him* as an adolescent. When he was her age, he *lived* at Jack & Jill after school!

"God. There's just *no way* my dad is gonna be cool with this..." Devon said softly with a frown. The numbers before him started to swirl.

Boldness, was all he sensed in his heart.

His uncle popped his head in the office at noon, startling Devon from his deliberation with God.

"All done. I think those windows are gonna be good. You can tell your dad he's welcome." James winked at Devon, indicating that he knew how well that would go over with his stubborn brother. "And when he wants to thank me himself, I'll be waiting for the call." He held up his phone as proof.

Devon laughed. "You not about to get me involved!" he said, figuring that was the best response. Right when he had spoken the words, the desk vibrated from his phone. Jasmine was calling. Devon held up a finger to his uncle.

"Hey, baby," he answered, clicking the accept button to her video chat. Instead of her usually fresh, bubbly face, she looked tired and worn out.

"Hey," Jasmine said, sounding unenthused. "I saw you called me earlier..."

"Yeah. I was trying to catch you before things got crazy here. I'm at my dad's restaurant."

Devon peered at her closer. "You hung over?" In lieu of her usual put-together hairstyle, it was disheveled as if she had forgotten to use her head scarf last night. Her eyes were also blood red. "Late night?" he added, not wanting to sound judgmental. *She is on vacation.*

Jasmine sighed. "I definitely overdid it last night," she admitted, brushing her forehead with the tips of her nails. "You mind if we talk later?" The light came on in the room, and she squinted before looking behind her. Antonio had slid inside, saying something about brunch.

Damn, did he knock? Devon wondered.

"Sure, baby. Ok. Just hit me later. Love you," he said, intentionally fast this time to make sure he got it in.

"Ok, baby," Jasmine mumbled and ended the call.

Devon sat, drowning in a mix of emotions, not sure which one to address.

His uncle, still holding up the doorway, slanted his head to the side. "Woman problems?" he asked. Without waiting for a reply, he stepped inside, closed the door, and dropped into the seat across from Devon.

Devon blew out some air and tossed his phone on the desk. "I got engaged, unc."

His uncle looked surprised. "Umm, what you say? Engaged? Like, *married* engaged?"

Devon bobbed his head.

"To who? That broad, I mean, female you been datin' like two seconds?" He looked bewildered, and Devon immediately regretted telling him. His uncle wasn't necessarily a well of wisdom when it came to love, having been divorced three times and playing the field in his mid-40s.

"Her name is Jasmine," Devon responded, fighting annoyance.

"I'm sorry, son. I'm just caught off guard. Ok, so you got engaged to—Jasmine. And now, what? You feeling insecure cuz you here and she—where she is?"

"Cancun. She's in Cancun," Devon said through gritted teeth. He looked up at the ceiling and rubbed a frustrated hand over his brow.

"Oh, right. That's right. You went there on your trip. Well, isn't Darion there?" His uncle looked at him with a question mark in his eyes.

Oh yeah. Darion. The weight on Devon's shoulders lifted some. "You right, unc. Darion is there."

His uncle looked pleased with himself. "Glad to be of service," he said before heading out to tackle his next assignment.

Devon owed his brother a call anyway. He had just been waiting to have more time to talk to him. He shot him a quick text.

> D, be free at 6 pm. I'm gon call after work.

A few moments later, Darion replied.

> Bet.

Devon already felt better just knowing he had actual boots on the ground. Now he could do what he needed to, and that was run his father's business.

Everything's gon be cool, he told himself. *Just a few more days and we'll be back together, and I can stop buggin'.*

Still, even with his inner pep talk, the tightening in Devon's stomach remained, and six o'clock couldn't come soon enough.

NINE
LEARNING HOW TO PRAY

"Bro. Now you *know* ain't *nothin'* going down on *my* watch. Antonio would be crazy. I mean, he crazy, but he ain't *that* crazy," Darion said. "And you know they both like to flirt. But as far as *I know,* we all just havin' a good time."

A long sigh of relief oozed from Devon. He knew his brother would keep it a buck and wouldn't try to sugarcoat anything if he had peeped something.

"But for real though. You sure you ready for marriage?" Darion asked, lifting a brow. They were on video chat, so Devon could see the doubt in his eyes.

Devon smacked his teeth. "Of course. Why would you even ask me that?" He felt insulted. If the closest person in the world to him didn't believe he was ready, what was that saying?

"I mean. You sure you trust her? You tweakin' about her dippin' out on you after just a few days..." Darion shrugged as his gaze drifted.

Devon was silent. He could see his brother's point. Clasping his neck with a hand, his face scrunched in thought. "I've never felt like this about anybody before, D. You know that. And I'm ready to start my life."

Darion said, "I know. I know. I got you. Just chill. We gon all be back at campus and everything's gon get back to normal."

Devon appreciated his brother's words. Then, within the hour, a much sober Jasmine called. She seemed back to her normal chipper self, filling him in on the day's excursions.

This time, before they ended their call, she said, "Love you. Talk soon, babe."

Ok. So it was all in my head. Feeling at ease, Devon stretched out his limbs while on his bed and smiled. He was getting married! A slow realization then dawned on him. Now that his anxiety over Jasmine had dissipated, the message from God that he received while at the office was loud and clear. God was telling Devon that he had something else for him. He was telling him that Jack & Jill was not in his future long term. Devon lay there for a second, meditating on this revelation. For decades, he had been preparing to inherit his father's dream. Now, suddenly, with his newfound faith, he felt strongly that he was being led in a different direction. Devon wasn't entirely sure whether that direction included L.A., but he had this urgency that it for sure didn't include Jack & Jill. Trepidation sank fangs deep into his stomach. In response, once again, that unction came to him: *Boldness.* Devon gulped, but then, love erupted in His heart. And this time it wasn't from God. It was from him. Devon was realizing that this new relationship with God wasn't just about God loving him, it was about showing God that he loved Him back. For the first time, God was asking Devon to do something for *Him.* He was asking Devon to trust Him with his future. Love danced in Devon's belly, spiked up to his chest, and exploded in his heart. He loved God!

"Ok, God. I got You. It's me and You," Devon said out loud.

Still, he sat, taking a moment to ready himself. Nervously, he teased his bottom lip with his teeth. He also needed to tell his father about the engagement. Anxiety stroked the back of his neck. *Boldness,* he told himself, strangling the cotton duvet. Finally, Devon forced himself up and endured the long walk to his parents' bedroom. As he approached, the sound from the TV spilled into the hallway, stirring up a cluster of butterflies in his gut.

Chill, Devon told himself. *God is with you.*

It was one thing to break the news about the engagement to his mother, who he was closer to, but his father was a whole different brute. Especially when it came to Mr. Woods's expectations for Devon to take over the family business. When he reached the door, Devon rapped on the opening with a few knuckles.

"Hey," his dad said, still staring at his laptop and pounding on keys. "How'd it go today?" He took his time looking up.

Easing inside, Devon decided to sit in the corner rocking chair his mom often used when she was knitting. Trying to make himself physically comfortable, even if he wasn't internally, he stretched out his long legs dressed in joggers.

Rocking a little, he said, "It went well. Everyone showed up for their shifts. Reggie's back from vacay. I had an issue with the inventory numbers, but I got it figured out. Oh, and Uncle James fixed the windows."

Mr. Woods rolled his eyes. "Well, it's the least he could do after what he said to me," he grumbled.

Devon smothered a smile. "Where's Mom?"

"She went out to run some errands with your sister. I guess she has this party she wants to go to and needs a new outfit."

"I doubt that, but whatever," Devon said. His sister could clothe a small country with the amount of outfits she had in her closet. "She was supposed to show today, but of course flaked," he added, not telling his father anything he didn't already know.

"I'm not surprised," his dad confirmed. "And I don't know why she think she needs another damn outfit. I'm gon get on Carla again about making her do her spring cleaning. Why she think that girl need all them clothes is beyond me. She needs to give *something* away."

Devon nodded to his father's rant, then cleared his throat. *Best to start with the lighter topic...* "So, umm. There *is* something I wanted to talk to you about," he said timidly.

Mr. Woods peered up with a concerned expression, but Devon hurried to appease him. "No, it's nothing with the restaurant."

His father breathed an audible sigh of relief. "Ok. Cool." Giving Devon his full attention, he dropped both meaty hands on his pot belly. "Wuz up?"

In an attempt to remove the moisture protruding from his palms, Devon rubbed his thighs. "You know I been dating Jasmine for a minute."

"Jasmine. Yeah. The cute chocolate sistah. When we gon meet her? You think it's gettin' serious?"

Devon fought a snort, "Uh, yeah. It's gotten pretty serious," then licked his lips. "I proposed to her."

Mr. Woods blinked. "Proposed? Like, *marriage* proposed?" He stared at him, confused.

Devon swallowed a laugh. His father sounded just like Uncle James. "Yeah. Like marriage."

"*Why?*" Mr. Woods blurted. "Is she pregnant?"

"No!" Devon quickly said.

"Sooo, why would you commit yourself to someone you hardly know?" Mr. Woods put a hand to his receding hairline. "You're about to finish college. You're about to run the business. You're about to start your life."

"Exactly. Jasmine *is* my life, Dad. She and I are going to share a life," Devon quickly defended.

"Son." His father stopped to inhale and searched for words. "I know hormones and sex clouds a man's judgment. Your girl is a looker. I'll say that. But you barely know her." His dad's new approach only got under Devon's skin.

"*You* don't know her. And, respectfully, sir, I understand that's why you're having a hard time with this. I'm springing this on you and probably not at the best time." His eyes fell to his father's encased leg. "But time is short. We'll be married after she graduates, which gives us a year. I have a plan in place to make sure we're good when she does," he finished, his voice steady. In the stillness of the room, Devon then added, "Sir, I'm not asking your permission. I'm telling you my plans."

Mr. Woods sighed again, this time long and hard. "Devon, we raised you to be responsible, and I appreciate you coming to me man to man. But we've been preparing you since you were a kid to take this torch. How does this new *marriage* affect you running Jack & Jill?"

Devon went quiet. *Ok, God. I really, really,* really *need You right now!*

Boldness. The reminder from earlier echoed in his heart.

"I'm telling you that there are a lot of things I'm certain about, but running Jack & Jill forever isn't one of them." There. He had said it. A supernatural peace kissed Devon's heart. Even though he had been scared to death to poke the bear, he had to be honest that there was simply another path for him to walk. Maybe L.A. was in his future after all.

"But you want to run *my* business while you stack up paper for this girl you want to marry, who you barely know?" his father asked, punching out each word in hurt. "You basically want me to pay for your damn wedding."

Devon's heart sank, and the peace he had just experienced fled the scene. Hurting his father was the last thing he had wanted to do.

"Jack & Jill is *your* dream. Not mine," he stated softly. It was a startling realization for him *and* his father. Devon had never really thought about his own dreams until now. He had always assumed that his father's dream was his. Now, God was hinting at something else. Something Devon couldn't quite see, but he needed to take this stance as a step of faith into an unknown promise.

The two men sat in silence with only the TV speaking. A gulf of lifelong expectations separated them, threatening to drown their entire relationship. Devon was too afraid to even look at his father, so he drilled his gaze into the beige carpet. He had never been this honest with his dad before, especially about something so near and dear to his father's heart. Devon had no clue what to even expect from him, as this was unknown territory.

"The problem is you kids are spoiled. We spoiled the hell out a you. You don't know what it's like to go hungry. Have your lights turned off. Walk to school in a blizzard, in subzero temperatures, with holes in your shoes and socks. You don't know what it's like to share one toilet with *five* siblings. That's the damn problem. You can't appreciate parents having a pot to piss in and giving you one to piss in too…"

Devon tightened his jaw. He had heard his father's horror stories of growing up poor more times than he cared to count. Anger burst in his heart. Out of all of his siblings, Devon was the most responsible. He was the most grateful for his parents' sacrifices.

"Hell, *legacy* wasn't even something we were taught in my generation!" his father's voice boomed on. "Cuz they ain't have shit to give! James and I had about two shirts we shared every other day, and you know what the kids said to *us*?"

Devon tried to keep his eyes from rolling to the ceiling while finishing the sentence in his mind, along with his father.

"Y'all ever gon get a new shirt? If you turn it inside out, you'll have another one!"

Devon cringed. His heart went out to his dad. He had never wanted him to feel like he didn't appreciate the opportunity to even have an inheritance. To continue their legacy. Gathering all of his courage, he cut in to his father's rant.

"Dad. I get it. I know you sacrificed a lot for us. I know both you and Mom did. I know you hustled and busted your ass trying to give us something better. I just want you to understand that I want this because-because—I'm just like you. I-." He stopped, searching for words. "I need to build something myself." Even as Devon spoke the words, he realized how true they rang. Whatever it was that God had for him, it would be something that he would build.

His father went silent. His eyes stared unseeing at his laptop. His jaw worked before he took a few deep breaths. It seemed he was calming down. Devon breathed an inward sigh. But his relief was short-lived.

"Fine. It's your future. I won't require you to help with the restaurant anymore. Your last day was today."

Devon's head whipped up. "What? You're, you're *firing* me?"

Mr. Woods put his reading glasses back on, keeping his gaze on his computer. "You fired yourself."

———

"Yo, son. Wuz good? You miss me already?" Darion answered the phone that evening on the first ring. When he saw Devon's face on the video chat, he glanced over his shoulder.

"Aye, y'all, I'm a take this in my room!" he shouted to his friends. As he started moving, parts of the beach house's interior flooded the screen.

Longing caressed Devon's heart. *Just a few more days*, he told himself. He wanted, no *needed*, to see Jasmine.

It was after 10 o'clock, and for the past hour Devon had been sitting in the dimly lit room, imprisoned by his father's words. When his mom came in and asked if he wanted dinner, he pretended to be asleep. When his sister knocked on his door and then texted him to ask if he wanted to see her new fit, he ignored her. Finally, he decided to call Darion.

"Bruh. Wuz going on?" Darion looked worried, peering at Devon's somber expression. "Dad ok?"

"Yeah. I mean, *physically* at least," Devon spat out. His heart was heavy, and that heaviness seeped into his tone.

"Then what? You look like somebody died."

"I think something did die. I told Dad I wasn't running Jack & Jill forever, and he told me I don't need to run it ever again."

Darion's eyes bugged. His mouth gaped. "Whaaaattt. Damn. That's crazy."

Devon said, "I know." He swallowed. "I mean, I have a strong sense that I'm supposed to do something different. You know?"

"Foreal? You never told me," Darion said, sounding surprised.

"Well, it's more recent. But I can't deny that it's the truth. And you know how Dad is. It took everything in me to get the words out. And then he went ballistic. Now in fairness, he was also already trippin' on the engagement."

"Wait. Dang. You told him about the engagement *and* about not taking over Jack & Jill?" Darion's face was wild with shock.

Devon nodded slowly. "I know. I know. It was a lot. And maybe I shouldn't have dumped on him so much at once. But you know, with the wedding…I just needed to lay my cards out so I can start fresh after graduation. Which is only two months away. So, I don't have a lot of time…"

"Whew. That took a lot of guts to tell Dad. I mean, he may cut you off financially, so mad props. Deadass. But…" Darion stopped, and Devon stared at him.

"What?"

"Um…this ain't you changing your plans cuz of J.T., is it?" Darion said quickly.

Devon bit his lip. Maybe initially he was willing to change his plans for his girl, but this intense need to do something of his own definitely came from God.

"No. I mean, there was some influence there, with Jasmine wanting to move to L.A., and I was trying to figure out how to do that while still running the business. But no. This is…This is something else. This is…" Devon's voice trailed as he tried to figure out how to explain his new spiritual revelation to his brother.

"It's what?"

"I just think I have something *else* I'm supposed to do. Like, a *calling.*"

Darion looked at Devon like he needed to get his head checked. "Calling? You mean like be a monk or something?"

Devon couldn't help but laugh. "Bro. Get serious. Obviously, I'm not about that monk life if I'm getting married. No, like something else that's important. But not necessarily as radical," he clarified. Yet even *he* didn't know what that something was, so it was hard to verbalize it to his brother.

Darion was the listening ear Devon needed and gave him props for sharing his truth. "You know I got you. No matter what," his brother assured before they ended the call.

Darion's sentiments were a well of comfort. He understood more than anyone the pressure Devon had been under his whole life to take over the family business. *And* he knew their father. That man hated when anyone disagreed with him. Especially when it came to something he had had his heart set on for decades. It was truly a miracle that Devon had stood up to him. He marveled at the fact and at God's strength to do so. Still, the sadness from letting down his father and not continuing his legacy wouldn't leave.

Devon's eyes roamed around the dim room. The decor was the same as when he was in high school. Posters of athletes hung on the wall. A few trophies he had won in chess tournaments graced his bookshelf stocked with collections of his favorite authors. Even a certificate he received from a win on the debate team floated above the shelf in a shiny silver frame. All his life, he had done what he was supposed to. Followed the right path. Achieved the right grades. Made the right friends. Now that he suddenly wanted something different from what someone else wanted for him, what his parents wanted for him, he was being punished.

"God, what am I supposed to do?" The words tumbled from his lips after he'd barely formed the thought. The quick answer that came rested on his heart like a newborn.

Pray.

Prayer was something Devon hadn't done for real since he was a kid. When they used to go to Sunday school, they would pray. Now praying like, on his own? That was a foreign concept. Well, with all of the ways God had been going out of *His* way to speak to him, the least Devon could do was try to meet God halfway.

Why not? Devon thought. He slid off the bed and fell on his knees. Awkwardly, he bowed his head and clasped his hands. At first, there was nothing. Just the droning of his wall clock as the hands ticked away. The discomfort didn't leave, but he pressed on, letting his heart lead him in this budding connection with God. Peace slowly emerged, along with that same feeling of love. Devon found himself thanking God for all the good things in his life. Yes, he was struggling with the outcome of his future and hurt by his father, but he was still taken care of. Still loved by his loved ones. He still had his dad, even if his dad wasn't his favorite person right now. Then, out of nowhere, a vision appeared.

Devon saw himself. He was in a suit, speaking. A group of young people surrounded him and eagerly jotted notes on what he had to say. The scene switched. He had an apron tied around his waist and was serving. That scene vanished, and a new one appeared. He was with a little girl in his arms, probably around three or four. She was gorgeous, and she looked at him with a smile. Love burst in his heart as he gazed down. Then the vision was over. Once again, he was in his bedroom.

Devon's heart raced. "Whoa!"

He had never had a vision before and didn't even know that he *could.*

"God. What does this mean?" he asked out loud.

Only the beating of his heart responded. That's when Devon decided he would spend the rest of the evening praying and fell back onto his knees.

That's when Devon learned how to pray.

———

IN THE MORNING, Devon told his mom about God's instruction not to take over Jack & Jill. She was surprised but understood and encouraged him in his obedience. Her response both comforted and amazed him. What shocked him even more, though, was her response when he shared about how his dad had taken the news.

"Don't worry about it. You want some eggs with your coffee?" Mrs. Woods was cooking breakfast and held up the pan of scrambled eggs.

"Ma. I don't think you heard me. Dad basically fired me. I don't even know if he's speaking to me right now. I don't even know if I should go in today." Devon looked at her glumly. "He took back the keys to the restaurant."

His mother came over and scraped the eggs onto his plate. "Your dad is just hurt. He'll get over it. Besides, he needs you for as long as you're willing to help. Who else is gon run the business? James?" She smirked since the brothers were still at odds.

"But. I mean. You know Dad is not one to back down on something he believes in."

"Baby. Your father loves you. And if anything, him being in that cast coupled with his love for you *and* him being in this clutch with Jack & Jill will be enough to bring him to his knees. Literally. Let's just keep on praying for him, shall we?"

She winked, and Devon marveled. His mother had really changed. In the past, she would have been just as wrought and torn up about the situation. She would have been upset at his father for being so stubborn and even upset at him for getting engaged without talking to her first about it, or that she hadn't even met his future wife beforehand. Yet the very things that would have had her up in arms before, she was letting just roll off her back.

I make all things new.

There was that word again.

"Has God ever given you a dream, or a vision?" Devon asked his mother. She had taken a seat at the dark oak kitchen table. The wide-open space and stainless-steel appliances oozed affluence. The Woods had a wall knocked out to make the kitchen larger and carved out a nook in the corner that hardly anyone used, except his mother. The white-tiled floors, cotton-white blinds, and matching chalk-white plates and cups all screamed Martha Stewart. His mother was a die-hard fan of Ms. Stewart.

"Yes," she answered slowly. "I've had a few. Why do you ask?"

Devon opened up to his mother about both his dream and vision from last night. She folded her hands and listened carefully.

When he finished, she said, "Give me a sec to pray," then closed her eyes and started murmuring to herself. After a few moments, she spoke.

"The dream was a warning, but it was also encouragement. There are some hard things coming, Devon, but you'll get through them. That's what the storm represents. But you were safe during the storm. The house is a symbol of you, and the bedroom is a symbol of your heart. God is giving you a new heart. His heart. God is making you a new creature in Him. It's both a picture of what's happening now and even a long-term picture of His work in your life overall. The sun represents His Son, Jesus."

Wow. Devon was stunned. His mother got all of that out of one dream? Who was this woman?

Oh, but she wasn't finished.

"The vision was about your future. God is showing you some of the things He has for you. I can't say I fully understand what they are, but I think He wants you to be encouraged that you made the right decision walking away from Jack & Jill. Because you're right, He has something else."

Goosebumps speed raced up Devon's arms. Whew! His eyes enlarged as he stared at the woman he had known his whole entire 23 years of life. Mrs. Woods had always been a powerhouse. She had always set the tone and standard for success and accomplishment, and even morality and the treatment of others. Yet, even with all of that, this new version of her was even better. Finally, Devon asked her the question he had been wondering about since their night at North Star.

"Mom, how come you never shared more about religion and spirituality with us? I mean, we did go to church on the important days, but you said you always had a relationship with God. How come that wasn't really instilled in us?"

His mother took a thoughtful sip from her coffee before speaking. Her face was somber when she spoke. "I had a super religious upbringing with your grandmother, Nana Jean. One that really scarred me. For a while, I ran from religion. When you guys came along, I knew you needed some kind of foundation, but I was so scared to push it on you like it was forced on me. I guess I was on the other extreme of things. I didn't want to push, but I didn't express its importance."

Her shoulders shrank before she reached a hand to cover his on the table. "I'm sorry."

"No. I understand. There's nothing to be sorry about. If you had made it more of a focus, I may have felt burdened by it." Devon enclosed his hand over hers. "Now I get to discover God for myself." Then he added, "Now we can do it together."

His mother grinned and got up to hug him. Suddenly, she said, "Hold on a sec," before leaving the room.

Devon took her absence as an opportunity to eat his eggs and finish his coffee. When she reappeared, she held out the keys to Jack & Jill.

"You'll need to eat fast if you want to get there on time."

TEN
THANK YOU FOR SAYING YES

The last two days of Devon's time at home sped by. Though his dad wasn't talking to him outside of a few grunts and head nods after he reported daily updates on the restaurant, a supernatural peace Devon couldn't verbalize accompanied him. It was like Christmas morning, gift-wrapped with his birthday, topped with a bow of love. He felt indescribably, undeniably *special*.

Friday evening, he attended the bake-off with his mother at North Star (his mother had made Nana Jeans' famous pound cake) where he got a chance to reconnect with Lena.

When approaching her, Devon's eyes sparkled. "God is so good!" he practically yelled.

Lena grinned. "Yes, He is!" She squeezed him into a warm hug.

Lena was probably the first young woman Devon had met who lived unabashedly for the Lord. She was attractive, down-to-earth, and hip, yet wore her spirituality as a staple of her outfit.

During the fellowship portion of the event, they talked for over an hour, and Devon soaked up Lena's wisdom and insight. She had been a PK (preacher's kid) and had taken the road a lot of PKs did. Rebelling against the stiff, structural environment and overbearing rules of her parents' beliefs, she went her own way for a while.

"But then, I met the wrong man, married him, and all hell broke loose," she confessed. A sad expression imprinted her pie-shaped face.

Devon's heart pinged. He could almost visualize the pain she experienced as she dove into the abuse that unraveled her marriage. She described both verbal and physical abuse, which caused her miscarriage. Then, her countenance changed, and she smiled.

"God used all of it to bring me back to Him. That's when I knew he was calling me. He was calling me to live for Him. And it wasn't because it was something my parents had told me my whole life or what my father preached across the pulpit. It was because He told me Himself."

Devon knew exactly what she meant. He was now wondering how he had ever lived without the voice of God in his life, especially concerning life decisions. It was like God was a GPS to his life!

"That's exactly how I feel," Devon said. "I told my dad I wasn't taking over his business, and it was one of the craziest things I've ever done. I've been preparing to be the owner since I was a kid, but I knew without a doubt God was telling me to do it." Devon swallowed, and Lena's eyes widened.

"Wow, Devon. I can't imagine how difficult that was for you. I'm so proud of you for being obedient to what was on your heart." When she spoke, she rubbed a hand over his, and Devon's heart fluttered.

"Thank you. It actually wasn't as difficult as I would have expected because there was this supernatural power giving me strength. What was more difficult was my father's response to my decision," he admitted. He dropped his eyes and studied the bench they were sitting on. The two were off in a corner of the sanctuary near the back.

Lena said, "I'll be keeping your dad in prayer. I'm sure once he sees what God has for you instead, he'll come around."

Devon said, "Thanks. That in and of itself will be a miracle! My dad is pretty tunnel-visioned when it comes to his own views, so him having a change of heart will *only* be God."

Lena gave him a sweet smile and said, "Well, prayer works miracles. My parents prayed for *years* for me to get to where *I* needed to be. And it worked." She leaned back, and peace seemed to ooze from her features.

Devon gazed at Lena in awe. He became smitten by the love and intellect that radiated from her. It wasn't the kind of intellect typically associated with academia or professionalism. It was *otherworldly*.

While assessing the ruby-red dress and matching lipstick she wore, for the first time, Lena's outward beauty was illuminated. Her pixie-cut, curly hair danced freely atop her head, then fell over the edges of her face, framing it perfectly. A smile or laugh always seemed to be resting beneath her thick, smooth lips, ready to burst on the scene at any moment. Her huge, almost perfectly symmetrical eyes batted with natural, long lashes, somehow without being flirty. It was a talent that rarely appeared in their generation. The longer Devon observed her, the more he wanted to keep observing her. A tinge of guilt emerged.

You're engaged, he thought, and sat back a little so they weren't so huddled up.

"So, how do you feel about going into a new direction, now that you aren't taking over your dad's business?" Lena asked, coming out of her quiet moment and facing him again.

Devon pondered her question. "Well, I feel nervous because I've never *not* had a plan before. But excited because God has been blowing me away with His supernatural ways. I mean, having visions and dreams, prophesying, and speaking in tongues. All of it has been wild! And it just proves how real He is. You know?" Devon was sure the large smile framing Lena's face mirrored his.

"Yep. I know exactly."

"So, He *has to* have a plan. But honestly? I feel like I'm on some kind of high. Like I'm getting addicted to Him."

Lena's melodious laugh flooded his ears. She tilted back her head in joy before saying, "Ahhh. Yes. Jesus is the best addiction!"

Mrs. Woods interrupted their deep fellowship and said it was time to leave (she had come in third with her mother's delicious pound cake). Devon admitted to himself that it was hard to go, so he followed Lena on social media to keep in touch. Social media was way safer than swapping actual phone numbers.

That evening, Devon lay on his bed with a smile glued to his face. So much had changed in just a few days! Excitement swam laps in his belly about whatever it was that God had planned for him, and a freedom he had never experienced before did breaststrokes in the hemispheres of his mind. His life was like a whirlwind, and it was just the beginning. Sure, it had some bumps along the path, like his dad freaking out about his engagement and his decision to let go of Jack & Jill. Yet nothing could compare to this overwhelming experience of being loved and safe. His plans were now God's plans. Devon was learning how to walk by faith.

God, thank You for calling me, he thought. A huge wave of gratitude washed over his chest. And right before drifting off to sleep, Devon heard in his heart as clear as day:

Thank you for saying 'yes' to the call.

———

SUNDAY EVENING, after the hour-and-a-half flight from Brooklyn Heights, Devon returned to school. He'd chosen to stay an extra day to help with Jack & Jill by training his uncle and updating his mother on the admin side. Both would try to fill his father's shoes until he was back on his feet. Or at least, until Mr. Woods got annoyed enough at being bound to the bed and forced them to let him return to work.

When Devon stood in the doorway to say goodbye to his pops, he received the same grunt and head nod. It stung, but Devon wasn't surprised.

His mother said, "He'll get over it," when she embraced him, and he exited the beautiful brick brownstone.

Devon hoped she was right. He hated being at odds with his father, and if it wasn't for his mother's support, he may have given in to his dad's way of thinking. After all, he was springing this whole marriage thing, *and* not taking over Jack & Jill, after *years* of being groomed for it, all at the same time. It made sense why his father was upset. Plus, it was a huge risk for Devon to share his truth when he was counting on the money from Jack & Jill to stack for him and Jasmine. Should he really have cut off the hand that fed him?

I have something else for you, came the still small voice whenever Devon revisited his decision.

So Devon chose to focus on that as he took the elevator up the three flights to his dorm and crammed his luggage into the intimate space. Most students had already arrived and were settled in their rooms, probably preparing for Monday's classes, so he didn't have to share it.

During the short ride, Devon's thoughts slid to the events of the last week. His emotions were tied into a bundle of exhaustion, excitement, and nervousness. Who knew his trip would take such a turn? And that the sacrifice he made to leave Cancun and go home to help his father would result in his father's ungratefulness. That was the part that also hurt. Not only did Devon feel unsupported, he felt *unappreciated*.

When he got inside his dorm room, it was clear Darion had arrived, even though he was nowhere in sight. His brother's clothes were strewn all over his bed and bursting out of his wide-open luggage, as if he had been searching for something to wear that he had packed. Since he had kept his original flight, Darion had landed the day before, on Saturday, along with everyone else. Devon had touched base with him on one other call, but all other communication was via text. It had been the same with Jasmine. It seemed they kept missing each other's calls the last couple of days.

It's cool. I'm 'bout to see my baby soon, Devon thought with a giddy grin. Diligently, he started unpacking his suitcase.

Devon's side of the room was in stark contrast to his brother's. Whereas his desk, bed, and closet were immaculate and painfully organized, Darion was lucky to find a pen in his pen drawer. That was one thing Devon would not miss when he graduated.

No more messy roommate!

Within moments of finishing sorting his dirty clothes and putting back his clean ones, his phone rang. Jasmine. Devon was surprised she didn't video chat him like usual.

"Hey, baby. I was just thinking 'bout you! Wanna come over? I miss you," he rambled in a husky tone.

Jasmine said, "Yeah. Hey. I was hoping we could talk. I'm not up for it tonight, but didn't want to leave you hanging. You wanna meet tomorrow? My day is jam-packed. I won't be free til around 6 pm."

Devon said, "Oh. Ok," and tried to dim the disappointment in his voice. "Yeah. I'm sure you're beat. I am too for real." He ran a hand over his fade. "You wanna do the cafe at Tyson? I know they have that Key lime pie you like. We can do a dessert date," he said.

Jasmine responded, "Ok, see you then," before hanging up.

Devon stared at the phone. *Maybe she's just tired,* he thought, trying to shake off his disappointment. *Shoot, I'm exhausted myself.*

Since he had to TA Marx's 8 am class, Devon decided to turn in early. With all the activities, he realized he never checked his emails to see the professor's response when he told him he could meet on Monday. Immediately, he pulled out his laptop to review the email thread:

Devon, please let me know when you're available for a chat. There's an important matter we need to discuss in person as soon as you're back on campus. Talk to you soon. -Marx

Devon's response:

Sure thing. I'll be free after my last class Monday, around 4 pm.

That was when his eyes fell on Marx's last reply. Somehow, he had missed it.

4:30 pm works. Meet in my office. Also, in light of our pending conversation, I won't need you to come in for my early morning classes. Schedule accordingly. Talk soon. -Marx

He doesn't need me to come in to assist his 8 am? Devon's brow furrowed. *That's weird.*

Marx hated early mornings and was normally super grateful for Devon's presence to assist for that very reason. Even when he presented the job to Devon, one of his requests was that he help with the morning classes.

Apprehension wrapped Devon's gut like a spiral staircase. He typed out his response.

Ok. I'll see you at 4:30.

He wrestled with what to say next, then settled on,

Talk to you soon.

As much as Devon wanted to stew on what in the world his favorite professor needed to talk to him about, drowsiness was kicking in. After checking out the remaining grades that were finally posted from his midterms (all A's and one B), and then catching a text from his brother: **"I'm spending the night at Kimberly's"** (*Ok, Darion!* he thought), Devon discarded the urge to dissect all the reasons as to why Marx needed to see him.

Whatever it is, I'm sure it's not that big of a deal, was his last thought before drifting off to sleep.

————

ONE GREAT THING about Marx telling him he didn't have to help with his morning classes was that Devon got to sleep in. With a deep yawn, he stretched his way into the late morning sunshine. It was beaming through his window, and it seemed that Spring was giving him her best smile.

"Good morning to you, too, Spring!" Devon said, feeling cheesy but still upbeat.

After starting his morning cup of coffee in his Keurig and warming up some Pop-Tarts stashed behind his brother's side of the food crate, he scrolled through his texts.

Antonio:

Yo. Let me know what you up to later...

Once he left Cancun, Devon had barely spoken to his friend, other than a few comments on social media. That wasn't that uncommon for them on breaks. It was just different this time because they'd been on vacation together. With running Jack & Jill, dealing with his dad, juggling his relationship with Jasmine, and even his newfound relationship with God, Devon's friendship with Antonio had been put on the back burner.

I need to do better with all these transitions, he chastised himself. His gaze landed on the picture on his desk of him and his friend taken two years ago at a Knicks game. They had been elated when Antonio's uncle, Dave, the team's manager's financial advisor, scored them tickets for Antonio's birthday. The Knicks had lost that one, but neither of them had cared. They were just happy to be in the house!

"I definitely need to make sure my boy knows we tight, especially when I graduate," Devon muttered to himself while hashing out a text.

> What up, bro. I'm under the gun today, but what about tomorrow? Let's hoop at the rec.

Without awaiting a response, Devon gobbled down his Pop-Tarts, swooped his coffee in his trusty reusable to-go container, swiped his messenger bag, and headed to his first class. He had back-to-backs until his meeting with Marx, which was cool. As long as he had his coffee, he felt energized for the day. It was just something about that fresh morning cup that did the trick.

The afternoon zipped by with one lecture after another. Devon tried his hardest to pay attention, but his thoughts either roamed to whatever this meeting with Marx was about or to daydreaming about his wedding. Jasmine in a white mermaid number. Him in a fly black tux. All of their friends would be there. Even his parents. The ring was on its way and would arrive in a couple of days. Devon couldn't help himself and kept peeking at the tracking information in his emails.

Jasmine is gonna love it! he thought excitedly during Intermediate Business Operations. He had to make himself shut off his phone to pay attention to the discussion.

Finally, it was after 4 pm. Devon was already in the building that Marx's office was in since his previous class was held there, so he started up the stairs from the first floor. When he approached the door, he was surprised that Marx wasn't alone. The back of Professor Clark's blond hair, streaked with grey, peeked out from above the chair across from him. Marx abruptly stopped talking, met Devon's eyes, and motioned him inside. Professor Clark turned her head also. Her gaze seemed to be speaking a message Devon couldn't interpret. She was cordial when greeting him, which, if it were someone he wasn't as favored by, would have been fine. But Professor Clark had always been super friendly towards him.

What's up with her? Devon wondered, easing into the room and slipping into a chair next to her. Nervously, he rubbed his khakis as he greeted the professors.

"You're early. We were just uhh, wrapping up," Marx mumbled. His gaze slid to Clark.

Marx's salt-and-pepper hair made him look older than he really was. Adding to it was a square, firm chin that sat beneath dark brown wire rims. He always wore some kind of grandpa-looking cardigan over a plaid shirt. His whole getup was intentional to demand a respect he had yet to achieve from tenured professors. Clark was one of those tenured professors. The no-nonsense type, she openly bragged about how she had paid her dues, trudging through the male-dominant field of the business world. Back when the rights of women in leadership were at their peak of oppression, Clark was burning her bra and screaming her war cry, leading the pack. In her quest for equality, she frequently shared with her students how she'd stumbled upon a passion for teaching and decided to hit the men where it hurt: train up the next generation of leaders in predominantly male industries and equip them with the mindset that all men *and* women were created equal. She was a tough cookie, though fair. Any student she showed an ounce of attention to had to be worth their salt because of the high bar she always had set. Devon had somehow hit that bar and made it into her good graces. But something was different about her today, and maybe without him knowing it, he had somehow fallen from grace.

Marx rose. "Let me get the door," he uttered before taking long, quick strides across the small office.

Once the lock clicked and he made his way back to his seat, Devon wondered, *What the hell is going on?* He fought the urge to get up and run. Or at least, pull out his phone and record the conversation. The room suddenly felt like a scene from "Get Out."

If Clark whips out a cup of tea and starts tapping a spoon, I am out, he thought, and chuckled internally.

"Would you like something to drink?" Professor Marx offered. "Water?"

Devon was so caught off guard that he just looked at him.

Marx cleared his throat. "Ok. Well, Devon, I'm sure you're

wondering why you're here. Thank you for taking time out of your day to come."

Would you just get to it already? Devon was starting to feel annoyed.

"I had a reason for not wanting you to assist with my morning classes." Marx paused, took a swig from his water bottle, and struggled with meeting Devon's gaze. Finally, after a moment, he said, "We have a situation."

Devon couldn't take it anymore. "What situation?" he asked, irritation winning over confusion in his tone.

"You—You've been accused of sexual harassment," Marx said faintly. It was as if he couldn't even bear tasting the words.

Devon blinked. "What?!" He frowned. "By *who*?"

"Monica Jones." Clark suddenly spoke up. She had been quiet up until this point, letting Marx take the lead. Even Devon could tell he was fumbling the job worse than a virgin on prom night.

"Monica…Monica. The Monica in your 10 am?" Devon was trying to place her as various students' faces flashed through his mind's eye. He assisted Marx with three different classes. "You mean, Monica, who asked *me out*?" Devon's face was flabbergasted as his shocked gaze shifted from one professor to the other.

"You're saying she asked you out?" Clark looked at him, skepticism dripping off her high cheekbones. "I saw her crying in the restroom after you were with her the Friday before break. That child was shook. She said you tried to take advantage of her when she turned you down for a date."

"*What*?!" Devon couldn't control the volume of his tone. He had practically yelled.

Marx tried to demonstrate some type of leadership role in the conversation. "Calm down, son."

Devon inhaled. *Oh my God. No, this broad didn't*! He was livid.

"You expect me to believe she lied to my face when she had literal tears rolling down her cheeks and was deeply embarrassed?" Clark said. "I walked in the bathroom, and she was a mess." Clark's voice waded in passion. It was as if her old protest days were upon her. Far be it for her to allow yet another sister to be the victim of oppressive male chauvinism.

With every ounce of dignity and self-control Devon had, he looked Clark in the eye and said through gritted teeth, "She's lying."

"Well, son. It's your word against hers," Marx said, trying to regain control of the discussion. "And at this point, because there are no real witnesses, we have to follow school protocol."

"Which is?" Devon asked tightly. His arms had crisscrossed his chest. He squeezed his balled hands beneath them. Blood pumped through every part of his being, threatening to unleash in an emotional explosion.

"You'll be under investigation. You'll be interviewed. You may need to go in front of the school board. And I can't have you helping in my classes until we get this thing straightened out," Marx hurried to say.

Devon shook his head in confusion. He couldn't believe this was happening. "So, someone *falsely* accuses me of something I *didn't* do, and basically, *I'm* guilty until proven innocent? My credibility, my work, my pristine academic record, leadership positions, honorable dealings with these students mean *nothing*?" Each word flew out, as Devon's arms drew circles in the air in wild disbelief.

"Because of our history in this country of women suffering at the hands of men and the many sexual victims who've been mishandled by our judicial system, we need to take these precautions," Clark stated. She didn't seem as harsh as she had before, but her eyes were still cool as cucumbers.

"What about the many *Black* men who were *falsely* accused of wrongdoing by our *judicial system* who've sacrificed *decades* of their lives rotting in prison for crimes *they* didn't commit? Who's their savior? Who fights for *them*?" The words shot out of his mouth like a cannon before Devon could even think. He glared, daring her to refute his statements.

Clark just sat dumbfounded. She was suddenly faced with the hard truth that the Black fight against systemic racism was out of her territory.

Devon tossed his head in disgust. It was clear her concern was more for his female accuser than for him.

"So, what do I do now?" he finally asked, his tone biting. He took a deep breath to try to calm his racing heart.

Marx sighed while placing both hands on his desk. He removed his glasses and pinched his temples. He looked older. Devon felt it wasn't because of his age, but because there were so many things in this life he had probably never had to deal with until he got into this position. Things like gender equality and systemic racism. Being a white man in America was like using a FastPass at Disney World. You got to cut the line and ride all the rides first with no questions asked.

"For now, just keep going to your classes," Marx finally answered. "You won't be able to assist me with the TA position, but the school has already started the paperwork needed for the investigation. They were a little delayed because of the break. They'll email you and schedule interview times. Until then, you wait."

Until then, you wait.

The words echoed in Devon's mind. Just a few days ago, he was rejoicing on the beach, proposing to his future wife, and preparing for graduation.

Graduation.

He grew worried and looked at his former favorite professor. "Will this affect me graduating?" Devon made himself ask. Steeling himself for the answer, he clutched both chair arms like a dying man in the electric chair.

Marx looked at him with a grave expression. "It could."

ELEVEN
THE POWER OF THE WORD

Devon took the long way to Tyson Hall. It started raining as he walked, but he didn't care. He needed to take it slow. Besides, getting wet couldn't possibly dampen his mood more than it already had been. He ran and reran the events in his mind that had taken place in Clark's classroom about Monica.

Did I lead her on? Did I flirt in any way? Every time he did, he came up empty. *Was it something I said? Was it something I implied?*

The relentless thoughts swarmed Devon's mind like bees, even as he finally reached the hall and swiped his phone against the QR code reader.

"Yo. Bruh. You look horrible!" His brother was there, and Devon realized he was working tonight. He glanced down at his drenched polo, jacket, and khakis, and blinked.

"Oh. Yeah. I got wet," he mumbled.

Though Darion's arms flanked a large grey tub piled with dirty dishes, smooshed against his green apron, he hurried to set it atop a nearby trash can. Examining Devon, he asked, "You ok?"

Devon shrugged quickly. "I just got some bad news. That's all. I'll talk to you later," he said, barely meeting his brother's eyes. He didn't want to get into it since he was meeting Jasmine.

Darion stared at him, uncertainty staining his almond-colored face. He cocked his head. "Yo. Hit me on my phone. I work 'til eight, but we can text."

Devon's head bobbed with glazed eyes. Darion still looked concerned, but he had to get back to work. He swooped up the bin and disappeared into the kitchen.

When Devon searched the dining hall, he didn't see Jasmine. Since he was a little early, he decided to get a cup of coffee. He hadn't really eaten other than the Pop-Tarts and a quick sandwich in between classes, but he didn't feel hungry. Coffee seemed to always make things better.

The evening crowd was thick, as lively chatter cluttered the space, and dishes and silverware clanked. Watching Darion bus tables and clean up after students, it once again, dawned on Devon how different he and Darion were from their sister.

Hopefully someday she'll get her act together, he thought briefly, stirring creamer into his coffee. He then found a table near the back. It wasn't until he took his first sip that Devon remembered how much he hated their coffee, but he was desperate. It was all he had. He forced a swallow.

Glancing at his phone, he saw that Jas was on her way. It was 5:52 pm. Devon sighed. *How in the world did I get into this mess?* After taking another unsatisfying sip, he pushed it down, then read and re-read the emails from Marx. It was obvious *now* that something was up; Devon just couldn't have fathomed what it would end up being. He felt *blindsided*.

To distract from the incessant eating of his brain, Devon switched to his social media. For the first time since receiving the horrible news, he smiled. It was a small smile, but a smile, nonetheless. Lena had popped up on his news feed. She was grinning ear-to-ear, her countenance shining bright. The post was a picture of her and a few of the faces he recognized from North Star, including his mother. Lena was wearing that bad red dress she had looked amazing in. It was the day of the bake-off, and each of the winners held up their ribbons. Ohh, his mother would be *hot* if she knew she was posted online! She hated social media.

I should send it to her for kicks. Devon laughed at the thought.

"What's so funny?" Jasmine peered down before sinking into the chair across from him.

Clearing his throat, Devon closed the app. "Uhh, nothing. I was just…" he fumbled. "Looking at something."

He leaned in then and reached over to stroke her hand. "Hey, baby."

Jasmine offered a smile that didn't quite reach her eyes. "Hey," she said softly. Her mood seemed dim, and he wondered if she, too, had received some bad news.

Jasmine ran her eyes over him. "You got wet?"

He shrugged. "Yeah. Got caught in the rain coming over here."

"Let me get you some napkins." She shot to her feet before returning with a handful of paper towels.

Grabbing a few, Devon wiped his forehead, "Thanks." He sighed. "I must a forgot to dry myself." Nodding to her black and white polka dot umbrella and pink poncho, he said, "I guess you were prepared, huh?"

She had already dropped her umbrella to the floor, but now removed her poncho, then folded it on the seat next to her. "I guess so…" Her gaze drifted away.

There was silence then, and it wasn't the comfortable kind that sometimes happened when people close to each other didn't need words because being together was so much better. How people in love usually are. How people engaged often were.

How they should be.

A tightening clenched Devon's stomach.

Jasmine licked her lips. "You gonna eat?"

The clacking from her heels on the floor echoed softly as she rocked her knee under the table. Devon always wondered how she managed heels on campus, and now, even in the rain.

Women are a mystery. The thought shot his ponderings back to the student, Monica.

"What's wrong?" Jasmine asked.

His face must have given away his thoughts. Devon inhaled loudly, drawing his hand away from hers, then slid it back to his coffee. While clasping his mug, he took a sip, desperately wishing he had a cup from his mother's French press.

I don't even think I can get the words out, Devon thought, in terms of telling Jasmine what was wrong. It made him sick.

"How was your day?" he asked instead.

Jasmine looked surprised by his deflection. "It was. It was ok," she answered slowly. Cautiously. "Look. Uh. There's something I need to talk to you about…" Her voice trailed as her eyes searched the table.

She looks nervous. Devon realized something was weighing on her. *I've been too caught up with me,* he scolded himself.

"Bruh, you not answering my texts." Darion was at their table, holding another grey bin. This one was empty. "Yo, wuz up, Jas," he said offhandedly. "Make sure you text me asap and let me know what's up!" Darion said, pointing at Devon with a finger before skirting off.

Peering at his phone, three missed messages from his brother glared at him.

Jasmine looked confused. "What's that about?"

Devon bit his lip. "I got some…bad news today," he admitted.

Concern instantly flushed her face, her doe eyes turning sympathetic. "What's up?"

"Remember that girl I told you about from Marx's class who asked me out?" Jasmine nodded.

"She says I-I…sexually harassed her."

Ugh. Just saying it made him want to throw up.

"*What*?!" Jasmine's jaw hit the floor. "You're not serious."

Devon nodded painfully. "Yeah. She said after I hit on her, I couldn't take the rejection and tried to force her to kiss me." His voice grew hard, and he grimaced, his eyes swimming with anger.

"That little b—" Jasmine was the type to use her fists over her words when someone she loved was hurt, and Devon knew it.

He reached across the table and took her hand. "She's just a kid, Jas. She don't even know the jeopardy she's putting me in."

"No. She don't know the jeopardy she putting *herself* in!" Jasmine seethed. "What's her IG?"

Devon knew better than to give her that information. "I don't want you doing anything stupid. It's not even worth it. She's just a kid," he said again. It was weird defending this girl when she was literally causing him so much drama. After a second, he added hesitantly, "But the other thing is I don't know if this is gonna hinder me graduating."

"What?" Jasmine said again. Her face dripped with shock, as she had no clue all this was going on with Devon.

"There's going to be an investigation. I may need to go before the board. They could suspend me…" He looked away, his eyes burning. He didn't want his girl to see him this emotional.

Jasmine was on her feet and jetted to his side of the table. After removing his wet jacket from the chair next to him, she sat in its place. Pulling him into a hug, she nestled her face into his neck and started stroking her long nails up and down his back.

"I'm here. Everything's gonna be ok," she murmured into the thick of his neck.

Devon gave up the fight on bottling his emotions and squeezed his arms around her, pulling her close. The familiar fragrance of some kind of fresh fruit soothed his nostrils.

It's gon be ok, Devon repeated to himself.

"As long as we're together, remember?" she whispered, sending tingling sensations along his skin.

"As long as we're together," Devon murmured back. He squeezed tighter.

———

THAT EVENING, Devon gave up studying and checked his phone. It was almost 9 pm. He'd called his mom earlier and was hoping she would call him back. When there was still no call, he moved to his bed to play a chess game on his laptop. Chess was usually very therapeutic, except when Devon lost three times in a row, it was obvious his head wasn't in the game. He switched it up and pulled up a show to watch. The show faded into the background of his thoughts, and the day's events flashed before his mind's eye.

At the dining hall, Jasmine had stayed with him for about an hour, but she had a Black student meeting to get to. "I'll hit you up after," she promised.

Once he filled Darion in on what happened, his brother offered to keep him company, but Devon had to study and didn't want to interrupt Darion's plans to study with Kimberly.

"So things are getting serious wit' y'all, huh?" Devon had said in a teasing tone to his brother.

Darion half-smiled. "Yeah. Kimberly has a lot of great qualities that I guess I wasn't paying attention to before," he admitted sheepishly. "I'm definitely starting to feel her." He paused. "I'm sorry about your situation, man. It's crazy." In sympathy, he shook his head while undressing, then threw on his robe. "Ain't no *way* I can see them kicking you out after this *one* incident though. And she ain't got no proof!" Darion exclaimed as he stood to face Devon, seated at his desk.

"Yeah. But these days the "Me Too Movement" is ramped up. And when has our country ever cared a lick about a Black man being wrongfully accused of something?" Devon huffed.

"Facts. But your professors trusted your character enough to hire you as a TA *and* give you keys to their classrooms. That has to mean something, dawg."

"I don't know. Clark has this white feminist lens that seems impenetrable. You know they only know their own oppression. All she sees is a poor victimized woman and a large predatory man." Devon grunted, leaning back in his chair and throwing his hands behind his head. "So the man *has* to be the monster. I guess I should just be glad it's not a white girl. You know they would have lynched me by now and hung me out to dry!"

"Bet. You wouldn't get *no* due process. Yo ass would a *been* gone," Darion cosigned.

"Anyways. I can't be worried about it cuz I got studying to do," Devon said, then revisited his marketing book.

"Well, hit me if you need me to come home at *any* time. We going to the library, so I'm not gon be out all night."

"Bet," Devon said, but he wasn't going to take his brother up on his offer. This was the first time he had seen Darion pursue a real relationship, and Devon was intrigued. He definitely didn't want to distract him from that.

Devon's phone vibrated, interrupting him from his reverie. His mother was finally calling him back.

"Hey, Momma."

"Hi, sweetie. What's going on? Sorry I missed your call! I had a great conversation with Lena after our Monday night prayer call. We were talking about coming up with ideas to get more youth involved in the church."

At the mention of Lena, Devon's heart warmed. "Oh yeah? Cuz you so young and hip, you know what will engage the youth?" Devon couldn't help teasing her. His mother's laugh hugged his soul.

"Honey, you just don't know how *fly* your mother was and *still is*!"

At that, Devon cracked up. He could probably count the number of times he had heard his mother use slang in his entire life on one hand.

"But, baby, what's goin' on? You good? Or were you just checking on your father?"

"Oh. Yeah. How *is* dad?" Devon asked. Guilt that he hadn't once thought about his dad since he got back surfaced. "How are things at Jack & Jill?" he added.

"Everything is fine. Your Uncle James is a Godsend, and your father *has* to see that, given if it wasn't for *him*, the restaurant wouldn't be open. And you, of course," she added quickly.

"I appreciate you saying that," Devon said. "I definitely feel like dad didn't see the sacrifice I made in coming back." He tried to keep his tone from sounding bitter.

"He will, honey. He will. Give him time. We're all learning patience on this journey, I'll tell you that much!"

His mother's loving tenderness saturated Devon's heart, and he was glad he had called her. "You're right, though. There is something I needed to tell you," he said, before unleashing the nightmare of today.

When Devon was done expelling all the gory details, it was clear that his mother was grieved and appalled.

"This is so disheartening. Especially since this young woman is manipulating a very much-needed advocacy for women in our country. And to be a *Black* woman doing it. She doesn't realize that she's making us *all* look bad."

Devon nodded even though his mother couldn't see him. "And I just keep running it back and forth in my mind like, what did I do to mislead her?"

"Oh, honey. You're experiencing what it's like for most *real* victims of sexual abuse. I know because I've had some things happen myself. As well as people close to me."

Devon's brows rose. "What? Ma, you've been sexually harassed?"

"Sadly, Devon, I don't know too many women who haven't been. It seems like, as a young woman developing, you start encountering catcalling and men lusting after you simply by walking down the street. Some of them are even crazy enough to put their hands on you."

Devon was quiet as he took a look at life through his mother's lens. "Wow. I didn't think about catcalling being harassment. I guess, because some women like it." His thoughts turned to Jasmine and Sheila, who ate up all the attention.

"Yeah, well, a lot don't. And then you have the real victims who try to share their story and get justice, and sadly, aren't believed. Or don't have the proof. That's why what this girl…Monica, you said her name was?"

"Yeah. Monica."

"That's why I can see even more how Monica is being used by the enemy. She's not just coming after you. She's coming at the system that's put into place to protect real victims. The school has that protocol for a reason, and that's because *real* women have faced *real* violations and *their* perpetrators went *scot*-free with no consequences."

His mother's voice was now dripping with passion coupled with a vengeance he had never heard from her before. Suddenly, Devon could see her on the front lines of the same women's movement that Clark probably led back in the day. Thankfully, her experience as a Black woman widened her perspective because she knew that the justice system had failed them both.

"Baby, take a look at the story of Joseph," his mother suggested. "I think it'll resonate with you and what you're going through right now."

Devon wracked his brain, trying to think back to his children's church days when they read Bible stories.

"Is that the one where his brothers threw him in a pit?"

"Yeah, and a whole lot of other stuff happened to him, too. One of those things was a woman falsely accusing him of sexually harassing her and trying to take advantage of her."

"What!? That's in the Bible?" Devon sat up on his bed in surprise and searched his computer for the Bible passage.

His mother chuckled. "There's a lot of relatable stories in the Bible. Remember what Lena said? These aren't just stories, Devon. They are *real* lives of *real* people."

Devon now had the passage pulled up to a section that read, "Joseph A Slave in Egypt."

"Hey, Ma. You think you can send me a Bible? I wouldn't know which one to buy…"

His mother's sweet voice responded on the other end, "Of course."

They talked a little longer, and Mrs. Woods agreed to keep Devon in prayer. She requested that he keep her posted on updates every step of the way. She was also going to reach out to the family lawyer and see what his next steps should be. Additionally, she asked his permission to share his situation with her prayer group, to which Devon wholeheartedly agreed. He needed all the prayer he could get!

Before they hung up, Devon said, "Ma, did you know you were on social media?" He just couldn't resist.

"What?" His mother sounded alarmed.

Devon cackled. "Calm down. Calm down. Lena put up a picture of you guys from the bake off."

"Oh," his mother said. "Well…I guess that's ok. Since it's for the church."

"Mmhmm…but, Ma. You know a way to get the youth more involved at your church?"

"Huh? What's that?"

"Make a social media page for the church." Devon cracked up, and his mother smacked her lips.

"Now you know that's not my territory," she replied.

"Hey, you the one that said you was fly!" he reminded her.

"Well, I'll talk to Lena about it…good night, *son*," she said.

"Love you, Mom."

"Love you too."

After they hung up, for additional spiritual safety measures, Devon decided to send Lena a DM:

> Hey. I hope you're doing ok! My mom will probably reach out to you soon, but just wanted to give you a heads up on a situation I'm facing…

After explaining everything and hitting send, Devon felt lighter. For some reason, it had never dawned on him to ask for prayer about what he was going through. He was grateful that his mother had suggested that others pray for him. When he started reading the passage of scripture she had referenced, he was even more comforted. Devon had become so engrossed in the story that he didn't hear his phone when it buzzed. He didn't know he had missed Jasmine's call until it was close to midnight, and it was too late to call her back.

I'll call her tomorrow, Devon decided, turning in for the night. His brother had made good on his word and was snoring loudly across the room.

As Devon unwound by processing his day beneath the covers, he assessed everyone's response to his bad news. Even though Jasmine had given him a shoulder to cry on, which was comforting, what really seemed to be giving him peace was reading the Bible.

That's when Devon started learning the power of the Word.

TWELVE

ME TOO

"Yo! I'm open!" Devon waved his hands wildly back and forth until Antonio finally outsmarted his opponent, a big dude with a curly fro.

Two dribbles and a fake shot left, Antonio spun right for the pass.

Devon's man had been on his heels, but Devon was just too quick. He lunged forward right in the nick of time, caught the ball, and went up for the layup.

Swish!

The game was over.

"Yeah boyyeee!!!!!" Antonio cheered and galloped shirtless in his Lebron 13s across the court to chest bump Devon. They concluded the moment with their special handshake.

Devon beamed.

"Yo. You *called* it! That's what I'm talkin' bout, son!" Antonio hollered, balling his shirt in his fist and pumping it in the air.

Devon tossed his head back and laughed. Then he remembered his manners and untangled himself from his friend. "Yo. Good game!" He went to give the other dudes hand slaps, and Antonio did the same.

"Yeah. We got y'all next time," the short, skinny dude who was guarding Devon said. "Y'all just caught us on an off day."

Devon snorted. *Shoot, if anybody should be saying that, it's me*, he thought, but pushed the dark musings away. He wanted to soak up this moment of something good happening. Something fun.

"Yeah yeah. You always say that, Rob," Antonio said. "Every time I beat you, that is!"

The other man rolled his eyes, and the foursome ambled out of the basketball court stationed on the east side of the campus recreation center.

Devon fell back while the three trotted ahead, reviewing the highlights and plays that led to the outcome. Antonio was suddenly an NBA draft pick, giving pointers to the men. Devon chuckled to himself while watching. It wasn't until they were at the entrance when the other guys left that Antonio calmed down.

"Yo, man, that was, like, *epic*. Yo whip skills done really came up," he marveled, looking at Devon, impressed.

"My guy, you know I *been* had these skills," Devon said, popping his t-shirt. "But, playing more with you has helped," he admitted.

"Yeah, you betta give me my props!" Antonio said. "You hungry?"

"I could eat," Devon said.

The boys headed to the pizza shop perched right off campus. It was a long walk, but they made it quickly, adrenaline still pumping, mingled with the high of the win.

"Yo, I got this," Antonio said, and he whipped out his wallet to pay.

Devon faked a shocked expression. "*You* paying for *moi*?" His eyes widened as he flattened a hand over his chest.

"Don't start. You done covered me enough. You know I owe you." Antonio's voice turned deep and thick. While lowering his gaze, he swallowed, handing his card to the cashier.

"Dude. You don't owe me a thing. We brothers. That's what brothers do," Devon said.

Antonio sniffed while grabbing the pizza.

Man, I guess we haven't really had bro time, Devon thought. Guilt taunted him for neglecting his friend. He could count the number of times he had ever seen Antonio emotional. One of them was when his uncle had died, which was completely understandable.

I'm a do better, Devon resolved while trailing his Day One out of the small parlor. They had gotten the order to go since the restaurant was closing. It was almost 8 pm.

"Let's take this to my crib since it's closer," Antonio suggested, clutching the box of the extra-large meat-lovers pizza.

Devon nodded. "Say less."

When they made it to Antonio's, Devon remembered why he rarely hung out at his friend's. His spot was just as messy as Darion's side of the room. Probably even more so because he didn't have a roommate. More than likely, Devon living with his brother caused Darion to at least *try* to keep his mess contained.

"Bruh. You should just have your dad get you a maid or *something*." Devon's lip curled up. *And what's that smell?*

"Dude! I done *tried.* I asked that man *three times* if I could get a maid! And every time he responds, 'Isn't it enough I got you free tuition and board?'" Antonio scrunched up his face while spouting out a stern, deep voice, imitating his father. "I ain't sayin' I disagree with the man, but clearly ya boy needs help." Antonio threw up his hands in surrender before shoving some clothes off the bed onto the floor to make room for the pizza.

Devon, who tried not to pay attention to what else fell on the floor, followed his lead. He removed a few wrinkled jeans and crumpled shirts until there was enough space to eat.

Not wasting any time, the two dug in. For the first time in two days, Devon felt his appetite return, and he was making up for it.

"Thanks, bro," Devon mumbled with food still in his mouth when Antonio handed him a Sprite from the mini fridge.

"Yep. Yo, did you grab napkins?" Antonio peered at Devon with eyes of hope after scarfing down three slices. Both hands dripped with sauce.

Devon cheesed. "You know it!" Reaching over at his feet, he confiscated several paper towels from his gym bag.

"My man!" Antonio grabbed a few and started wiping.

After his fourth slice, Devon called it quits and fell against the wall that the bed slightly brushed against.

Antonio's room had the same layout as his own but was a smidge smaller since it was a single. Still, because his father was on the board for the school, Mr. Johnson did his big one and got him one of the more spacious singles.

The walls were plastered with posters flaunting either athletes or voluptuous women of all shades. Antonio, as he said, did not discriminate when it came to females. The only thing that all the women had in common was their body types. They were all thick.

Devon's eyes grazed some of the posters, and he chuckled to himself. His boy was never one to hide who he was, and that was another thing he admired about him. With Antonio, you got the good, the bad, and the ugly. But at least you knew what you were getting.

"Man, it's been a rough few days. I definitely needed to let loose," Devon said after a while.

Antonio lay stretched out against his headboard with the pizza box slid between them. He was patting his six-pack when Devon had spoken, having removed his shirt so his tattoos were on display.

From time to time, Devon had thought about getting a tattoo, but whenever he did, he could hear his mother's voice.

You're going to have to live with that decision for the rest of your life.

Her pragmatism had stuck with him, so he refrained.

"Yeah, man. I'm really sorry about everything," Antonio responded. For some reason, he looked deeply grieved. His lips had sagged into a frown, and his eyes drilled into his feet.

Devon frowned. "You heard about the Monica thing?" He was surprised. He hadn't had a chance to tell Antonio about it, but maybe his brother had.

Antonio's face pinched in confusion. "Monica?"

"Yeah. The girl who's accusing me of sexual harassment," Devon stated. "That's her name," he clarified, just in case his boy didn't know that part.

Antonio flew up from the headboard and sat upright. "Dawg. What are you *talking about* right now? You being accused of sexual harassment?" He gaped at him.

Devon sighed. "Yeah. It's a mess. This chick in one of Marx's classes said that after the study group I led, I asked her out. Then tried to kiss her when she turned me down."

"What? You not being serious right now." Antonio's face oozed disbelief.

Devon nodded, feeling the weight of the situation all over again. "I wish I was. The wild thing is, *she* came on to *me*. She asked *me* out, and I turned *her* down. She straight flipped it."

"See. That's the shit Michael Davis be talkin' 'bout!" Antonio ranted. "Women crying about oppression and inequality, and look at the bullshit they on. Using the system to lock us up. Steal our authority!" His face contorted into spite while spewing his words. "They taking over, man. I'm *telling* you," he said in an eerily conspiratorial tone.

"It gets worse," Devon said, staring off into the distance. "I may not graduate." His voice was even, but his eyes were stinging.

"Bro. I can't believe this. What the hell. How they gon just threaten your future like that over one b—'s accusation. I mean, what rights do *you* have? Is it just all about *her* rights?!" Antonio was livid. He huffed and puffed about the injustices of the system for the Black man. How the world was against them, and how the only safe spaces they had were in each other.

It was obvious he was repeating the rhetoric he had digested from the podcasts he constantly dined on. Even though Devon didn't agree with everything they said, he did feel like he was getting the short end of the stick in this situation. He was being made to be the abuser, and *he* was the victim.

"I'm telling you, in another ten years, if we don't rise up, we gon lose *all* of our rights!" Antonio shouted, fuming with anger. His light skin had turned a rouge-like red that flushed to his neckline, causing his splotchy birthmark to gleam even darker.

"My mom is supposed to talk to her lawyer to see what my rights are and what steps we should be taking," Devon shared. To this, Antonio dove into his heartfelt cry about lawyers being all about the money, and who can really trust *them*, either?

"I should know. My dad's a judge!" he ranted.

Devon just felt sad. He didn't know what to think. Monica had always seemed quiet and sweet in previous study sessions. She couldn't have had a clue as to what she was doing to his future and how she was, as his mother had said, "being used by the enemy." It just didn't seem fair.

Then, after a few moments, Devon realized something and he turned his head to look at his friend. Antonio was still going off about the injustices of the Black man when Devon said, "Yo."

Antonio paused, mouth midsentence, and replied, "Wuz up?"

"What did you *think* I was talking about?" Devon asked.

Antonio looked at him, perplexed. "What chu' mean?"

"You said you were sorry, but you didn't know about the Monica thing," Devon said thoughtfully. "What were you sorry about?"

Antonio sat still, then fidgeted around, suddenly appearing very uncomfortable.

Fear started creeping along Devon's insides, wrapping its fingers around his midsection.

His friend dropped his gaze, then asked, "Didn't, didn't you talk to Jasmine yesterday?"

Jasmine? Why does that matter? Devon thought. The fear began growing limbs and started crawling along the back of his neck, making the little hairs stand up.

"Yeah," Devon answered slowly. "Why?"

Antonio's facial expression looked pained. The previous passion and aggression he had minutes prior seeped out like a balloon.

He looks like a little kid, Devon thought, disconcerted.

"Didn't. Didn't she tell you?" Antonio asked in an uncharacteristically soft tone. This time he leaned back against the headboard and started tapping his fingers on the bed near his thigh.

His boy's behavior was beginning to freak Devon out, along with the fear mounting his insides.

"Tell me what?" Devon asked in the calmest voice he could muster.

Antonio gulped from his Sprite can, swallowed deeply, then whispered, "We slept together." His eyes glazed over as he stared at his basketball socks, unable to meet Devon's gaze.

The room tilted. Fear morphed into panic, crashing in in waves. It was drowning him, and Devon went underwater. His ears started ringing.

I didn't hear what I thought I heard.

His breath came faster.

I can't breathe.

Then, after moments of silence, he forced the words out of his mouth.

"That ain't nothin' to play about, bro. S-stop playing." His jaw clenched while trying to breathe through his nose.

The ticking from Antonio's clock echoed in the stillness. The chatter from students in the hall subtly reverberated through the door. Devon's own breathing chanted to the ringing in his ears. His chest rose and fell faster as air shot in and out of his nostrils.

Antonio stared at him, his eyes glistening. "I'm so sorry, man."

That's when Devon knew. He was telling the truth. He sat stunned, as tears welled up in Antonio's eyes. His mouth was moving. He was saying something, but Devon couldn't understand it. All he saw was red.

Like a pit bull, he lunged at him, swiping the air with his fists and aiming for his neck. Antonio attempted to run but fell on the floor and banged his leg on the desk chair. It rolled away, fleeing the scene as the two young men entered a match comparable to any WWE fight.

Devon was on top of him. Antonio was larger in build, but Devon had always been faster.

"You asshole!" he screamed while taking shot after shot, blow after blow.

Antonio wrestled against him, trying to push him off, but Devon was in an angry frenzy. He wouldn't let go.

"I'm sorry, man! I'm so sorry!" Antonio wailed, attempting but failing to avert Devon's fists and keep his hands from choking the life out of him.

Expletives Devon didn't even know he knew flew from his mouth as his body took the lead, unleashing all his pent-up pain and enmity.

"I'm sorry!" Antonio kept screaming in between gasps of air.

Near the end of the beatdown, Devon's own tears masked his face. He looked down at Antonio, whose pathetic body lay bloody and bruised beneath him. His lip was busted. His eye was already swelling. His tan skin was turning purple around his neck. The indentations from Devon's fingerprints still stained it.

Devon breathed heavily as more tears ran rapidly down his cheeks. Both fists still tightened at his sides, he sniffed up the liquid pouring from his nostrils. He then wobbled to his feet. After grabbing his belongings, he swung his Nike gym bag over his shoulder. When he looked back at Antonio, the image burned in his mind.

"I'm sorry." Antonio was sobbing in a fetal position, hands wiping his face like a child's.

"Me too," Devon said before opening the door.

I'm sorry I ever called you my brother, he thought, then slammed it closed behind him.

———

When Devon made it back to his room, Darion was nowhere in sight. It was his night off work, so he wasn't sure what his brother was up to. At that point, it was hard to care. Devon's heart was shattered. He was a zombie walking to his dorm room and had no real remembrance of stripping his clothes and getting under the covers. Somehow, he must have because when he decided to check his phone for a text from Darion, he realized that's where he was. Naked under the covers.

Darion:

I'm at Kimberly's tonight. Text if you need me!

His brother had also sent a colorful emoji. Devon also had some messages from Antonio that he quickly deleted without reading. There were some missed calls from him, too. Jasmine had also called. Devon went back and forth about calling her back. He finally did.

"What do you want?" he asked when she picked up. His tone was hard.

She paused, then said, "Baby, I'm sorry. Antonio told me he told you. I wanted to. I was *going* to. You just—had a lot going on. It was *one* night, and it *won't* happen again. We were drunk out of our minds. Baby, please believe me. Please. Let me come over."

Jasmine was begging better than the 90s R&B group *Jodeci*. She sounded desperate and had probably been crying. For the first time in their relationship, Devon put his feelings before hers.

"Don't ever call me again," he said coldly, then hung up.

Devon blocked both his girlfriend and his best friend on his phone, before crying himself to sleep. He had never been more heartbroken in his entire life.

———

THE NEXT DAY, Devon missed all of his classes, choosing to hide beneath his quilted covers and cotton sheets rather than brave the campus of happy-go-lucky students roaming the earth. While staring into the thick fabric of the inside of his blanket in utter shock, the birds chirped outside his window on the tree.

What the hell are they so happy about? he wondered.

Devon blinked a tear away. It was the most hurtful thing that had ever been done to him. His girlfriend and his best friend.

Classic. He smirked.

Then rose this insatiable need to see how he had missed it. He swiped open his social media and drilled his eyes into every picture or video of him, his best friend, and his girlfriend. No. Scratch that. His fiancée. His fiancée had cheated on him. After examining and analyzing every single image, all Devon saw was him and Jasmine happy and in love. Jasmine, with her doting eyes on him, and Antonio being his normal life-of-the-party self. The flirting Devon caught last week was the first time that any suspicions had surfaced that there could be something more between them. But even that fact alarmed him.

How long has this been going on?

Because it may have meant they were *experts* in hiding the affair.

Devon took down the engagement post and deleted every single picture he could find of Jasmine.

The engagement is off.

Deleting the posts did nothing to remove the heartache, though, so Devon just went back to sleep.

It wasn't until sometime that afternoon that the door creaked open. *Darion*.

"Yo. You still in bed? You feelin' ok?" his brother asked. The banging of shoes against the wall echoed, then tumbled to the floor. "Bro, you got a package in the mail."

Darion set something on Devon's desk, then went quiet, other than the small sounds of him moving on his side of the room. Suddenly, he said, "Man, I was hoping nobody noticed me wearing my fit from yesterday at Stats class this morning. I didn't get a chance to get back here before class to change."

Devon stayed silent, too weak to respond.

"Hello. Earth to Devon," Darion said, now in his bathrobe.

More silence, so Darion walked to Devon's bed and shook his form. "Bro. Wuz Up? You good?"

Finally, Devon stirred and flipped over to face him, but he still had the covers pulled to his ears.

"I'm not goin'," he mumbled.

His brother pulled away the covers. "Dev. What is goin' *on*? You trippin'. Why you not going to class?"

Devon snatched the covers back up to his chin but pried his eyes open.

"Yo. Your eyes are bloodshot!" Darion said in alarm.

"Jasmine cheated," Devon said simply, and saying the words made them more real than he ever wanted them to be. His heart trembled.

Darion dropped onto the hardwood floor in his terry-cloth robe, crossing his legs Indian-style. "Word?! What are you talking about? With who?" His eyes bugged out of his face.

"Antonio," Devon said thickly.

Darion inhaled. That mother f—!" he said. He started shaking his head back and forth.

"Naw. That can't be right. You not tellin' me it was in Cancun!" He started breathing hard and rubbing his knees fiercely.

Devon nodded slowly. "He told me yesterday," he croaked.

His brother started going off about putting hands on Antonio, and how he was gon beat the mess out of him. When he saw the pain mask Devon's face, he stopped.

"Dev. I'm so sorry. Man, I *promise* you I ain't see *nothin'*. I'm so sorry, bro." Darion sat on top of the covers and patted his form. Devon's body shivered from his quiet tears beneath the covers.

"Me too," was all he could say.

———

IT WAS LATE EVENING. Darion had brought Devon some soup earlier and put it on his desk for when he was ready to eat.

"I need to go to this study group for Psychology, but I'm only a text away if you need me. I'm a be back *tonight*," Darion said, putting an emphasis on the word "tonight" so Devon knew he wasn't staying at Kimberly's.

Devon had nodded his head beneath the covers but wasn't sure if his brother even saw it. He grunted just in case. Now it was hours later, and his belly rumbled.

I should probably eat, he thought. *And use the bathroom.*

Gathering all of his energy, he swung his body off the bed. His eyes fell on a crumpled t-shirt and basketball shorts. It was what he had played in the day before when he and Antonio won at the rec. That game seemed like forever ago. Devon slid on the shorts and grabbed his room key. After using the bathroom, he trudged back to his room. He had avoided as many people as possible on his trip to the restroom. It was a co-ed dorm, so he felt a little weird being shirtless, but he didn't have the energy to put one on.

When he entered his room again, his eyes fell on the container of soup on his desk. Saddled right next to it was a small package. It was then that he remembered Darion had said a package arrived in the mail. A sinking feeling grew as Devon stared at the brown paper-wrapped box as if it contained a bomb. Slowly, the fog in his mind dispersed as he tried to remember what day it was.

He grabbed his phone to look at the date. Wednesday.

God, please don't let this be it.

A silent, fleeting prayer. One he hadn't even intended to pray. It leaped out of the depths of his soul, like a Hail Mary tossed from a losing team in the final moments of a football game.

Ignoring the soup container entirely, Devon grabbed the box, found a pair of scissors in his drawer, and started cutting. Like lightning, he unraveled the paper, butterflies clawing his gut the whole time. The shiny, smooth, elegant black box peeked through. He gripped it, freeing it from the Styrofoam casing with shaky hands. Slowly, nervously, he popped open the lid. A beautiful diamond ring, princess cut, white gold, size 5, ½ a carat, sparkled in all her glory. Once again, his heart shattered. His knees buckled.

Devon cradled the box, sank to the floor, and bawled.

THIRTEEN
RIGHT ON TIME

THE REST OF THE WEEK BLEW BY IN A HAZE AS DEVON FORCED HIMSELF TO shower, put on clothes, and drag his body to classes. Eating was an accomplishment when it happened, but mostly, he lived off coffee. He even succumbed to the bitter tar substance on campus. Wherever he could get it, he drank it. He just added more sugar.

His brother kept bringing home bowls of soup from Tyson each night and slept in his own bed instead of Kimberly's. "I'm here, bro," he said. When Darion started cleaning his side of the room, it had to be a sign that Devon must truly be in dire straits. Regardless of whether it was out of pity, Devon appreciated the support and the clean room. He needed all the help he could get. It was so hard to pay attention and concentrate. Even completing minor tasks like walking to class winded him, as if he had just enough energy to breathe. And every time he took a breath, his heart raged against the pain it caused.

Devon had never felt so out of sorts. The closest he had ever come to being this out of it was when Nana Jean had died. They had been really close, and he was so young he didn't understand that she was dying. He only knew that whenever he was around, she was shooting herself with needles. Turns out they were insulin shots for her diabetes. When she passed, Devon slept in his parents' bed for a week straight, and his mother rocked him to sleep. Now he wondered when she had ever found time to grieve since she was so busy comforting him. Yet even that loss paled in comparison. Because at just ten years old, Devon understood that his grandmother had been in pain and was finally free from that pain. There was at least some solace in that.

But what solace was there in *this*?

I AM your solace, came the still small voice.

The blinking cursor on his laptop mocked Devon, yelling imaginary profanities at his failure to produce. He had been trying to focus on the tax form he was completing for his Federal Taxation course. It had been thirty minutes, and the incomplete form stubbornly glared back at him.

His thoughts tore him away from the image. *What does that mean?* he wondered, repeating the phrase in his mind: *I AM your solace.*

An impression sat on Devon's heart, and he picked up his phone to swipe open his social media. There was a missed message from Lena that had been sitting there for days.

Lena.

Devon had forgotten all about the DM he had sent her Monday evening. So much had happened even since then. He swiped open the message thread:

DEVON:

> Hey. I hope you're doing ok! My mom will probably reach out to you soon, but just wanted to give you a heads up on a situation I'm facing...

Lena:

> Hey there! Oh, Devon, I'm so sorry to hear that.
> It's heartbreaking to say the least. Yes, I will
> definitely be praying and keeping you lifted. In
> the short time we've known each other, I can
> tell you're a man of character and integrity.
> Similar to Joseph in the Bible. You should
> probably check out his life story if you're not
> familiar with it. May be of encouragement to
> you. Another good one to read is Moses, who
> experiences God as THE I AM. God will be all
> that we need in times of trouble. I can share
> that from personal experience. Please reach
> out if you need to talk, and keep me posted.
> Below is my number. I'm agreeing with you
> that God's justice will prevail, in earth as it is in
> heaven.

Wow. Devon sat blinking. He read and re-read Lena's message several times, yet couldn't get over the accuracy of her words. Not only did she confirm the scripture passage his mother wanted him to read, but she also confirmed the word on his heart about God being "The I AM."

Since Lena had left her phone number, Devon used that for his reply after making sure it wasn't too late. It was after 8 pm.

> Hey, Lena. It's Devon. I got your message.
> Sorry for the late response. My week was
> crazy. I wanted to thank you for your
> encouragement. It confirmed some things my
> mom said. No updates on the false accusation
> situation. I'm still waiting to hear from the
> school, but I do ask that you pray for another
> situation...

Devon paused. He felt embarrassed thinking about telling her that he had been cheated on and betrayed by both his best friend and his girlfriend. It made him feel like a fool. Then he remembered how vulnerably Lena had shared about her own heartache and betrayal. That her ex had cheated on her multiple times with different women. He proceeded to text her:

It's too long to type out, but if you're up for a call, maybe tomorrow I can discuss with you then? Thank you again for everything. I'm so grateful we met when we did. I can see now it was right on time.

Devon re-read the message before hitting send. He decided to look up the scripture Lena had referenced and searched the Bible app on his phone. Just as he was reading, a response from Lena rolled through:

Hey, Devon. It's good to hear from you. I'm free now if you are.

Devon's heart fluttered from excitement. He was also surprised she was available and open to talking on a Friday night. Lena was an amazing woman who had to have plenty of date options. Either way, Devon was thankful she was making time for him. He hurried to dial her before it got too late.

"Hey, Lena."

"Devon. How are you?"

Lena's voice was just as sweet and disarming as he remembered. It was like she had this ability to make others feel completely comfortable and willing to tell her anything.

She'd make a great pastor, Devon thought. Suddenly, a strong urge to share that with her surfaced.

"Hey. I'm doing ok," Devon replied, then chuckled nervously. "Thank you for being available for me."

"Of course. We're friends now. Anytime I pray for a brotha, and he falls out under the anointing of the Holy Spirit, that makes us friends."

Devon laughed, and Lena joined in. The sound further brought him peace and clarity. Just hearing her voice was already lightening his mood.

"Uhh. This is probably gonna sound strange, but have you ever thought about being a pastor?" Devon gave in to the intense pressing on his heart, nudging him to share. He was thinking he would wait until further in the call, but the burden was increasing by the second.

"Wow. That's crazy. The funny thing is, I'm actually considering theology school. My dad has been on me about it for a while, but I just wasn't sure if I was ready, you know? With everything I've been through, I guess I didn't feel qualified to be officially pastoring folks. Teaching Bible study is one thing, but a pastor? It's a lot of responsibility."

Lena's sharing her insecurities was surprising. Devon realized he had put her on a pedestal because she was a couple years older and further along spiritually. Yet her vulnerability made her feel more human. More relatable.

Another great quality in a pastor, he thought.

"You giving me that word is definitely something I need to take heed to," Lena added. "Thank you."

Devon said, "Wow. You're welcome. I wasn't even sure if I should tell you, but I couldn't shake the need to. It was like growing by the second that we were on the call," he admitted.

To get more comfortable, Devon moved to his bed and stretched out on his back, keeping the phone to his ear. He felt relaxed in a pair of joggers and was shirtless, since he had absolutely no plans to go out that evening.

"That's your prophetic gift working, Devon. When you get a chance, you should take some classes that'll help you grow your spiritual gifts. Particularly your prophetic gifts."

"Whaattt? There are classes on spiritual gifts?" Devon was shocked. He had never heard of such a thing and wasn't even sure that he fully understood what spiritual gifts were.

And what does 'prophetic' mean?

"Yep. Sadly, many churches don't train their members in spiritual gifts, especially prophetic gifts. So the members either have them and don't know it, or don't believe in them and aren't open to receiving or developing them. Or they misuse them by misleading or abusing others."

"Wow. How do you abuse God's gifts? I mean, they are gifts, so they're inherently *good*, right?" Instantly, Devon was intrigued. It was like this whole other world that existed that he had no clue about. It was a spiritual world.

"Well, some people use their spiritual insight and knowledge to mislead others. Say, for instance, you were discerning that I was called to be a pastor, but you didn't believe women should be in leadership in the church or be pastors in the church. You could encourage me to be a teacher or lead a women's group, but you wouldn't say the word pastor. And then I wouldn't be able to walk fully in my calling because I couldn't shepherd the full congregation like I was called to. Then those folks I was called to grow wouldn't get what they needed either. Another scenario is a prophetic person drawing people to themselves and their gifts instead of to God. Even charging others to give them a word. Now maybe they won't call it a fee, but instead they'll call it an offering."

"Whoa. So what does being *prophetic* mean?"

"Well, a basic meaning is a person who's able to see in the future. But the Bible teaches that we only see in part (1 Cor 13:9). So even those who have a gift to see in the future are only seeing a snippet. They're only getting insight into what God is *allowing* them to see. And it's not always spiritual sight with your spiritual eyes. Sometimes it's a knowing, or a feeling, or a hearing. Either internally or even audibly. So when I prayed for you, and gave you that word, that was me only hearing a *part* of what God had for you," Lena explained.

Devon flashed back to her encouragement to him when he first visited North Star.

"But He gives us that gift to encourage others," she continued. "It shouldn't be used to condemn or make them feel bad. Even when it's to rebuke, the hope is that they'll repent, *and* the prophetic person should only be speaking the truth from a place of love. They should have that same hope for the person they're speaking to."

Whoa. Lena was blowing his mind, and even more questions rapidly stirred in Devon. There was so much to learn. He hadn't even thought about people having an issue with women being in leadership or pastoring. Then, he thought about Antonio, who would definitely not be feeling having a female pastor! Devon chuckled internally at the thought, but his humor was soon snuffed out by pain when remembering his friend's actions. If he could even still call him a friend.

Devon cleared his throat. "Wow. Thank you for sharing all of this. I feel like I should be taking notes!"

The sound of Lena's laugh sent a ripple of pleasure through Devon.

Their connection was heady and a little overwhelming, but overwhelming in a good way. It seemed to be hitting him in so many different ways: mental, spiritual, emotional, and physical. It was like eating a wonderful stew, and everything tasted amazing, and you kept looking forward to the next bite, not knowing what you were gonna get but knowing it was gonna be good.

"Well, you have plenty of time to learn," Lena said. "Take your time and enjoy the ride. There's no point in rushing because we'll always be learning."

"Yeah. I definitely feel like I'm learning a lot right now. I already shared about what was happening at the school with this girl, but I've had some other crazy stuff happen." Though Devon was enjoying their discussion, he figured now was a good time to go into things.

It was then that he poured out his heart in a way he hadn't since he found out Jasmine had cheated. Even though he had spoken to his brother a little, talking to Lena was a whole other experience. She was so wise and had been through her own heartbreak. Darion's greatest love was his latest pair of Jordans. He loved Devon, but there was no way he could relate to the feeling that his heart had been ripped out of his chest, decimated into a million pieces, and each piece stomped on repeatedly. Every morning when Devon woke up, dread met him. The memory of Antonio telling him slammed into his psyche as soon as his eyes popped open. In class, he repeatedly fought daydreams of Antonio and Jasmine having sex. His mind was his greatest enemy, filling in the gaps of what happened. How it happened. Where it happened. How many times it happened. It took everything in Devon to face the day.

After Devon finished unloading, Lena was quiet, but he could sense her compassion even before she spoke.

"Devon, I'm so sorry this happened to you. As you know, I've been through some similar stuff. It's never easy when someone you love hurts you, especially someone you've been that intimate with. You were ready to share the rest of your life with Jasmine. Maybe you still will. Only God knows. But you also have the added pain of losing a close friend. Someone you called your brother. I can't imagine the level of betrayal you feel. Right now, the healing and restoration that needs to happen can only be divine. And more than likely, it's going to take you time."

Devon nodded on the other end, his heart weighing down his whole being. Lena was such a timely friend. He was so thankful to be able to talk to someone who understood. Someone who had walked through similar pain and made it out on the other side. The fact that she was full of joy, love, and life gave Devon hope that maybe, one day, he would be, too. Before talking to her, fear about his future had begun creeping up again. Now that Jasmine was out of the picture and he had walked away from Jack & Jill, what did God have for him? Right now, it was taking everything in Devon to keep going to classes and face the fear that he would run into his perpetrators at any moment. He let out a deep breath.

"I want to send you a copy of a book that helped me after my divorce. It's called *How to Overcome Heartbreak: Recovering from Misguided Love*," Lena said. "The author vulnerably shares how difficult her first heartbreak was, but how God used it for her purpose. He used it to reveal His love for her and teach her who she was to Him."

Devon then remembered how God had said it was time for him to learn his identity. "Yes. Please do," he said.

"The author was actually a college student just like you when this heartbreak took place, *and* she was engaged at the time."

"Wow. That definitely sounds like a book I should read!" Devon said.

The rest of the conversation flowed just as effortlessly, and it was almost 11 o'clock when Lena admitted she needed to call it a night. "I have choir practice in the morning," she explained. "God only knows why Minister Felix insists we have it at 8 am on Saturday. Like folks don't want to sleep in."

"Oh. Yeah. Of course," Devon said. He glanced at the clock on his phone and immediately felt bad. "I'm sorry I took up your whole evening. Thank you so much for your time. I definitely needed it."

"The pleasure was all mine. We need each other. You gave me that word, which I know is God beating me over the head like, 'Girl, would you do what I said already?'" Devon laughed. "Besides, I didn't have much going on tonight, so you were needed company."

Devon was surprised to hear it, but didn't want to pry, so he just said, "Ok. Cool. Well, if it's okay with you, then I'll hit you up some other time. Learn more about those spiritual gifts…" When he spoke, his eyes were closed, and a small smile played on his lips. Devon felt bathed in comfort.

"Sounds like a plan. And in the meantime, look at 1 Corinthians 12 & 13. Oh, and the whole book of Acts. That'll help get you started."

Whew! The whole book!

Opening his eyes, Devon hurried to punch the passages into his notes app before he forgot.

Man, I got so much to catch up on, he thought, thinking of all the scriptures that had been given to him just that week alone. Then he remembered Lena's encouragement to take his time.

"Good night, Lena. Thanks again. For everything," Devon said.

"You're welcome. And thank you. G'night."

For a while, Devon lay there with the phone on his chest, meditating on his conversation with Lena. He was in awe of how good it made him feel and how refreshing it was. Before he knew it, he was drifting off to sleep with a supernatural peace wrapping him like a cocoon.

That was when Devon began to learn the power of fellowship with other Believers.

FOURTEEN
ANTONIO

I FORGIVE YOU

Cancun was the escape from life that Antonio needed. He had been avoiding checking his midterm grades every day since being there. He knew it wasn't going to be a pretty picture and dreaded hearing yet another sermon from his father.

Maybe I need to enroll in the military. The depressing thought invaded his mind. School just didn't seem to be his jam.

Sighing deeply, sprawled on the queen-size bed Antonio had claimed in the bonus room of the oceanfront home, he reached for his vape on the nightstand. It was early in the morning, and everyone was knocked out from being up late celebrating Devon and Jasmine's engagement. Just thinking about it made Antonio take a hit of his vape. As the smoke, once again, blinded him, his stomach churned.

What the hell is Devon thinking? he fumed, coughing on smoke.

Proposing!

Yet Antonio knew what Devon was thinking. Jasmine could put it on a brotha. Not that he knew that from personal experience. Only rumors. He had a few homies who had smashed and lived to tell the tale. He himself had only had one encounter with Jasmine. It was her freshman year, and she was on the prowl. They hooked up at a party one night, and she was good and drunk. When it was about to go down, she said no because they didn't have protection. Antonio was a little caught off guard, said he would pull out, but she was adamant. He wasn't one to force a female. He had had too many conquests to do that. Still, he would be lying if he said he left that night not feeling slightly rejected. Antonio shook it off, though, the way he shook everything off. When she started kicking it with Devon, his rejection resurfaced. Then it really messed him up when she got serious about him. Jasmine was known for running through 'em. How in the hell did his boy manage *that one*? Eventually, Antonio's sincere love for Devon won out, so he figured, *Shit, if he's happy, I'm happy.*

Deep down, he thought their love affair would run its course; Jasmine would move on and do her one-two, and Antonio would have his boy back. Little did he know she would put it on him so good the brotha would propose!

Antonio took another drag of weed. The smoke filled the space, quickly blurring his vision. His heart ached. It wasn't that he wasn't happy for Devon; he just was also quite jealous. Jealous that he seemed so sure of everything. Devon got the grades. He got the girl. He was about to inherit his father's business. His future was airtight. Antonio had been floundering throughout his whole academic career and had only enrolled to appease his father. Plus, tuition was free, so who says no to that?

Reaching for his phone, Antonio scanned their group chat until pictures from last night appeared. Devon was cheesing in all of them. Antonio took another puff. It just didn't seem fair. Then later that afternoon, Devon's love for him shone through as they talked on the deck. It was clear that Devon was truly the brother Antonio had never had. Being an only child and always the life of the party, there weren't too many men who stuck by his side once the party ended. They were usually in and out, passing through like a revolving door, depending on their mood. Or his. Even Antonio's uncle, who he had been the closest to, passed away the year before. His mother had been walked out when he was just two years old. Everyone seemed to leave. Yet

Devon was the stick-to-it-type. Everything he did was laced with commitment.

Watching Devon's eyes sparkle with love and hearing him say he was making him his best man (along with his brother) moved Antonio to tears. Deeply inspired, he resolved to live up to the standard that Devon had set. Or at least, give it his all in trying.

Then Devon left, and things started heating up between him and Jasmine. At first, it was subtle. A leg brush here. A lingering hand there. All of a sudden, her big brown doe eyes started hinting that *something could go down*.

Or had they? Maybe she was just flirting?

Regardless, each night they found themselves on the deck, hitting the vape and cracking up about everything. Jasmine was a good time, and Antonio could even see why Devon was on her. Over the last several months, they had developed a camaraderie, with Devon as their middleman. Now Devon's absence seemed to unleash the more raunchier sides of their personalities. Jasmine laughed at every nasty joke Antonio told and started confiding in him about her fantasies. It was turning him on more and more, and he knew she knew it. One of her fantasies was to do it in water.

During this time alone, Kimberly and Darion would be doing their thing, which left Antonio and Jasmine to their own devices. The night she suggested they go skinny dipping, Antonio knew what it was. He had a decision to make. The twisting in his gut wrestled with the enlargement of his gym shorts.

Maybe this will show Devon who she really is. The bitter thought snaked the smoke from his vape. Taking another hit, he stroked his jaw and passed it to Jasmine as they walked along the shoreline. They'd made sure to go down far enough so they'd be hidden from any random passersby, though there were only a handful still on the beach. The moon was illuminated, pulsing light almost loudly. It seemed to be yelling at Antonio.

Don't do it!

His eyes betrayed him and devoured every inch of Jasmine's curves when she started removing her cover-up. Then her swimsuit. His sockets bugged out of his head. *Damn!* She was gorgeous; cocoa skin shimmering and radiating like a goddess. The moonlight became her crown. She giggled and laughed, high off her ass. They had been drinking all night, too. That was the other thing. Antonio knew he was out of his mind right now. He always knew when he was past his limit; he just had very little care to stop.

Don't do it.

There was that voice again. His heart squeezed at its presence. It was like in the cartoons when an angel and a demon sat on each side of the person's shoulders. Antonio stood watching Jasmine frolic in the water. She kept waving him in.

"You comin'? Or you gonna leave me out here by myself?" she teased, bouncing in the waves completely naked.

Antonio swallowed, but his eyes stayed glued to her figure. Her breasts were perky and taut. Her body was ready.

F it, he thought, and dropped his shorts. He had never done it in the ocean before.

————

AFTER INDULGING THEMSELVES, Antonio and Jasmine returned to their respective rooms and passed out. The next morning, he awoke to an inky black horror at the realization of what he had done. Intense vomiting and nausea followed. He spent the whole morning puking his guts out. Their flights were scheduled for 10 am, but he couldn't get off the damn toilet. It was coming out at both ends.

"Leave me. I'll re-book my flight," he huffed out to Darion between puking fests.

It was probably for the best. He couldn't imagine facing Jasmine anyway. When they got back to campus, Antonio hit her up. They both agreed it was a horrible mistake and would never happen again. They blamed it on the liquor, the weed, and Cancun.

"I'll tell him," she said.

Antonio sat in his room, gripping his phone and staring blindly at the ceiling.

"You sure? Maybe it's best if he doesn't know..."

He had been struggling with himself for days. How could he play his boy like that? He had done some foul shit in his life, but this was the lowest of the low.

"Yeah. I-I really do love him," Jasmine said, her voice teary and waddling with grief. "I still want us to get married. He needs to know."

That made Antonio feel even worse. This woman really loved Devon. How could he jeopardize both of them like that? He knew she was lit. He knew she was high off her ass.

I should have said no.

Guilt and turmoil took turns punching Antonio's gut. He waited at school, anticipating Devon. Devon had stayed longer in Brooklyn to help his family out.

During the wait, Antonio tried to get his story together, hoping there would be some way to salvage the friendship. Although he didn't deserve forgiveness, he desperately wanted it.

When Jasmine said she would tell Devon on Monday, Antonio figured that if Devon agreed to meet him for basketball, then he had forgiven him. If he was a no-show, then their brotherhood was more than likely over. When Devon showed up, he was elated. Then they played the best game they had ever played. It had to be a sign that their friendship would remain intact. They were meant to go the distance.

Antonio was floored when he found out Jasmine hadn't told Devon, angry that she hadn't given him the heads-up and sorrowful over how much he had hurt his friend. The beatdown he took was completely deserved. If he believed that it would restore their relationship, he would take another one.

The week of their fight, Antonio had been holed up in his room, consoling himself with weed and brown liquor. When he looked in the mirror, his left eye was still slightly shut, and his lip puffed out like a cloud. Even still, the wounds to his heart were worse. At least he had assurance that his physical wounds would heal.

God, I messed up! his heart cried out. Antonio didn't expect a response, but one came anyway.

That's why I sent my Son.

Whoa. Antonio popped up in his bed. Did he just hear what he thought he heard? His heart quickened as he searched for his phone. His screensaver was a picture of him and Uncle Dave. Uncle Dave had always talked about God. He was a minister in his church and frequently sent Antonio encouraging messages.

Hurriedly, Antonio flipped open his text thread from his uncle. He had saved every text and voicemail. There was one in particular that stood out.

> Tone, just remember that no matter what life brings, God loves you. That's why He sent His Son.

Antonio gulped. When he read it at the time it was sent, he figured it was just another way his uncle was showing him *his* love. He hadn't really thought of God's love directly. Uncle Dave was the bright light always shining, always rooting him on. It was *his* love that Antonio never doubted. But God's love? He wasn't so sure.

How could God love me? Antonio thought, then took another swig from his bottle.

He was heartbroken, not just by his actions but by this over-whelming feeling that *nothing he did was right*. When he looked at his future, all he saw was darkness. When he thought about his present, all he saw was the same.

How could God love me after how much I've failed? Depression sank in. *I betrayed my best friend!*

In a drunken stupor, Antonio fumbled to his feet with an unex-pected burning intent to get dressed. This sudden urge to see Devon took over. Previously, when he had called Devon several times, it had gone to voicemail. He figured he was blocked, so he kept leaving voicemails. He also tried social media, but nothing. He was blocked.

Maybe if I beg him, he'll forgive me, Antonio thought despairingly, zigzagging to his closet and throwing on clothes.

It was Saturday night. He didn't even know what time it was. It had to be well after midnight, but he couldn't stop himself. He grabbed his room key and headed for the door.

The late partiers were out. People stacked in groups or pairs, laughed, and caroused their way into the evening. The rowdiness of campus on the weekend was a stark contrast to the studious environment of the week.

Taking fast, long strides across the quad, Antonio ducked his head beneath a baseball cap and popped jacket collar. He didn't want to run into anyone he knew who could ask him about his bruises. When he made it to Devon's dorm, he posted outside, waiting for a drunk student to let him in. He didn't have to wait long. A rail-thin kid with a red shirt and skinny jeans was teetering by the QR code reader.

"Yo. You need help, my man?" Antonio asked, not feeling too sober himself.

After several failed attempts at swiping his phone, Antonio held Red Shirt's slender arm steady for him.

"Thanks," Red Shirt slurred, and they stumbled into the building, holding on to each other.

Antonio assisted him up the stairs while clutching the railing with his other hand.

Damn. Maybe I was just there for this kid, he thought with an internal smirk.

"I got it," Red Shirt said, once they made it to the third floor. It also happened to be Devon's floor.

Antonio watched as Red Shirt zig-zagged in the opposite direction of the hallway before he started moving towards Devon's room. Somewhere in the back of his mind, he knew this wasn't a good idea.

But I gotta try, Antonio thought, grabbing the wall to steady himself. The Hennessy and weed were in full effect. It was a wonder he had made it across campus.

Finally, the numbers that he needed shimmered on the door, and, using all of his focus, Antonio knocked long and hard. After several moments, there was shuffling on the other side before the door swung open. Devon's expression was a mixture of exhaustion, startlement, and confusion. He had clearly been asleep.

"Hey, man," Antonio slurred. "Can we talk?"

Realization danced across Devon's features. He huffed and scowled. "Do you know what time it is? I thought you were my *brother*. I thought something was wrong." He sounded angry, and Antonio rushed to explain.

"I know, bro. I'm shorry it's sho late. I jush. I jush. Want to apologhize. For everyshing."

Devon held up a hand. "Look. Save it. I need to move on. So do you."

The door slammed, causing tears to sting Antonio's eyes. Burning pinched his nostrils. Invisible hands bowed his head to the floor.

God, he doesn't want me. He sulked while walking away.

But I do, came the still small voice.

That was the first time Antonio could definitively say that he had really heard God. It was such a clear message on his heart, seeming even to wipe away the fog of his substance-induced intoxication.

God wanted him?

The thought stuck with Antonio as he trekked back across the campus to his dorm room.

God wanted him.

The moment Antonio entered his room, he popped his phone back open and started reading all the messages his Uncle Dave had sent. The thread went back to a year before his death. Every message was saturated with love and care for his nephew.

> I'm praying for you, Tone. I love you, Tone. God has a plan for you, Tone.

Uncle Dave had been the most devout Christian Antonio had known, but what made him so dope was that he was relatable. He didn't try to pretend to be super saved or perfect. He was real. He wasn't a hypocrite like so many Antonio had seen in the church. He actually lived what he preached behind closed doors.

Dropping to his knees with his head in his hands and his phone next to him, Antonio prayed. All this time, he had been believing he wasn't lovable. He couldn't do anything right. He wasn't worth a damn. Now, suddenly, his eyes were open. The scriptures Uncle Dave had been sending for years finally seemed applicable. They seemed *real*.

God sent his Son for me, he thought. The thought blew his mind.

I'm sorry, God!

Antonio cried out that night, alone in his dorm room, tears from ancient hurt rushed unapologetically down his face. His room echoed with the sounds of his sobs. His mind was cleared even of all the darkness that had been engulfing him from his attempts at staying high. The response that night in his bedroom was the most magnificent thing he had ever heard in his entire 22 years of life.

I forgive you.

FIFTEEN
CHESS MOVES

ON TUESDAY, DEVON FINALLY RECEIVED AN EMAIL FROM THE TITLE IX Coordinator of the school in regard to the sexual harassment accusation.

Dear Mr. Devon Woods, it has been brought to our attention of an accusation of a sexual nature that will need your prompt response. Ms. Monica Angela Jones has advised that you pursued unwanted physical contact on March 23rd in Professor Sharon Clark's classroom. As we are gathering evidence to support or dismiss these claims, we will need your personal statement. Below are the dates and times you need to select to be interviewed regarding this matter. You may have legal representation present during your interview, though it is not required. Our hope is that you will be forthcoming with providing the needed information for this investigation to avoid further legal consequences. Please reach out directly if needed using the contact information below.

Sincerely,
Cory Heart, Chief Title IX Officer
Office of Student Protections and Title IX

Reading and re-reading the email, Devon took a shaky breath. His hands clasped the phone tighter as he stared at the screen, as if it would somehow change the message. The part that made him want to laugh out loud was the instruction to respond promptly. A prompt response could have been warranted had they sent the email promptly! He had been waiting over a week since his discussion with Marx and Clark. They had disrupted his life for a whole week. This chick, Monica, had disrupted his life, and now, suddenly, they wanted a prompt response! If the whole situation hadn't been so devastating, it would have been comical.

Devon drew in another trembling breath. After diving into the scriptures Lena had referenced and talking to his mom, he had finally gotten to a place of peace about everything. Now this email had caused anxiety to return with a vengeance.

This is really happening, he thought in stark disbelief. His eyes roamed to and fro on the phone screen.

"Woods, you're up!" It was their chess coach, Timothy.

In a robotic state, Devon shoved his phone into his pocket and took a seat opposite his opponent in the rickety wooden chair.

Chess club was held bi-weekly at Java's Cafe. Timothy was close to the owner, who let them use the back room for practice. For the last two years, Timothy had been running it, but it was a student-led organization, so he was looking for someone to pass the torch to. Timothy was graduating with Devon in June.

"I wish you weren't graduating and could keep this thing going!" Timothy had said to Devon one day. He had always been after Devon to take on more of a leadership role in the club. Devon declined, already having too much on his plate. Also, if he became a leader, the added responsibility would steal the joy he received from being a member.

As Devon sat awaiting the buzzer, he reflected on Timothy's words about graduation.

I may not *be graduating,* he thought grimly. Sadness crushed his heart.

It was his love for chess and its incomparable stimulation that had Devon looking forward to chess practice all day. Chess had been his go-to way to decompress since his mother taught him when he was younger. He had fallen so in love with the game that when Darion was involved in summer sports camps, Devon opted for summer chess camp. Ignoring the teasing from his peers and even his brother calling him a geek, Devon relished the enlightenment received from outsmarting his rival. While a decent chess player could think four or five moves ahead of their opponent, Devon could think eight.

Now his stomach sank at the news from the Title XI Coordinator, and he regretted coming to practice. Instead, he wished that he could wallow in his room, huddled beneath the covers.

I can't believe this is happening.

"Bzzzz!" rang the buzzer, and Devon drew on all his energy to focus.

The kid across from him was pretty good, and Devon couldn't afford to hold back if he wanted to win. Thankfully, this wasn't a timed match, and there wasn't the added pressure of having to move quickly. Still, even those were fun for Devon. He tended to thrive under pressure.

The kid took the lead, moving his white pawn. The game started out slow and safe. Devon held back most of his power pieces for as long as possible, except for the knight. He loved his knight. The strategy he used depended on the skill level of the opponent, but one thing that stayed the same was that Devon was going to use his knight. The knight was appealing because it was unique in making a move that no other piece on the board could make, including the queen herself. She was the most powerful piece, but not even the queen could do what the knight could do.

"Check," his opponent said.

Wait, what? Devon blinked. They were ten moves in, and he had missed it. The kid had him cornered. He had brought out his knight too soon. He had left his king vulnerable. Immediately, Devon started scanning, looking for any opening that would get him out of this mess. Then he saw it. He moved his bishop into a position to block the rook that had him cornered. She was protected by a pawn.

The kid sat there, looking confused. He made another move that worked to Devon's benefit, and Devon pounced on him.

"Checkmate," he said after four more moves.

Whew! That was close.

Disappointment stained the kid's face, but they both shook hands and said, "Good game," as was their custom.

"That was a close one!" Timothy had watched them play as he circled the room, checking out all the matches. He patted Devon on the arm. "Don't seem to be at your best today. Something on your mind?"

Devon was a class A player and technically more skilled than the kid he had just played, who was ranked class B. Under normal circumstances, Devon would have never let him get the drop on him, even for a moment. Apparently, Timothy had noticed.

Lowering his gaze, Devon half-shrugged. "Yeah. Just got some bad news. That's all."

Timothy's face exuded concern. "Hey. Bro. Let's chat afterward, ok? I'll be available after practice."

Devon nodded. Timothy was cool people. He had a huge heart to help others and was graduating with a doctorate in counseling. His plan was to one day open a counseling center. Devon had had a handful of one-on-one conversations with him, and they were always helpful. He definitely felt like Timothy was in the right field. They weren't close, but maybe that was best. People who were closer to a situation tended to be more emotional about it. People like his mom. Devon could still hear her going off in his head in their last conversation a few days ago.

That so and so! We'll show her! Mr. Right is definitely gonna put a stop to all of this. You mark my words.

Mr. Right was their family lawyer who had agreed to take on the case when Mrs. Woods had phoned him.

"Sounds good," Devon replied to Timothy. "I'm gonna cut out early from practice and get some coffee up front. I know I won't be able to give my best today."

"Ok, I understand. I'll meet up with you soon," Timothy said. His large blue eyes swam laps of care.

Devon nodded before heading to the front of the cafe. It was late afternoon, and lots of students were either studying or chatting in small groups, along with some locals. The ambiance had a classic, soothing feel. One that Devon always preferred over noisy, rambunctious spaces, such as restaurants and bars. Such as Jack & Jill. The thought made him frown a little as he sat on a barstool.

"Hey, Dev. Thought you'd still be back there claiming your victims," Frank, the owner, said. He was working the coffee bar.

Devon forced a smile. "Not today. I'm just gonna drink my sorrow away with coffee," he said. He had tried for a joke, but the pain still seeped through his tone. Frank seemed to catch it.

"Ah. I see. Well, sounds like something my famous freshly ground French roasted, hint of almond and hazelnut, can cure." Frank gave him a sympathetic smile, and Devon's eyes lightened.

"You always got what I need, Frank," he said. "If it wasn't for your coffee, I don't know how I would have made it on campus these five years."

A hefty fellow, Frank's jovial laugh resounded above the chatter of the cafe. "Oh, I do what I can!"

When he started on the order, Devon whipped out his phone. He had a missed text from Lena.

How are things?

Just when he was about to text her back, a hand rubbed his shoulder. Turning around, his brows rose in surprise.

"Hey. I—I was hoping you would be here."

Jasmine. Devon hadn't seen her since the evening they met at Tyson's. She looked the same, except her eyes were muddied with pain and regret. His heart squeezed, but he reminded himself *she* was the one in the wrong.

She should *feel pain.*

The angry thought snatched him to attention, and Devon turned a little to face her more. When doing so, his phone fell onto the coffee bar.

"What are you doing here?" he asked. He tried not to let her appearance shake him, but it was hard. Her eyes were so sad that he wanted to swoop her in his arms like a doll and tell her everything would be ok.

She bit her lip, shifting from side to side in a pair of old school Adidas.

"I remember you had practice today. Was hoping I could catch you," she said softly.

Hearing the pain in her tone tore him to shreds. Then his gaze dissected her from head to toe. When had he ever seen Jasmine wearing tennis shoes? Devon couldn't remember. Now that he took a closer look, her whole ensemble was unusually chill. She wore a pair of joggers, a baby-fitted T-shirt, and an oversized jean jacket. Her hair was in a simple high bun. No makeup. Not that she ever really needed it. Her skin always glistened, her lips exuded a natural rose-colored pink, and nature had dressed her eyes with long, thick lashes.

"You look…" he started, then stopped. He didn't want to insult her. She was still beautiful, just not her usual done-up self.

Jasmine grimaced. "I know. But it's been hard to get dressed since…" She let the sentence hang, and Devon finished it in his mind.

Since you slept with my best friend?

He didn't say the words out loud. No. He was too much of a gentleman for that and didn't want to put her business out there in front of all these people.

Maybe if we were alone in private. The thought pricked his heart.

"One famous gourmet freshly brewed, French roast, almond, hazelnut concoction for you, sir!" Frank, oblivious to the awkwardness sitting between the two, presented a large white mug with a strong, flavorful smell. When it sailed the short distance to Devon's nose, he inhaled.

"Frank. I already know this is about to be good!" Devon said eagerly. "Just by the smell."

Then the intentionally shaped foam Frank had created on top of the liquid came into view.

"What?! It's a horse!" Devon was in awe. "Man. You're *amazing*." He looked at him with appreciation.

"Hehe. Glad you like it. I remember you said the knight was your favorite chess piece, so figured I'd add a little touch." Frank winked, then noticed Jasmine. "And what can I get you, little lady?"

Jasmine fiddled with her hands clasped in front of her. "Oh, umm…"

Devon interrupted, "She's not really a coffee drinker."

"Oh. Well, how about water? Or tea?" Frank offered graciously, his striking silver hair shining in the sunlight from the window.

"Umm. You know what. I think I'll have a cup of coffee. I've been trying to do things different lately," Jasmine said with an anxious smile.

Devon chose to ignore her comment and sipped from his mug. All of his senses stood on end. It was the most delicious thing he had ever tasted!

"Frank, you been holding out on me," he exclaimed, wonder dripping from his tone.

Frank grinned, then turned to start Jasmine's order.

"Seriously, you gotta give me the recipe," Devon begged as Frank moved like lightning behind the bar.

"Aww, honestly, it's something I just came up with. I knew you liked all those flavors and figured I'd try something for you."

Devon sat on his stool, amazed. "You made that up? Just now?" He gaped at him.

The older man shrugged like it was nothing, then handed Jasmine a special blend of nutmeg, steamed milk, and honey in a medium roast.

"Since you're a newbie coffee drinker, I figured I'd take it easy on you," Frank told her. "Let me know what you think." He smiled kindly before he went off to serve the next customer.

"Umm, can we find a table to talk? I mean, if you don't mind…" Jasmine cupped her mug with both hands and peered at Devon with longing.

His heart tugged at his chest, and he glanced around the intimate space. "There's a spot in the back," he relented, cocking his head.

As they passed the small round tables of coffee lovers, Devon sifted through his emotions. He didn't really want to talk to Jasmine. He was still mad as hell. But he also couldn't deny this desire that clung to him as soon as he was in her presence.

It's like she still has this damn spell on me, he fumed.

When they sat across from each other, Devon intentionally kept his gaze low. Drinking the brew Frank had made did provide some comfort. He made a mental note to talk to him again about the ingredients. Jasmine sipped hers also, and Devon couldn't help himself. He asked, "So, how is it?" Even now, he still cared so much about her. Even wanting her to be happy with her damn drink.

She looked at him, surprised. "It's actually really good. It's like semi-sweet and warm and soothing." She marveled. "Not bitter or blah, like at campus."

Devon smiled a little at her description. "Yeah. That's how mine is." He took another sip and watched Jasmine fidget in her seat. She looked like she was trying to figure out what to say. Yet what could possibly be said? Nothing would change what she did to him.

"Devon. I'm sorry," Jasmine started. Her voice trembled, but her eyes remained fixed on him. "I know I can't undo what's been done. I just. I just..." She paused.

"You just what?" Devon said, his voice cracking. He hated himself for wanting to even know what it was she wanted to say. Hated that he still loved her.

"I just want you to know, I really did love you." She stopped herself and licked her lips, gathering courage. "*Do* love you." Her head slanted to the side as she stared at him pleadingly. Devon took another sip to hide his pain. He loved her so much.

"I don't know if you know what love is, Jasmine," he said softly after he had swallowed.

"I think you're probably right." She leaned back and sighed. "The truth is, I've never been loved like this before. Never been this serious about someone. Never thought I could even feel this way about a guy or have him feel this way about me." Her eyes fell to her hands in her lap, and when she peered back up, they shimmered with tears.

Witnessing her sincerity, agony gripped him. But her genuine feelings only made everything more confusing.

"Then *why?*" Devon said, his voice hard as wood. "Why, if you loved me, would you..." Instead of saying it, he took a drink of his coffee.

Jasmine bit her nail and then studied the table. "I guess...I just...I think I just was *scared*. Scared I was about to have everything I ever wanted. In you."

When she looked back at him, a yearning deep inside caught in Devon's throat.

"I can't handle this right now. I got a lot going on." He was thinking about the email he had just received from the school.

"Right. I'm-I'm sorry. I didn't mean to intrude. It's just that you blocked me…" Jasmine looked off.

"Yeah. Well. We know why," Devon said, keeping his voice even. He shot his gaze at the wall as he spoke.

"I just wanted you to know that I love you. It's not like I don't. It's just, I made a horrible, horrible mistake," Jasmine said, and this time she looked him in his eyes. "But it's never gonna happen again. I promise you. I won't *ever* let it happen again."

Devon was surprised at how much he wanted to believe her and how sincere she had sounded. He had truly believed it was over between them.

How can I ever forgive her? he wondered.

Then she did something that made him second-guess himself. She reached over and stroked his hand resting on his mug. Her touch was light. Gently, she rubbed his thumb and forefinger, sending a shiver down his spine. All the while, she kept her eyes steady on his, determination reflecting in them.

"I love you, Devon. I'm going to wait for you," Jasmine declared amid the clatter of the cafe chatter.

It was a tone that Devon was very acquainted with. It was the one she used when she had a goal, set out to pursue that goal, and then achieved it. It was the one she used when she wanted to ace an exam, get a campus activity approved for the Black student organization, or get her chapter to be on board with whatever campaign she was championing.

Devon's heart fluttered. Now she was using that tone with him. She wanted him.

"Jasmine, I…" His voice faltered.

He wanted to refute her. Wanted to tell her she shouldn't waste her time. That she had hurt him in the worst way possible. Then, just as he was trying to find the words, she leaned over and kissed his lips. It was a quick, sweet kiss. If it had been on his cheek, it could have been considered chaste. But the fact that it was on his lips sent the message she had intended. She would wait for him because he belonged to her.

"I love you," Jasmine whispered. She got up, grabbed her purse, and added, "Just hit me when you're ready," before leaving him there speechless.

SIXTEEN

FORGIVING YOUR EX

When Jasmine left, confusion, anger, anxiety, love, and even lust swirled in Devon's mind. How could she do this to him? It's like she waltzed in and out whenever she pleased. He had to let her know this was unacceptable. Yet the other side of him pined for her, wanted to be with her, wanted to believe her. Devon took another swig of coffee and then sat there staring at a painting on the mantel. It read: "Mornings are for coffee" above a happy coffee drinker watching a sunrise.

"Frank said you were over here." Timothy popped up in front of him, blocking the painting. It was a much-needed interruption from Devon's hamster wheel thoughts about his exes' brazenness.

"Hey. Yeah. Have a seat." Devon nodded toward the empty chair, and Timothy slipped into it with his own mug. The man was half a foot shorter than him, with silver frames and a wiry build.

He even looks like a counselor, Devon observed, chuckling within. All Timothy needed was a pipe, a notepad, and a leather couch.

"How did the rest of the match go?" Devon asked.

"Oh, the gang seems to be doing well. I think we'll be ready for our final match with Winsor next month." Timothy was referring to a rival school that they typically lost to.

"Oh yeah? I hope so. We need a win with Winsor!" Devon

remarked. His eyes drifted to his phone. He had never texted Lena back and had left her on read.

"So, what's going on with you? I knew something was wrong when Billie almost won that match," Timothy said, peering at Devon with an earnest expression.

Devon blew out a weighty puff of air. "I got a *lot* goin' on, man." He dove into the sexual harassment allegations, and Timothy's blue eyes widened behind his rims.

"Whoa. That's heavy stuff. I'm so sorry you're going through this. Obviously, this young woman, Monica, has a lot of deep-rooted insecurities to boldly lie like that. Could be she's experienced some sexual violations and is projecting them. Whatever it is, she clearly can't handle rejection," Timothy informed. Leave it to Timothy to psychoanalyze her.

"Tim, have I ever told you you're in the right field?" Devon looked at him with humor in his eyes.

Timothy smiled. "Thanks, bro. I better be! I'm graduating in less than two months!"

The statement sent a slice of pain through Devon, and he must have looked it because Timothy's face fell.

"Hey. Bro. I'm sure you are too! Everything's going to be alright."

Devon nodded, the words echoing in his mind. Where had he heard them before? He took a sip of his quickly diminishing coffee.

"Well. There's more I have to share," Devon said, then opened up about his situation with Jasmine.

In the process, folks started disappearing from the cafe, and the music overhead abruptly stopped. "Guys, take your time. I'm just closing the joint," Frank called a few feet away with a broom in his hand.

Devon peered down at his phone. It was five o'clock. Turning his neck over his shoulder, he said, "Thanks, Frank. We're wrapping up."

"Now, you said she *just* came here? *Today*?" Timothy asked. His eyes were large, round pools of fascination as if Devon's situation was prime meat for a psychological case study.

"Yeah, man. She came and she, she…" Devon swallowed. "She kissed me."

"Whoa. That's wild. I mean, how do you feel about it?" Timothy said, quickly reeling in his own opinions.

Devon shrugged his left shoulder. "I hate to say it, but I still love her. I still long for her. I just don't know how I could possibly ever trust her again." His eyes dropped to his palms, lying lifelessly on his lap.

I feel like a fool.

Timothy reached over and patted his shoulder. "Bro. We've all been there. I've been there. Love is complicated. No one does it perfectly. But you hit the nail on the head. Trust is key. What boundaries would she put into place to keep it from happening again? Her not wanting it to happen again doesn't mean it won't. She said she got cold feet about marrying you. It sounds like she has her own issues with self-value. If she doesn't believe she's worthy of your love, she'll self-sabotage again."

Whoa. Devon sat with Timothy's insights. *This brother really knows what he's talking about.*

"It's crazy because Jasmine comes off so confident." Devon stroked his chin, his forehead creasing. "She's so full of life and gorgeous and spunky and energetic. That was why I was so drawn to her. It's hard to think of her, of all people, not having a strong sense of self-value." Devon began processing his growing insight into his ex. Though it was hard for him to think of Jasmine as not valuing herself, he couldn't deny what Timothy had said. Clearly, she had self-sabotaged the relationship. Maybe even what he perceived as her being sexually free was really her trying to fill some kind of void. Whew. Now it felt like Timothy's gift of counseling was rubbing off on him!

I AM a Wonderful Counselor, came the still small voice. Immediately, Devon typed the words into his notes app. He had been trying to do that whenever he felt like God was speaking to him.

I need to look that up later, he thought, then redirected his focus on Timothy.

The boys chatted for a few minutes before flipping their chairs on the table so that Frank could clean beneath it.

"Thanks for the space, Frank. Appreciate it as always," Timothy said to his friend on their way out.

Frank beamed. "Of course! It's my pleasure."

"Yeah. And can I get that recipe from you? I know you made it up, but I at least want the ingredients," Devon said. "I can try to get my mom to recreate it when I go back home."

Frank bellowed a laugh. "Sure." He reached for Devon's phone and started typing. "As much as you love coffee, Devon, you would make a great barista," he commented.

Devon looked at him. "You know, I never thought about it. I mean, I make coffee for my dad's restaurant sometimes. But it hasn't been anything I ever really figured I would make a career out of."

"Well, as you can see, I'm short-handed." Frank waved a hand at the empty cafe. "If you want to get some experience, I'm here. Normally, there are at least two other servers helping, but it's hard to find college students who are deeply committed to serving jobs." Frank gave a small chuckle.

Devon thought about it. "You know, I do have a pause on my current job and could use the extra money..." He peered around the cafe as something stirred in his heart. He just wasn't sure what it was.

"Well, the pay isn't the best. But there *is* an unlimited supply of coffee I can throw in to sweeten the deal." Frank's eyes twinkled.

Devon grinned. "Man, you should a led with that!" They both laughed.

Frank said, "You can start whenever. I'm here from 9-5 pm, Monday through Saturday.

Devon ran over his schedule in his mind. *I can at least work the hours I would normally be working for Marx,* he thought. Now that things were off with Jasmine, he had even more free time.

"I'm in!" he agreed, and Frank shook his hand to seal the deal.

"Aww. I love it! Now I have *another* reason to hang out at Java's," Timothy said.

As Devon and Timothy headed to the dorms, Devon couldn't help but notice how much better he felt. It was like Java's had been a source of comfort and therapy. When he and Timothy separated, going to their respective dorms, he quickly called Lena. To his surprise, she answered on the first ring.

"Hey! I didn't expect you to be free. I figured you'd be preparing for Bible study." It was Tuesday, and in the short time that they had been talking, Devon had already learned her schedule.

She chuckled on the other end. "You know me well. I am. But I wanted to make sure you were good." Her voice was saturated with concern, and Devon's heart melted.

"I appreciate that." When he entered his dorm, he stopped by the row of mailboxes. His eyes lit up as he opened the shared mailbox with Darion.

"Looks like I got a package from Lena Williams in my mail!" He beamed, removing the 6 x 9-inch, large brown envelope.

"Yay! It's there. That was another reason I was checking in," she admitted.

Devon said, "I'ma open it when I get to my room," before starting up the stairs.

"Great. How was your day?" Lena asked kindly.

With a sinking feeling, Devon remembered the email he had gotten. "Well, I did hear from the school. I have to make an appointment for the interview." He made sure to keep his words generic so that no passersby in the dorm understood what he was saying. Finally, he made it to his room and flanked one side of his bed. Darion was probably at Tyson. Devon tried to ignore the mess that was already piling back up on his side of the room.

"Ok. So, the next step is happening." Lena's soothing voice stroked his ear. "But remember. God has already gone before you. Whatever happens, He has you."

Warmth met him with her words, and with the phone sandwiched between his neck and shoulder, Devon started unsealing the package. "Thank you for that. This is definitely a situation that's building my faith." Devon's eyes gleamed as the sky-blue cover with a heart on the front peered at him. "Yes! You sent the book."

He could hear Lena's grin through her response on the other end. "I hope it helps. I just want you to know you're not alone through all of this, Devon. But I do have to go. You were right, I am working on the lesson for tonight. Hit me later if you're up. I'll be free after 8 pm. Unless, of course, the Holy Spirit shows up." She giggled, and the sound plastered a smile to Devon's face.

"Bet. Yeah, I got you. I don't want to get in the way of you preparing your sermon." He cleared his throat. "I mean, uh, your *lesson.*" He was kidding and alluding to her calling as a pastor.

"Yeah yeah. I see you," Lena said back. "Oh. Speaking of the Holy Spirit. How's the Book of Acts coming?"

Devon's eyes enlarged. "Man. It's *lit*! I mean, *who knew* there was this whole other supernatural world with supernatural powers. It's like Christians are superheroes on the low."

Lena laughed. "I love it! Yes, Devon, you are a superhero. No matter what comes in this life, know that you have the victory."

More warmth enclosed Devon at her words, and he clasped the book in his hand.

"Wow. Thank you. I really needed to hear that." Devon then thought of the kryptonite of Jasmine Thomas. "I'm definitely gonna need all the supernatural power I can get."

After hanging up, he spread out on his bed to start reading *How to Overcome Heartbreak.* As Devon consumed the author's experience, God's presence saturated him. About halfway through chapter four, Devon was inspired by the end-of-the-chapter questions and decided to write out the things brewing in his heart. Opening his laptop, he wrote:

God, I know I'm going through some really hard things right now, but thank You for showing me I'm not alone in them. You sent my mom to North Star, which led her to Lena, who You keep using in my life. Now You've sent me this book through her. And You even sent me Timothy to help me process my emotions and gain insight. Please help me to be the man You want me to be. Please show me my identity. Please turn my pain into purpose. And please, please, please have a plan for me after graduation! I'm trusting You with everything I have. I'm trusting You to provide.

Devon sat with that last thought. Walking away from Jack & Jill was a huge step of faith and standing up to his father could only have happened with God's supernatural boldness. Never before had he stood up to his dad like that. Yet, now that Jasmine was out of the picture, Devon was faced with the sharp realization that he had hoped God's redirection meant that he was going to L.A. *Clearly, that's not happening.* Then what in the world did God have for him? Devon's stomach turned again. Disappointment that his life plans had been bulldozed over by his best friend and his girlfriend sat on his chest. He was torn up that his first love had hurt him in the worst way possible and scared to death that he couldn't see his future. Devon re-read his letter, and the goodness of God shone in each person He sent to help him in his hardship. God was meeting him and building his faith. Just like He had done with Lena.

"I trust you, God," Devon murmured, then typed the date and saved the letter in his folder labeled "journal." While intentionally meditating on all of God's gifts, Devon remembered Timothy's words: "Everything is going to be alright." Suddenly, it dawned on him. Those were the words he had said on the plane on his way to Brooklyn! His spiritual eyes of understanding were opened, and he realized that God had been speaking to him even before he had needed the word. That thought rocked him. Devon was learning that God was not only a Wonderful Counselor, but He was omniscient.

———

BY THE TIME Darion busted into the room, Devon had switched to his homework. His Operations Management quiz was fast approaching, and he needed to buckle down to get ready for it.

"Yo. Guess who was looking straight *pathetic* at Tyson's tonight?" Darion boasted while flopping across from Devon onto his bed.

Devon glanced up from his textbook. "Who?"

"Your girl. J.T." Darion gave an ugly smirk.

Devon's heart pinged. He tried to look unfazed. "Oh yeah?"

"Yeah. She came up to me with these big puppy dog eyes, practically begging me to put in a good word to you for her." Darion rolled his eyes. "She lucky I didn't dawg the mess out of her. But I had to keep it professional, you know, being at work and all." He popped the green apron trimmed in white that he still wore.

"Word? She came to my chess practice today," Devon revealed.

Darion's face exploded with surprise. "Whattt? Dang. She must really got it bad."

Devon frowned and dropped his highlighter, lifting himself on his side to face his brother. "I don't know. I just know the way she played me is crazy."

"Facts. I mean, who comes back from *that*?" Darion made a disgusted face. "What did you do with the ring anyway?" Then he started removing his jacket, apron, and shoes.

Devon swallowed. "Nothing. It's in my desk drawer," he admitted.

"Aww, man. You gotta get yo money back. That ho ain't worth it. The sooner you move on, the better."

Devon sighed. His brother was right. He had to move on. He just didn't seem to know how.

"I heard from the school today," Devon said, changing the subject.

"Oh yeah? What'd they say?"

"I got an interview with them this Friday at 11 am. It's gon be in the Office of Student Affairs' building. I'm hoping Mr. Right can come. I'm waiting on mom to text me back."

"Bet. I wish I were free, but I got class. Hopefully, you can get off and put this whole thing behind you," Darion added, trying to comfort his big brother.

Devon rubbed a hand over his eyes, pinching the skin near his temples. "Yeah. That's the hope."

"You heard anything from yo boy?" Caution swaddled Darion's tone, as if he were tiptoeing on the landmine of Devon's heart.

Devon figured he was referring to Antonio, but was smart enough not to say his name. "Yeah. He stopped by here drunk the other night. I forgot to tell you."

"Whatt?! Damn. They gettin' bold ain't they?"

"Puh. I'll say."

"So what happened? You talk to him?"

"Pshh. I ain't got no holla for that brotha. He disrespected me in the worst way possible."

"Period. He ain't even worth the time. What they did was unforgivable," Darion cosigned before changing to meet Kimberly for their study date.

As Devon went back to studying, his brother's words rang in his mind. Was what Jasmine and Antonio did unforgivable? What qualified as unforgivable? His newfound faith was teaching Devon that God seemed to consider *everything* forgivable. Just because God did, did that mean he had to too? These thoughts circled his mind even as he studied, and Devon couldn't shake them. When he had the room back to himself, he pulled out the book on heartbreak again. His jaw dropped as he read chapter 5, "The Secret to Healing." It was in that chapter that the author disclosed one of the major keys to her healing: forgiving her ex.

SEVENTEEN
THE BEST THING THAT EVER HAPPENED

The rest of the week was spent carrying out Devon's typical student duties and learning the ropes at Java's. He was surprised by how much he enjoyed making coffee. As much as he loved drinking the stuff, never once had it occurred to him to work in a cafe. At Jack & Jill, they had the standard coffee maker, and at his parents', they had his mom's French press. But that was about it. The elaborate spread of espresso machine, coffee grinder, drip coffee maker, blender, etc, was like being at an all-you-can-eat buffet for coffee lovers. Devon felt like he was in coffee heaven!

"You're a fast learner," Frank had affirmed while training him.

By day three, Devon was completely at ease and even included his own added flair to some of the beverages they made. His background in running Jack & Jill proved to be a huge benefit.

Yet throughout the week, whenever he was in between classes or his shifts at Java's, his stomach churned. His mind corvette-raced about the outcome of his future and his heart fought perpetual anxiety. The interview with the school relentlessly clawed at the back of his mind. It did give Devon some comfort that his lawyer, Mr. Right, would be present, but no one else seemed to be available. His brother would be in class. His mother had to run the business, and his father was still in recovery. Well, that was one silver lining in this whole dreadful ordeal. Devon finally got a call from his dad.

"Hey," Mr. Woods huffed on the other line.

It was Wednesday evening, and Devon had been finishing up *How to Overcome Heartbreak.* He was surprised to see his father's name on his phone.

"Hey, Dad," he replied.

"You know I love you, right?" Mr. Woods said, his tone thick with emotion.

Devon's eyes burned. "Of course. I know." He shoved down the lump in his throat.

"Your mom told me about this sexual harassment thing."

Devon inhaled. "Yeah. I go on Friday to do the interview."

"Ain't no Black man safe in this world, Devon. I know you know that."

Devon bobbed his head against the phone. "I know, Dad."

"You call me right after, you hear?"

Devon sniffed. "Yep. I will."

"Alright. Love you," Mr. Woods said again gruffly. Clearly his dad was apologizing for reacting the way that he did. His father wasn't one to hash out his feelings, so this was the closest Devon was going to get to any kind of in-depth conversation.

"Love you too," Devon replied, before hanging up. He finished the book with a smile on his face. At least his father was back in his corner.

Thursday evening, Devon and his mother had a video chat with Mr. Right. The high-profile lawyer had flown in that day and was camped out at the Hilton near campus. The call was a preliminary. One in which he reviewed potential questions Devon could be asked, along with appropriate responses.

"The overall goal is for you to establish your credibility and capitalize on their lack of proof," Right said with an air of authority. "And of course, just be yourself and tell the truth," he added with warm green eyes inherited from his European ancestors. His skin tone landed somewhere between tan and the sand Devon had walked on in Cancun.

Just having him on the call helped calm Devon's nerves, but the morning of the interview, his nerves were back.

He was dressed in his best, "I'm a respectable citizen" outfit: classic, short-sleeved, stark-white collared shirt, blue slacks, and a matching blue tie and jacket. Mr. Right advised blue meant trustworthy. As his Nana Jean would say, Devon was casket sharp.

When he looked in the mirror and completed the task of tying his tie, he realized why he was so jittery. He needed to pray.

In the hush of the late morning, risking dirtying his slacks, Devon fell to his knees.

"Lord," he breathed. "Please go before me. Please help me to trust You every step of the way in this process." A tear escaped as he murmured the words to his Father. Yes, Devon was starting to know God as His Father. God would never not talk to him because He was mad at him. All the days his father had ignored him made Devon appreciate this eternal access he now always had to God through His Son, Jesus Christ.

Within a few moments, the peace he was becoming so familiar with embraced him. His heartbeat sped up at God's presence. The birds chirping outside of his window seemed to be rooting him on. Strengthened and resolved, Devon stood on his patent leather brown shoes, flattened his shoulders, lifted his chin, and headed for the door.

———

THE SECRETARY outside the meeting room led the way, and Devon and Mr. Right followed into the box-like setting. The sun did shine through the partially raised blinds. That at least was comforting. Other than that, the room was brisk and bare. Kind of like Cory, the Title IX Coordinator. There was simply nothing warm about this woman. Her muddy brown hair was cut short and wrapped behind two elf-like ears. Her full red lips stayed tight. Only a thin string of pearls gave Devon any sense of affability in meeting her. They reminded him of his mother.

"Would you like water?" Cory asked after their greeting. She said it less with kindness and more as a preliminary, but Devon still nodded. His throat was parched.

Once the secretary served them a few bottles of room temperature water, Cory said, briskly, "Ok. Let's get started."

The interview was in line with what Right had him prepared for. It was Devon recounting the events to the best of his memory. Devon sharing his reasons for wanting to take on the TA position. Yet when Devon stated that Monica had actually asked *him* out, Cory's red lips frowned. This was obviously news to her.

"And why didn't you tell Professor Marx about the incident if that was the case?" she asked, her tone disbelieving.

Devon swallowed. "I intended to. I-I was *going* to, but then we had spring break. And I guess I minimized the situation." His shoulders shrank as he spoke.

Sitting in the small room at the square table, Devon's mind rewound back to that day. He had been caught up with Jasmine. He had called her and was running around campus to get her breakfast. He was trippin' on Bruce. He was so focused on not wanting Jasmine to be jealous of Monica's come-on and dealing with his own jealousy over Bruce, that he literally forgot to tell Marx. After that, he had been more focused on proposing than anything.

"I see," Cory said, taking notes.

Her gaze homed in on her notepad.

Devon thought, *Lord, if You get me out of this, I promise I'll never get myself in a situation like this again!*

Cory hit him with a few other questions and 45 minutes later said, "Ok. That concludes our investigation. We'll reach out to you within a few days with an update. I'll be submitting my findings to the decision-maker. They'll determine the final outcome or next steps. This can take up to 90 days."

Devon's chin nearly hit the floor. "90 days! I graduate in less than two months."

Mr. Right said, "Surely you will include a speedy due process given Devon's particular situation, Ms. Heart."

Cory looked unmoved. "As I stated, I can only do my job. They will have to do theirs."

Right tried again. "Ok. Well, do you want Devon to submit a list of references who can vouch for his character? Maybe that will aid in your investigation."

Cory was hesitant, then shrugged. "Sure. Sometimes that can be helpful." In a begrudging tone, she said, "You can email them to me directly."

Immediately, Devon wondered who he would use as references. Ironically, the first two names that came to mind were Marx and Clark. They were literally his best sources, and yet Monica had turned them against him. At least Clark. He wondered about Marx.

"You'll want to send them as soon as possible," Cory added, already stuffing her belongings into a large leather Louis Vuitton briefcase.

Right squeezed Devon's shoulder. "You did great. Make sure you cc me on that email, and I'll call you and your mother later. I gotta hurry and catch my flight for a meeting with a client."

Devon said, "Thank you so much for coming out here to be with me. I definitely appreciate the support." And he meant it. Having Right prepare him for the interview had given Devon more confidence as he walked in. Still, he wished his mother were there.

I can't believe they up here talking about 90 days! he mused. His stomach sank.

After shaking hands with Cory, Devon trailed Right out of the room, trying to get himself together internally.

Mr. Right was a few inches taller and several inches wider than Devon, so he blocked his view as they approached the secretary's desk. When Right shifted to exit the door leading into the hallway, Devon's startled gaze met Jasmine's eyes. She was sitting in one of the two chairs in front of the secretary's mahogany desk.

"Hey," she said, hopping to her feet in a pair of jeans with a white T and pink blazer. She licked her lips, which seemed to perfectly match her blazer. "I came to support you, but they said I had to wait out here."

Devon was in shock and cleared his throat. Just when he was about to speak, Cory brushed by him to make her exit. She didn't say anything but looked between the two with a raised brow before disappearing out the door.

"How did-how did you know I was here?" Devon stuttered. He slid a hand behind his neck and pinched the skin.

"Don't be mad. Kimberly told me last night. She had hung out with Darion, and I begged her for updates on you and well..." When she shrugged, her shoulders reached her earlobes. "Don't be mad," she repeated with pleading eyes. Coyly, Jasmine began to shuffle in her heels while stretching both ends of her blazer in his direction.

Devon knew that he probably should be mad. What gave her the right to just pop in his life whenever she wanted to? Especially while he was dealing with such a crucial issue, such as his education being sabotaged. Yet his heart betrayed him. It burst with gratitude. He needed a friend.

"You want to get coffee?" he found himself asking.

Instantly, she beamed. "Only if it's at Java's."

Devon smiled.

———

THE COUPLE CAPTURED the same table near the back that they had when Jasmine had first come to see him. This time, Frank greeted her with familiarity, but he looked at Devon, confused.

"I thought you weren't coming in 'til 2 pm?" he said, scratching his salt and pepper hair. "And you know you don't have to dress up for this job, right?" he added, running his eyes over Devon's fit.

Devon had removed the jacket and loosened his tie after the interview, but he still looked super done up for school. "I see you got jokes, Frank. We just came to chill for a minute. If employees are allowed to still be customers, that is?"

Frank said, "Of course. But you're gonna have to serve yourselves cuz, as usual, I'm short-handed. Tiffany called off again."

"No problem. I can even start earlier if you need me to," Devon offered.

"No. No. You go ahead and enjoy your friend there." Frank's eyes darted to the back, where Jasmine was on her phone. He gave Devon a knowing smile.

Without waiting another second, Devon hurried to whip up their drinks and meet her at the table. "Voila," he said, presenting the mugs as if he were a magician.

Jasmine looked impressed. "You work here now?" She had seen him chatting with Frank and then jumping behind the bar.

"Yeah. It's filling in the time gap I would normally spend assisting Marx."

After Jasmine took a sip, her face shone. "Man. Devon. This is really good," she said. She sounded surprised.

Feeling pleased, Devon laughed. "I know, right. Who knew?" He took his first sip, and the flavors of cinnamon, oat milk, and a touch of honey did a funky line dance across his taste buds.

The cafe buzzed with easy conversation and the soft lulls of singer-songwriter types drifting in the background. Java's was starting to feel like home.

"So, how did it go?" Jasmine asked hesitantly. She seemed to be groping around, trying to feel her way into this part of his life again. Before, she had had full access. Now, things were different.

Devon leaned back and laid his hand on the table in thought. "Honestly? I don't know. They're saying it could take up to 90 days to decide, which is insane since I'm supposed to graduate."

Jasmine's eyes exploded. "90 days? What are you supposed to do about graduation? Does that mean they would let you walk? Would you just get your diploma later?"

That was something Devon didn't think to ask. He made a mental note to reach out to Mr. Right later.

He shrugged in response. "That's a good question. I'm not sure. But I'll find out. But the Coordinator, Cory, is the no-nonsense type. You can tell she don't play. That could be good or bad. Good, because if she's really about finding the truth, she'll submit her findings honestly, and I'll be cleared. Bad because she seems like one of those left-wing feminists Clark ran with back in the day and will probably taint the evidence." To that, Jasmine raised a brow. "You know what I mean.

Not like you…just like the type who thinks every man is a chauvinistic pig," Devon elaborated.

"Well. Your situation is rare," Jasmine said slowly. "You're a good guy. It's just that so many *other* men have taken advantage of women. It's hard to know who to trust and who not to."

More than likely, Jasmine was thinking of her personal experiences of being taken advantage of by men, but the comment reminded Devon of his difficulty with trusting *her*.

"Well, I can relate to that," he said.

Jasmine looked up then reached a hand on the table and stroked his arm. "I'm going to earn your trust back, Devon," she stated firmly, her eyes steeled. "You're the best thing that ever happened to me."

Devon's stomach swam laps of emotion. It felt like Jasmine was a part of him, and he had lost a limb. Ever since their breakup, he had been hobbling around trying to get his bearings. Even being in her presence fed something inside of him that he couldn't comprehend.

"I need time," he managed with a deep breath. "I just need to get through this situation."

Jasmine nodded. "I know. I told you, I'm going to wait for as long as it takes."

They talked for another hour until Devon had to start his shift. It was like when they first started dating. Jasmine updated him on her latest shenanigans with Sheila and the grades she got on her midterms. Devon was always so smitten by how the world looked through her eyes. There was always a cause she was fighting for or a party she was getting ready for. Life was always more fun with Jasmine. Well, until it wasn't.

After she left, Devon let the work at Java's sustain him. He started recognizing faces and learning the regulars, even their orders. At five o'clock, he stayed to help Frank close before agreeing to be back in the morning. He would work an eight-hour shift the next day. Even though the whole sexual harassment thing was a huge traumatizing disruption, if not for that, he wouldn't be working at Java's. While heading back to his dorm, the scripture that came to Devon's heart was Romans 8:28.

"And we know that all things work together for good to those who love God, to those who are the called according to His purpose."

It was one that Devon had committed to memory after Lena had texted it to him. She sent it the night before to encourage him for the interview with the Title XI Coordinator. They had agreed he would update her about how things went that evening when they had their chess date. Turns out Lena liked chess too. Of course, she wasn't as skilled as he was, so he would have to take it easy on her. Even so, Devon was excited about their first chess date.

When he got to his dorm, Darion was blasting music and dancing in the middle of the room. Devon took his time watching and cracking up from the doorway until his brother turned around.

"Bruhhh. You coulda let me know you was standing there!" Darion quickly shuffled to his phone to turn down the music on his Bluetooth.

"And stop the show?" Devon said, tossing his coat jacket on this desk chair and slipping out of his shoes. "Never."

"So? How'd it go?"

Devon held up a finger, "Hold up," he said, then dialed his mom on video chat. She answered right away.

"Hey, baby! Your father is right here." She positioned the phone so that his dad, sitting next to her on their bed, came into view. He was still in his cast, leg propped up and all.

"Hey, son." Mr. Woods's gruff tone blared through the video chat.

Devon let Darion get in the phone camera so their parents could see him. The brothers sat side-by-side against the wall on his bed, and the four chatted about Devon's day. Sans Debra, it was a family affair and one that rarely happened, given everyone's schedules.

"Well, son, you sound like you're in good spirits, so stay in good spirits!" Mr. Woods said.

"Yes, and remember what we talked about," his mother said, winking. She was referring to their conversation about having faith and trusting God. Devon thanked everyone for their support.

After they ended the call with their parents, Darion asked, "Yo. I'm taking Kimberly out tonight. You want me to come home? Or you good?"

"Ah, you good. I got a hot chess date tonight," Devon revealed, chuckling.

"Oh word? Who wit'? And what the heck is a chess date?" Darion gave him a funny look while spraying on cologne. He studied his reflection in their shared mirror.

"Not a date you would go on," Devon said, ignoring the first half of his brother's question. Matter of fact, it was time for him to call Lena. "Have fun with Kimberly," he said, and meant it. Maybe at least one of them would find love in this season of life.

When Devon called Lena, her beautiful face filled the video, and she smiled brightly.

"Ohhhh, Okkkkaaayy. That's the chess date, huh?" Darion said, peering over Devon's shoulder, trying to get a better look.

Lena laughed. "Who is that?" she asked.

Devon moved the phone so that Darion couldn't see her. "No one you need to meet any time soon," he said, then sent her the website link to their chess game. He was already in the virtual room with his laptop open on his bed.

"Y'all have fun with yo *virtual* date," Darion piped on his way out the door. "Maybe we can do a *real* double date sometime!"

Devon rolled his eyes and hoped Lena didn't hear the comment. Thankfully, she seemed busy signing in to their virtual room. They spent the rest of the night playing and talking. It was the first time Devon had played chess with a woman he was interested in. Lena was better than he thought, and a few times she actually almost beat him. Finally, she had to get off to turn in so she could get up early for choir practice.

"This was fun!" she said, and Devon agreed.

"I'll call you tomorrow," he promised, before wishing her goodnight.

Slipping on a pair of sweats, Devon checked his phone. It was still pretty early to go to bed, and he wondered if he should pull up a movie. Just when he was about to pick one, someone was knocking at the door. That was odd. Normally, anybody coming to see him would have texted. Maybe it was for Darion.

It bet not be Antonio again, he thought with a frown and got up to answer it.

Still clutching his phone in his hand and ready to cuss out his friend, Devon opened the door. Surprise flooded him. Jasmine stood, her eyes swirling with desire and intent, her hair wild and cascading over her shoulders, not like earlier when she had it swooped in a high bun. She was decked in a trench coat and heels. When she slowly undid her belt, part of a red lace bra peeked beneath the double-breasted collar. Devon knew then that she was only wearing her underwear.

"You want company?" she asked in a low, sultry tone. Her eyes pierced his, and all the blood raced to Devon's loins.

He swallowed hard, imagining the curvy figure beneath the trench. As if in a trance, he stepped aside and let her in.

EIGHTEEN

I DON'T WANT TO KNOW

THE NEXT TWO WEEKS FLEW BY WITH DEVON FINDING HIMSELF RETURNING to Jasmine time and time again. He told himself they weren't back together, yet each night he was either in her bed or she was in his.

"Bro. You good?" Darion had asked him one evening, looking worried.

Devon had been gone for days, and Darion wasn't even sure where he was one particular night until Devon randomly texted him.

"Yeah. I just. I just…" Devon couldn't find the words. It was like when he wasn't in class or at Java's, the longing was to be with Jasmine.

I feel like an addict! he thought wildly, trying to get his bearings.

Devon hadn't noticed it, but his communication with Lena had wilted. So had his connection with God. No longer did Devon feel addicted to God. Instead, he felt addicted to Jasmine.

One day, Lena texted to check in:

> Hey. Haven't heard from you in a while.
> You ok?

Devon was with Jasmine at the time and felt weird about texting back. Then, when he finally left her, he had forgotten all about it. *I'll call her later,* he thought. But later never came. Instead, he was in bed with Jasmine.

God. Help! Devon cried out one day when he saw he had gotten a C on his Operations Management exam. He knew then that he was distracted and going under.

Now, whether he couldn't hear God or he just wasn't listening, Devon didn't know. But the response to his prayer never came. Instead, he continued floundering. Floundering under the grips of Jasmine Thomas.

"I told you she was kryptonite, dawg," Darion said, shaking his head. Devon hadn't given him the details; he was too ashamed, but Darion had put two and two together.

"It's just hard because I love her," Devon admitted one night in their room while cradling his head in his hands. They were supposed to have a guys' night, but he ended up getting a text from Jasmine asking if he could come through. It was like he just couldn't say no to her.

Darion glanced behind him from his desk. "Bro. You are in lust. Not love."

It was probably the wisest remark Devon had ever heard his brother say, and he couldn't help but feel it was actually God speaking through him. Just when Devon was about to refute the statement, he got another text. Lena. This time, he knew he couldn't ignore her.

"Let me get this."

Immediately, he called. "Hey."

"Hey. I hope I'm not bugging you. I just never got a response to my last text and wanted to make sure you were good."

Devon fell back on his bed with only his boxers on. He was just about to shower before heading to Jasmine's. It was Friday night. He figured Lena probably wanted to chat before she had to go to bed for her early morning choir practice. Guilt struck Devon's heart. He had missed her last Friday, and now he had to blow her off again.

"Yeah. It's been…I've just been a little—off lately," he said, trying to find the words.

His brother snorted, and Devon shot him a look at his turned back.

"Yeah. I figured," Lena answered quietly. "This wouldn't have anything to do with your ex, would it?"

Whew! How did she know? This woman never ceased to amaze him. It was like her gift of discernment was magnified, reaching hundreds of miles away.

Devon paused but decided to be honest. "Yeah," he answered carefully. "Yes, it would."

Lena went silent. He couldn't tell what she was thinking.

"Devon, I know the season you're in," she finally said. "And I know we're in two different seasons. I just want you to know, I value our friendship. And at this point, I know that's all we can have. I'll be praying for you. I've been in a similar space, and my heart goes out to you. It's not easy to become the person God called you to be. The enemy wages war over our souls and tries to distract us time and time again from our purpose. It's a battle."

Devon sighed. *I definitely feel like I'm in a battle!*

"Have you ever heard of soul ties?"

Hmmm. *Soul ties. Soul ties.* And then he remembered. "Yeah, it was in the book you got me!" Sitting up, Devon searched for the heartbreak book on his desk's bookshelf.

"Right. Soul ties are a spiritual connection that happens between two people when they have sex. It can even happen when two people are emotionally intimate. One of the things I had to do when I left my ex was break those soul ties. You may need to do that, too."

Devon flipped through the book until he reached the section on soul ties. He hadn't really paid too much attention to it the first time he read the book. Now it seemed so applicable. His mind started to clear as he meditated on Lena's words. Holding the phone with his cheek, he said, "Lena, I think you may have just saved my life!" and she laughed. Relief flooded him at the sound. Devon was grateful to still have her as a friend, even if he couldn't have anything more right now.

"I can lead you in the prayer if you want," she offered.

A tussling within caused Devon to hesitate. Saying this prayer meant he would be giving up something he enjoyed and loved: sex with Jasmine. For the majority of their relationship, that experience was incredibly enjoyable. Now, it only wracked him with guilt. It was pulling him away from communion with God and distracting him from his academic responsibilities. It was also keeping him in a situation with his ex that he didn't want to be in. It wasn't healthy to be in a relationship with her right now, yet Devon couldn't seem to distance himself because of the sex. What once felt good now felt like his master. It was like he had absolutely no power when it came to Jasmine, and he was a puppet on her strings. Devon had to get his agency back.

After weighing his options, he finally said, "Yes. Yes, I'm ready."

Lena led him in the prayer, and Devon didn't even care that his brother was just a few feet away. He said it and asked God for forgiveness for succumbing to his desires.

Darion glanced over his neck with an odd expression, but turned back to his laptop.

Devon sniffed. "Lena, thank you so much for being a good friend. I already feel better. I feel—lighter, like something left me that was keeping me bound."

Lena said, "That's awesome. Now, it's still going to be a fight. God will give you the power, but we have to first submit to Him for the enemy to flee (James 4:7). When the enemy has ground in our lives, that's when he can wreak havoc. You need to stay in community and fellowship, Devon. Find a local Bible study or church. Find a mentor. I can only do so much not being there, but you need others who will walk with you as you fight for your purpose."

Lena's words washed over Devon.

"You're right." His hand squeezed the phone in gratitude. "I'm gon look for some resources right now!"

After they hung up, Darion looked at him with raised brows. "Bruh. Wuz up? You over there *praying*?"

Devon typed a few things into the campus search engine to see if anything was happening that evening. His eyes lit up at a Christian meetup being held nearby.

"I haven't felt this good in a while," Devon said, then got up and started putting on clothes.

"Where you goin'? You still gon blow me off for J.T.?"

"I'm going to church. There's an on-campus fellowship event happening at the chapel."

Darion looked at him in shock. "Uh. You not serious. You going to *church*? On a Friday night?"

Devon looked back as he zipped up his jeans. "Yep. You wanna come?"

That was when Devon saw the effects of his decision. His brother started to laugh, but then stopped. It was as if a light was illuminated and he eyed Devon strangely.

"Sure. Why not," he replied with a shrug. "I was gonna be bored here, anyway."

That's when Devon learned the power of supernatural deliverance.

UP UNTIL THAT POINT, outside of Lena, Devon hadn't fellowshipped with other young Believers. When he got to the chapel, he saw that there were so many! Even better, there was a mix of races, which was really dope. Someone was speaking at the front of the sanctuary, as many in the pews sat in unparalleled focus.

Since he had walked in first, Darion whispered, "Dawg, where you wanna sit?"

Devon's eyes scanned the room until his vision landed on a few empty spaces near the front.

Most of the folks were attentive to who was speaking, but as he and Darion looked for seats, a few turned his way and gave friendly smiles.

"Follow me," Devon murmured. As soon as his legs started moving, he was engulfed in that same loving euphoric feeling he experienced at North Star. It was the presence of God, and it was saturating the room.

The brothers whispered awkwardly, "Umm, excuse me," as they weaved through the knees of attendees and slid down the row of a pew.

Finally, when Devon sat, he was able to pay attention to the speaker. A small, Hispanic kid with glasses was confessing his struggle with alcohol. He had been on campus for two years, and when he first got to school, he used alcohol to make friends. Without alcohol, he felt awkward and found it hard to talk to people. When he went to parties and drank, he became the life of the party.

"But then I realized I wasn't just drinking on the weekends. I was drinking almost every day. If I went without a drink, I felt sick in the worst way," he admitted, his expression grieved.

Devon gulped. He could definitely relate to this brother's struggle. Except, it wasn't alcohol. For him, it was Jasmine. It was sex.

"But then, my roommate prayed with me. He started taking me with him to church, and it took a few months, but I finally surrendered my life to God. When I did, everything changed." His face brightened. His eyes glowed behind the rim of his glasses.

A young man who was in the front row said, "Amen!" and the kid smiled at him. It was like they were a family.

Devon marveled at how easily everyone supported the kid's message. There was no embarrassment. No judgment.

After he shared his story, the group went into a time of worship. It was the first time Devon had experienced corporate worship since North Star.

He could feel Darion's hesitancy as the group stood on their feet, and a few gathered at the front to lead. They gave instructions on where to find the song lyrics online.

Devon smiled at Darion encouragingly. Darion followed his lead, hopped to his feet, and popped open his phone for the lyrics. For the first time in two weeks, Devon had peace. This time, he was going to fight to keep it.

———

Saturdays were on another level at Java's. If during the week the ambiance was low-key and studious, it was because the rowdier locals and coffee lovers claimed the weekends.

"Yeah, Mr. R., I got chu'. Double latte, no froth, almond milk with a dash of cinnamon!" Devon called to one of the regulars.

The older gentleman smiled in wonder. "You got it, Devon!" he affirmed, before sticking his head back into his newspaper.

Mr. Roberts was a sweet older gentleman whom Devon learned had been frequenting the cafe every Saturday for the five years it had been open. Frank shared that the day before he opened the cafe, Mrs. Roberts had died. Frank had fixed one of his famous on-the-spot brews as he had done for Devon, and the man had been coming ever since. Devon's eyes lit up when he heard the story. His mind started spinning. It was like Frank had this power to brighten a person's day simply by serving them coffee. Devon had never imagined the concept and yet was a witness that it worked! He aimed to do the same thing when he served. He aimed to bring a smile to every customer's face. Devon was eager to soak up all the knowledge Frank was lavishing on him about running the café. Frank, in turn, was grateful for the younger man's consistency and genuine desire to learn the business.

"I just need four more of you, Devon, that way I can take a day or two off myself!" he kidded one day, and Devon laughed.

"I'm sure it's a lot of work. I've watched my pops slave over Jack & Jill and other restaurants since I was a kid," Devon said in an empathetic tone.

"Yeah. It is. But honestly, I thrive off of it," Frank admitted. A gleam clung to his eye. "I feel like it's a part of my purpose. You know?"

Wow. Purpose. Devon nodded thoughtfully. "Yeah. I do know." He had been praying more and more for God to show him his purpose.

Devon wasn't 100 percent sure whether Jasmine was in it. He had told her he needed space and that he couldn't be involved with her physically anymore. Even when she had suggested they fall back and focus more on the friendship, he declined. At one point, he couldn't see his life without her. Now he could see the error of his views. He should never have tried to make someone else his purpose. Only God could be his purpose.

"I just need to get myself together emotionally and focus on my future," Devon told Jasmine in their last conversation. "Then I'll figure out where you belong in it." She was quiet but agreed. What could she say? These were the consequences of her actions. That was almost a week ago, right after Devon attended the campus fellowship for the first time. He hadn't spoken to her since. She was finally respecting his boundaries.

Thank God! Devon thought while making Mr. Roberts' drink. As much as Devon was feeling good about breaking those soul ties, he didn't know how strong he could be if she pulled another one of her trench coat episodes!

In just that week alone, Devon was already seeing the benefits of keeping his boundaries. He pulled an A on his Accounting quiz and was tapping into a weekly Bible study led by the campus ministry he and Darion had attended. Apparently, they had Wednesday evening Bible study and Friday night fellowship.

How did I never know about this? Devon thought in awe while attending the Bible study. But the answer was obvious. It was because he was never seeking God before. It was wild, how, once Devon's eyes were opened to this spiritual world, the connections he was making with those on the same path flooded his life like a Tsunami. Even Darion seemed to be changing, whom Devon had never considered being affected by his personal transformation.

After they attended the first Bible study, Darion asked Devon, "So, what were they saying about that guy David in the Bible?" The study was on David being anointed king, but having to endure different trials before he actually became king.

"They were saying how young David was when he received his call," Devon explained. "But how he still needed to go through things to mature to be the leader he was called to be." Devon was surprised at his own acute remembrance of the lesson.

"Yo. Like, when you were saying you felt like you had a calling?" Darion asked, and Devon was floored. He had forgotten he had even said that to his brother!

"Yeah. I guess so. But not like to be king...just, something important God has for me to do."

Darion was sitting on his bed and peering at the Bible study questions on his phone. "Gotcha. Guess I'll have to see if I have a calling..." he murmured, his voice trailing.

Devon, who was also lying in his bed, beamed. God was on the move! The only thing he kept wrestling with was the sexual harassment allegation. The school had been quiet after he and Mr. Right emailed Cory his references. Other than her polite, "Thank You," response, it was crickets.

"You know God has you, honey," Mrs. Woods was quick to remind Devon whenever they talked. He appreciated her faith because his anxiety was giving him an ulcer.

"I know, Ma. It's just, what if God calls me to give up this degree?"

It was something Devon had been thinking about lately. It felt like God was asking him to give up sex with the woman he was still in love with. He had already let go of this lifelong preparation to run Jack & Jill. Could it be that God would have him give up his degree, too? So many of his plans had failed. So much of what Devon had been working towards seemed to be torn to shreds and thrown into an inferno. Yet even with his heart still grieving his breakup and wrestling with confusion about the future, his heart couldn't deny that he was loved by God. God's love was being demonstrated through his loved ones and their support. As if to confirm his inner thoughts, his mother replied, "If it's not God's will for you to graduate, Devon, then we will walk that road too, baby. We will walk it together."

Devon was amazed. His parents spent 10s of thousands of dollars on his and his brother's education. For five years, they had been funding the bulk of it outside of a few academic scholarships. Just like that, Mrs. Woods was willing to let it all go? That's when Devon realized, this wasn't just his test, it was his mother's too.

I wonder what Dad would say?

Mr. Woods was back at Jack & Jill, cast and all, and posted up in his office. He couldn't move around too well, but he didn't need to; he could dictate to everyone what they needed to do. He also had finally thanked Uncle James for manning things while he was out. Devon took that as a sign that, yes, God was even working on *his* heart.

By the time it neared five o'clock, Devon's inner thoughts simmered from bouncing around the various compartments of his life. The rat race of serving, making coffee, and cleaning behind customers was coming to an end, and he started assisting with closing the cafe.

"Good job once again!" Frank affirmed Devon as he worked to empty the trash. There were a few other students helping today, so thankfully, they would get out much sooner.

"Thanks, Frank," Devon said, dipping his head back over the stuffed trash bag.

Suddenly, Frank said, "Hey, there! We're actually closing up," to whoever had walked in. The bells had done their normal jingle over the entrance, but Devon had been too focused on the trash.

"No. Umm…we're here for him," Darion said.

Devon turned to see his brother with Jasmine. Confusion blanketed his vision.

"Ah, ok. Then come on in," Frank said, keeping the same friendly manner and hearty tone.

A weight sank its fangs into the pit of Devon's gut. When had he ever seen Darion and Jasmine together?

Alone?

Darion took a few steps closer, his eyes grave. Somber. Jasmine followed his lead but the evidence of her having been emotional lingered. Her eyes were watery. Her mouth was turned downward. Her gaze stapled the floor.

Devon cleared a lump in his throat and focused on tying the trash bag.

I don't want to know. An abrupt thought, but Darion kept drawing closer.

The echo of footsteps reverberated in the intimate space. The scraping of chairs being placed on tables, and the murmuring of the other students, joined the background.

Devon shook his head. "I don't want to know," he spoke out loud.

His brother was now in front of him. Jasmine wasn't too far away. She clasped her fingers together, but her head stayed low.

"I don't want to know," Devon repeated. This time, the tears were burning his vision, blurring the trash bag.

Darion's eyes, too, were misty as he grabbed his brother and pulled him into his arms. They sank to the floor together.

"There was an accident," Darion whispered into his ear, holding him tight. "He's dead."

I don't want to know! Devon cried out in his mind. But it didn't matter, because he already knew. Deep within, he knew.

Antonio was dead.

NINETEEN
GOD IS LOVE

"Untimely death always feels like a tragedy, but especially with the youth." Lena paused, swallowed, and gazed at the funeral attendees. "The only hope we can have is that God meets each of us in our own time on His own terms. God's plan for each of our lives doesn't always make sense. He's an eternal being, outside of time, but the peace we can have is that He is good. And so, even though we don't understand these circumstances, God's goodness will prevail in even the worst kinds of circumstances."

Lena went on to talk about losing her child through a miscarriage. Though her child was never born, the loss of hope she experienced was unfathomable. The darkness that ensued was only lifted from her encounter with God and His family, who wrapped comforting arms around her. She looked at Antonio's father when she said these words, encouraging him in his mourning.

Devon bit his lip to keep it from trembling. His legs rocked as Lena's words straddled his mind.

How could there be good from this?

How could God allow this?

How is this happening?

Devon was in a state of shock. The news of his friend's death had taken him under. It seemed, as soon as Devon found his footing, another storm hit.

Where is God in this? he thought again.

His mom's hand laced around his own, rested on his knee and stroked it, probably to still his shaking leg. His brother laid a protective arm around the back of his chair on his other side. They were his rocks. Mr. Woods, finally out of his cast, was on the other side of his mother. The rest of his friends were scattered throughout the church.

When Mr. Johnson, Antonio's father, had called to let Devon know about the accident, Devon had been so busy at work that he had barely checked his phone. That's why Darion and Jasmine showed up. Darion got a call, and so did Jasmine, since they were contacts in Antonio's phone. Both Darion and Jasmine had reached out to Devon, but he had missed their calls. Jasmine then called Darion, and when he told her Devon was at Java's, they agreed to let him know together.

After his breakdown at Java's, Devon called Mr. Johnson. He needed to hear it himself. He still couldn't believe it. Mr. Johnson's words were stilted. It seemed it took everything in him just to speak.

"He was on his way home from playing basketball with some kids down the way in Brooklyn, and a bus hit him," the older man disclosed. His tone was thick. "He had on those headphones y'all are always wearing. It was dark. He didn't see it coming. They said he died on impact."

Devon's stomach threatened to unleash the contents of the coffee and bagel he had consumed that day, but he stuffed it down. He had to keep it together.

Mr. Johnson continued, saying that Antonio had been home for the past month. After midterm grades came out, he was put on academic probation. Johnson said he was livid, laying into Antonio for wasting his education, but for the first time, Antonio honestly told his father that school just wasn't for him. He had given it his all, and he was ready for something different. Mr. Johnson said he needed to figure out something quick. That's when Antonio picked up a job in Queens near his home at the local YMCA. He started coaching basketball to young men. Turns out he was a natural, and the boys loved him. For four weeks, he coached, finding that he had a knack for it.

Mr. Johnson admitted to Devon that they didn't have a church home. What pastor would do the service? Devon knew one. At least, a soon-to-be-one.

"I got you," Devon replied and called Lena. She didn't hesitate, though she had never in her life given a eulogy.

North Star's welcoming environment was the perfect setting for this type of gathering. It didn't matter that no one in the ministry was very familiar with Antonio or his loved ones. All that mattered was that his family felt welcomed and cared for in their time of need.

The repast was held in the very room where Devon had attended their Bible study. Who knew in just a couple of months he would be there for a different reason entirely? Flashbacks of his first experience at the church flew past his mind, confusing his heart. That night, Devon had been overwhelmed with joy. Now he felt buried by pain.

"Baby, you want a plate?" his mother asked, tilting her chin to the spread North Star had provided for the repast. Members filled with the love of God shining through, stood like soldiers on the frontline, hands shielded by serving gloves.

Devon shook his head. He couldn't eat a thing.

"I'll get you just a little something," his mother said and patted his arm. Ignoring his response entirely, she sped to the buffet.

Jasmine was perched at a round table by the east wall near the entrance with Darion, Kimberly, and Sheila. Devon caught her gaze. Her eyes seemed to ask if he was ok, but he didn't know how to respond. Nothing was ok. He dropped his eyes and sank into one of the seats near the back.

"Dev, come meet my dad." It was Lena. She was standing nearby, but Devon had been so focused on Jasmine that he didn't even realize he had sat right in front of her. Obediently, he stood and held out a hand.

"Reverend Williams, thank you so much for opening your church to us," Devon said, shaking his hand.

The short balding man smiled with his eyes before it ever reached his lips, his generous spirit exuding easily. As soon as Devon laid eyes on him, he saw the resemblance. Lena definitely took after her father.

"Of course, son," Mr. Williams said. "What else are we here for than to serve others?"

Warmth hugged Devon, temporarily satiating the constant wringing of his gut. As he chatted with the two, some of the boys from the YMCA drifted over, as well as his mother, plate in hand. His father, Devon noticed, was at a table in conversation with Mr. Johnson and a few ministers. Antonio's dad seemed to be keeping it together as well as one could expect, given he had just lost his brother last year. He had asked Devon to speak at Antonio's funeral, but there was just no way that he could. Devon just wasn't the friend Mr. Johnson thought he had been. Darion spoke instead. Afterward Devon thanked him with a grim nod.

The boys from the "Y" started chatting and sharing stories about Antonio teaching them different basketball moves and boasting about how great of a coach he was. Hearing this almost brought Devon to tears. He had no idea his friend had been coaching kids, or that he would be so good at it. Then his last game with Antonio fluttered to his mind. How excited he had been about their win. How his bragging had always hyped up Devon, even when they were losing. Devon was no doubt a better player because of Antonio. Then the memory of Devon's last interaction with Antonio surfaced. His heart plummeted.

I should have reached out.

Lena had a hand on his arm and steered him away from the group.

"You wanna get some air?" she offered.

Devon couldn't get the words out, so he just bobbed his head. As they made their exit, he ignored Jasmine's questioning look. The pair drifted through the maze of long hallways until they reached the entrance of the church. Lena smoothed down her grey-blue dress and took a seat on the steps. Devon followed her lead. He sniffed, eyes burning, stomach weighed down by a ton of bricks.

"Thank you for doing the eulogy..." he croaked out, staring into the warm afternoon. Temperatures were finally rising as May peeked her way into their lives.

"And for everything," Devon added.

Lena said, "Of course. I just hope it offered some sort of comfort."

They sat in silence for a while as Devon battled all of the thoughts that kept haunting him. If only he hadn't slammed the door in his face. If only he hadn't blocked him. If only…All the if-onlys swirled like an internal tornado, becoming a storm of agony threatening to take him under.

"I-I wasn't talking to him," he finally said in a horse tone. "He-he did what he did, and I cut him off."

"Devon, you couldn't have imagined you didn't have time to make things right," Lena said. "I know people say this a lot, but you know my story. I can tell you firsthand, you can trust that God is going to bring good from this." Lena's voice was firm yet kind.

Devon kept his head squeezed between his knees.

"But what if I hadn't reacted that way? What if I had given him a chance…" he mumbled at his knees, then he thought of Jasmine. He had given her a chance. Why hadn't he given Antonio a chance? Weren't they brothers? Isn't that what he had said? A flashback of their embrace in Cancun when he asked him to be his best man shadowed his mind's eyes. He shuttered.

Lena slid a gentle hand along Devon's upper back and rubbed. "You were the best friend Antonio ever had. Isn't that what his father said? You stuck around when others didn't. And even when you put up a boundary, it was out of respect for yourself. Antonio was held accountable for his actions. His actions caused him to miss out on communicating with you."

Devon's mind ran over Lena's words. His glazed eyes stared ahead, unseeing. Folks ambled down the street chatting, and cars whizzed by as if it were just a normal day.

How could anything good come from this? he wondered forlornly.

How could God possibly work *this* for the good?

———

SEVERAL DAYS AFTER THE FUNERAL, Devon was still at his parents' home in Brooklyn Heights. Mrs. Woods called the school, reported what had happened, and received approval for a short-term leave.

Devon couldn't get out of bed. His mother came in, brought him food, or coffee, or just sat on his comforter and rubbed his unmoving body. One night, she read the Bible to him. It was about grieving with hope.

"How do we know Antonio is with God?" Devon whispered that particular evening. He had no idea what day it was.

His mother sighed. "We have to trust God, baby. We know that He has His own way of leading each of us. We don't know how He chose to draw Antonio."

Guilt resurfaced. *If I hadn't shut him out of my life, I could have led him,* Devon mused. The influence he had on Darion and his budding relationship with God was evidence that Devon was called to lead by example.

As if his mother knew what he was thinking, she said, "You're not God, baby. You aren't responsible for everyone. You have to trust His ways."

Everyone kept saying to trust God, but it was getting harder and harder. It was one thing to have his boy sleep with his girl, but then *this*? His boy to just be taken out like that? Before they could even reconcile? What sense did *that* make?

"No sense," Devon spat in response to his raging thoughts beneath the comforter.

One night, maybe because she had never seen him in such a state, Debra came to check on him. Darion had gone back to school. He had classes he couldn't miss and work, but he had called every night to check in with Devon. So had Jasmine and Lena. Sometimes he took their calls, sometimes he didn't.

After knocking, Debra entered the room, not waiting for an answer. Quietly, she slipped off her shoes and stretched out her legs after climbing onto his bed. Propped up against the bedrest, with one long leg over the other, she scrolled through her phone.

"What do you want," Devon said more as a statement and less as a question. He was curled on his side with his back to her. The light had been off, but she had turned on the small lamp beside his bed, emitting a dim haze in the room.

"I'm keeping you company," she said and kept scrolling.

"I don't feel like talking," Devon muttered.

"Then don't," Debra responded. But after a good ten minutes of silence and her being there, Devon sighed.

"You gon be bored, so you may as well just leave." He couldn't turn off his big brother role to care about her comfort if he had tried.

"I'm fine with being bored. We can be bored together."

That was a first. Debra, putting someone before herself? Yet she was going to be bored out of her mind just sitting there with him. Finally, Devon forced himself to roll over and peered above the covers pulled to his nose. His sister wore her school uniform, so it couldn't be too late in the evening. She would have changed into sweats by now. Even though he had switched his position, she pecked on her phone without a care in the world.

Devon coughed. "I need some water," he said. Part of him figured that if he started asking her to do things, she would leave. She got up immediately and the door opened before she returned moments later with a fresh glass filled to the rim.

It took everything in him to make himself sit up. Devon took the glass, mumbled, "Thanks," and gulped.

"What else do you need?" she asked, and her voice was so tender, so sincere that his heart caved.

"I need my friend back," he whispered honestly. Devon sniffed and bowed his head.

Debra sat next to him, opening her arms. "I can't bring him back. But I'm here."

Never in Devon's 23 years had he been able to lean on his little sister. Yet that moment had come.

"I just need a second chance," Devon whispered as she held his figure still wrapped in his comforter. "We—we weren't talking when he, he..." Devon couldn't say it. "I-I had him blocked." His breaths were coming rapidly as he fought to hold back the tears. His chest felt like it was about to explode from sorrow.

Debra stiffened. "You blocked him? On your phone?"

Devon nodded, still keeping his head low. "I-I blocked him on everything. On social media too."

Debra said, "Did you know that even if you block someone, they can still leave a voicemail?" and the words sent an eerie shiver down Devon's spine.

"What?" He raised his head and looked at her.

Debra said, "Yeah. If you check your voicemails and look for blocked messages, and somebody who was blocked left a message, it'll show."

Devon's reality started dancing around and becoming re-altered with this new information, like puzzle pieces rearranged and put together to show a different picture. He had never known about this feature on his phone before. Blinking, he sat up and reached for his cell on the nightstand. Carefully, holding it like a bomb, he looked at Debra.

She widened her eyes as if to say, "Hurry up!"

Slowly, Devon unlocked his phone. Some missed texts from his brother, Lena, and Jasmine appeared. Then he went to his missed calls. Then voicemails. After he scrolled all the way down, 21 missed blocked voicemails appeared. 21.

"OhmyGod," Devon uttered, and looked back at Debra. His stomach dropped. She grinned.

Wordlessly, Devon opened the first one and put it on speaker. It was Jasmine. She was apologizing profusely for the affair. There were three more like that from her. Embarrassment flushed Devon's cheeks since his little sister was now hearing all of the gory details about his breakup. Debra only looked sad and not at all eager for teenage gossip. There were a few more messages from spam numbers Devon had blocked. Then, it switched to Antonio.

"Hey, bro. I know I messed up. I know I did the unthinkable. I'm so sorry..."

The date was a few nights after Devon had found out and beaten him to a pulp. He flipped to the next one.

"I understand why you slammed the door in my face. I deserve it..."

Antonio had called after he tried to come over. His voice was still intoxicated and slurred. The next one, from a few days later, was different. He sounded clear. Lighter. Even *happy*.

"Dev, I'm so grateful for everything you did for me, bro. Being

the brother I never had. The love you always showed me. The example you were to me. The standard of work ethic, integrity, and brotherly love..."

Antonio was lavishing him with honor and praise. Devon was shocked. He had never heard his friend sound this way. Something had changed. And then, the next one.

"Devon, I been going to this campus Bible study. It's been dope. They talked tonight about close friendships. They talked about David and Jonathan, who weren't blood-related but loved each other like brothers. There was a time when they got separated, and they weren't close anymore. But then David found Jonathan's heir and put him on. He honored their friendship. I know God was speaking to me, man. Even though we aren't in each other's lives anymore, our friendship was divine. I know that type of connection lasts forever..."

Devon nearly dropped the phone. That's what was different! Antonio had found God! The next message confirmed it.

"Bro. I been in prayer about our situation and what I keep hearing is, 'I forgive you.' God keeps telling me He forgives me. I know you may not be ready to, but He does. And for now, I'm at peace with that. Still, I want you to know how much you mean to me and how I've always admired you, Dev..."

The messages led up until only a few days before his death. Antonio was updating Devon on his new job at the "Y", the boys he was coaching, and even being honest with his father about not wanting to go to school. He talked a lot about his uncle and how he could finally understand what his uncle had been telling him all those years he wasn't listening: *God is love.*

Devon's eyes glistened as he marveled at the phone in his hand. He looked over at his sister and was met with the same expression of wonder.

"He-he found God," Devon uttered. "He-he's saved."

TWENTY

BROTHERS ARE FOREVER

MR. JOHNSON WAS THE OLD-SCHOOL, NO-NONSENSE TYPE. THAT MEANT when you said you were going to do something, you did it. Devon understood that his friend's father was native to a generation when you worked a job for 50 years, got your pension, and basked in the security of retirement.

"Commitment, endurance, and dedication are just a few of my core values, son. And this new school thought of floating from one thing to the next, well, it just doesn't bode well with my worldview," Johnson told Devon while in his study. The ambiance of intellect blended with affluence mirrored the Woods's home. Mr. Johnson was a city court judge.

"So I was hard on him," Johnson continued. "Too hard. I just wish I'd made it easier for Antonio to tell me how he really felt."

His friend's father's face crumbled in sadness, and Devon's heart squeezed. Searching for the right words, he sipped more herbal tea before responding. "I know what you mean," Devon started, "I have a lot of guilt. Antonio and I... didn't-didn't end on the best terms."

Mr. Johnson lifted his unshaven chin, peering in surprise. He had no idea the boys had fallen out. "Really? Antonio never mentioned it..." Leaning back onto the leather sofa, Johnson sipped from his own mug, which consisted of more rum than tea.

"Yeah," Devon said. "There were some…things…that popped off in Cancun." He shrugged, studying the grey carpet that clothed the room. "I was having a hard time getting over them."

"Ahh…I see." Mr. Johnson scratched the low stubble wildly decorating his face. It had to have been days since he'd shaved.

"Well, I know how much you meant to him, Devon, so regardless of the falling out, he considered you a brother. And I know firsthand, brothers are forever." Johnson's eyes took on a far-off look, no doubt, thinking of his own brother.

That's when Devon remembered how much Antonio revered his Uncle Dave. He realized he could relay that information to Mr. Johnson in a special way. *The voicemails.* His eyes glowed as he reached for his cell in his back pocket.

"Mr. Johnson, I'd love to share something with you."

Devon had been replaying the messages on repeat since he and Debra had discovered them the night before. He pretty much had them memorized and knew which ones pertained to his friend raving about his Uncle Dave.

As Johnson sat and listened, his eyes shone. He leaned forward, still cupping his mug, and shook his head, shocked.

"My God. I can't believe it. He sounds the way he did when he found that job. It's like he found a new beginning for himself."

Devon smiled. "Yeah. That's what I thought when I heard it. You can tell he found…purpose."

Mr. Johnson's face suddenly sagged into a frown. "Well. Yea. But then why did he leave this earth so soon after?" His tone hardened. "What purpose could come from that?"

Devon said, "I've been wondering the same thing. I've only just started to begin seeing how sometimes we can make poor decisions, but even those can somehow be woven into a good outcome."

With a grave expression, he ran a hand over his fade. Devon was thinking of one of the voicemails in which Antonio said that when Devon slammed the door in his face, that act made him cry out to God. In a sense, their falling-out had brought Antonio closer to God. The fact astounded Devon, and it was just the beginning of him learning just how much higher God's ways were than his own.

"Wow, son. It sounds like you've got a lot of wisdom there," Mr. Johnson said, his eyes crinkling in surprise. "I definitely wish I had that kind of wisdom at your age."

Devon felt unworthy of the praise.

"I feel like it's hard-taught wisdom, you know?" he replied. "Like, wisdom you learn through pain and mistakes." Thinking about all the hard things that had been happening lately, Devon grimaced. This was the first day he had made it out of bed since the funeral, and that was because of the encouragement Antonio's voicemails had brought. Plus, he couldn't turn down Mr. Johnson's invitation to grab some of Antonio's things.

Johnson sighed, "Yeah. I definitely understand that. That's called life," and the loss he had experienced pierced his expression. His wife leaving, his brother passing, and now his son. What other hard things could life possibly throw at this man? These were the thoughts suffocating Devon as he gazed at his friends' father. He wished he could somehow offer him a gift. Some sort of… compensation. Yet what could possibly console him from all that he had been through?

He's like Job in the Bible, Devon thought, remembering the scriptures he had read at North Star's Bible study.

"Speaking of life hitting hard, I kept forgetting to mention that I'm the decision-maker for your situation with this sexual allegation at school."

What? Devon almost dropped his tea as he had just been about to take a sip.

"Umm, *really*?" Embarrassment flushed him. He started stuttering, "I-I didn't do it—" but Johnson cut him off with a hand.

"Son. I know you would never do such a thing. And I'm not even allowed to have told you that I'm the personnel for the case. I just wanted you to know, I got you." He winked then, and all of the fear and anxiety Devon had been dealing with for months flew out the window. Devon sat in a daze. All this time, he had been worrying, but God had already put an advocate in place ahead of him.

"These things tend to take time," Johnson continued, "with there being a lot of paperwork, bureaucracy, and such involved, but you should be getting an email soon with the final verdict. Typically, these cases are difficult to determine because they're 'he said, she said' situations, but I had some weighty evidence come through in your favor. Your references were a great help, also. I can't disclose too much, but know that everything is going to be ok."

Wow. Devon's mind was still reeling over the fact that Johnson was the decision-maker. He had totally forgotten that he was on the school board and could even be involved in the process. His being a judge was an added bonus. Johnson was a truth-teller and a justice-seeker, exactly what Devon needed. He was also his best friend's father.

Wild!

"Th-thank you, Mr. Johnson. I'm so thankful it's you. I've definitely learned a lot from the situation." Devon bit his lip, sliding his hands along his denims in relief. "Now I understand the need for boundaries better. Especially with women." When Devon made the statement, he wasn't just thinking of Monica and other students; he was thinking of Jasmine.

Mr. Johnson gave him a kind, fatherly smile. "It's the least I can do for you, Devon. You've been an amazing friend to my son. I look forward to seeing your success and accomplishments, and I'll keep in touch. If you don't mind."

Devon was flattered and thankful for Johnson's favor. Of course, he agreed to keep in touch. On his way out, gripping the box of Antonio's belongings, Devon opened his other arm to embrace the older man.

"I'm going to make you proud," he promised into his stubbled cheek.

Mr. Johnson murmured, "You already have."

———

"HOW DID things go with Mr. Johnson?" Mrs. Woods found Devon looking through the stash of Antonio's belongings in the living room. Some college pictures, his favorite jerseys, and his vape. Devon laughed at that one.

Probably won't be needing this, he thought, tossing it on the living room table.

As his mom sat by his side, Devon looked up. "It was ok. I just wish I could console his pain," he admitted. "He's been through a lot, and Antonio was the closest family he had left." Devon's voice caught in his throat, and he swallowed his sorrow.

Mrs. Woods placed a loving arm around his shoulder. "I know, honey. Your heart is so caring. But you have to trust that God has a plan. We just don't know the fullness yet."

That reminded Devon of the good news he had to share. "Speaking of God's plan. Guess what?"

"What's up, baby?"

"Mr. Johnson is the decision-maker for my case with Monica."

His mother's eyes lit up. "What?"

"Yeah. Can you believe it? He says I'll be getting an email soon, clearing me from the allegation!"

Mrs. Woods dove into a full-fledged praise dance. She literally got up and started shouting and praising God, hands in the air and all.

Devon laughed and raised his hands too, lifting his face to the sky.

"See! See, baby! I *told* you God had a plan! I *told* you God has you!" his mother cried. She nearly cut off his circulation from squeezing him so tight. They both fell back into the cushions, wearing large smiles.

"Yeah, you did. You were right. He had me the whole time!"

As his mother bubbled about the goodness of God, tears of joy streaming down her face, Devon sat in awe. He relished the moment before peeking back into the box Mr. Johnson had given him.

There was a picture of him and Antonio taken during his friend's sophomore year and Devon's junior year. It was the year they met at the school's rec center. Devon had decided to get a workout in, and Antonio was there to play ball, but the guy he normally played with was a no-show. Antonio had found Devon puffing along on a stationary bike in his own world, listening to Reggae. Since Devon was the only brotha around, Antonio figured he could hoop. The truth was, Devon wasn't that good at basketball. Little did he know that playing with his friend would make him better. After that first game, they were tight ever since.

Devon's fingers grazed over the picture, lovingly thinking back to the good times.

Seeing his sadness re-emerge, his mother said, "You know a way you can keep your friend's memory alive forever?"

Devon looked curiously at the gleam in her eye. "How?"

"Get a tattoo of his name." Mrs. Woods cheesed, and Devon snorted.

"Ma, you're not serious."

She nodded adamantly. "I am! Honey, I'll go with you. We'll do it together."

Devon shook his head. Wasn't this the woman who had drilled into his head to never get a tattoo because of how permanent the decision was? Yet her expression was dead serious.

"Mom. You're nuts," he said. But when Devon glanced back down at a picture of his friend, shirtless and tatted up, he couldn't snuff the desire to honor Antonio in a way that he would appreciate.

Getting a tattoo suddenly seemed like the perfect idea.

————

"I CAN'T BELIEVE you and Mom got tattoos!!!" Debra burst into his room later that evening and fell onto Devon's bed. Clad in a large, oversized t-shirt and yoga pants, she proceeded to whine. Devon was busy packing and getting his things together to return to campus.

"You ever knock?" he asked, folding a shirt.

"Let me see, let me see, let me seee!!!" Debra drooled, her eyes wildly searching his physique.

"Yo. Chill," Devon said, then pulled out his phone. Right after it was finished, he had his mother take a picture. Because it was bandaged, he couldn't show Debra in the flesh. On his upper right back, behind his shoulder blade, were the letters "AJ" engraved inside a basketball. The lines on the ball opened up in the middle to make room for the letters.

"Whoooaaaa. *FIRE!*" Debra raved. She hopped back on her folded legs and crossed her arms, his phone still in her hand. "Why y'all didn't wait for me?" she complained.

Devon said, "Short stuff, you were at school."

"So. Y'all could have waited!" She pouted, fluttering her long lashes. "I never get included in the fun stuff. Y'all want me to come to church, but you don't want to take me to get tattoos." She fell back on the bed next to his suitcase dramatically.

Devon cracked up. "You know Mom got a scripture," he said.

Debra rolled her eyes, her limbs still spread askew. "I *know*! BO-RING."

"I like it."

"You would."

"Ooooohhhh somebody's getting a call from Leeeeena!" Debra howled, Devon's phone glowing in her right hand.

When Devon reached his arm out too quickly to snatch the phone, pain shot up his shoulder.

"Hey! Give it to me," he said, trying to rub his arm from the pain. The tattoo artist had told him it would take a few days to heal, which meant no working out or sudden movements.

"Not until you tell me who Lena is!" Debra sang out. She jumped on his bed, waving the ringing phone in the air.

"Little girl, if you don't give me that phone!"

"Or what?" Debra cocked her brow and beamed. She clearly had the upper hand. Literally.

"Ok, fine. I promise to take you shopping before I leave for school," Devon muttered.

Brightening, Debra held out her hand, "Deal," then dropped the phone into his palm.

Ugh. Blackmailed by a 15-year-old.

"Hello," Devon hurried to answer before it went to voicemail.

"Hey. Am I…interrupting?"

Devon mouthed to his sister, "Get out!" and pointed to the door.

She rolled her eyes and stomped toward the doorway.

"No. Not at all. My sister is just being a jerk. How are you?"

Devon stopped his packing and sank onto the bed. It had been a few days since they'd talked. He had been thinking about her and wondered how she was doing, but had been so caught up in his own stuff. It was the same with Jasmine. She had reached out a few times, but they hadn't had a chance to connect.

"I'm doing rather well. I actually have some news…"

Devon's heart sped up. Was she seeing someone? He had to remind himself it wasn't his business. They were just friends.

"Cool. What's up?" He tried to sound casual.

"I applied for theology school and got in!"

"Aww, Lena, that's great! Man, I'm so proud of you." Devon's heart swelled with care. He was happy she was pursuing her calling.

"And I want to thank you, Devon, for being a part of the confirmation. I know God used you to not just give me that word but also for you choosing me to honor your friend's passing with his eulogy."

At the mention of Antonio, a tinge of sadness nudged Devon, but he could see, once again, how his death was being used for someone else's good.

"I'm just grateful you said yes. I didn't want just anyone doing it," he said.

"Yeah. I start classes in the fall. I'm also going on a missionary trip this summer with the church. We're going to Uganda, sooo, I'll kind of be MIA for a while…" Lena said.

Devon felt a little caught off guard. "Oh? Ok. Yea. I get it. You gotta focus on your purpose." Lena was clearly giving him a heads-up that she wouldn't be as readily available as she had been. Her season was changing. Then Devon realized *his* season was changing too. Graduation was coming!

"I have good news, too. I found out that Mr. Johnson is the decision-maker for this sexual allegation at school."

"What? Whoa. That's *crazy!*" came Lena's shocked response.

"Yeah. I mean, of course, he's ruling in my favor. He said I'll get an email soon from the school."

"Wow. Devon. I'm so *happy* for you! I mean, you just can't make this stuff up," Lena said, amazed.

Devon grinned. "I know. It's like God is before us, with us, *and* after us. He really does have a plan."

He continued chatting with Lena and promised to check in when he got back to campus. Devon understood that their lives were changing. God had swept her into a season of his life when he desperately needed her, but that season was vanishing. Just like spring was giving way to summer. Maybe it was because he still had feelings for Jasmine. Maybe it was because Lena was further along in her spiritual walk. Devon wasn't sure why, but what was clear was that Lena had been brought to hold his hand through a very dark season. Now she was moving on. He could only hope that she would find someone who could give her the gift that she had given him. The gift of brotherly love.

TWENTY-ONE
THE HARDEST LESSON

THE FIRST FEW DAYS BACK ON CAMPUS CONSISTED OF DEVON SINKING INTO a rhythm of school, work at Java's, grieving, and pondering his future after graduation. He had finally received that email Mr. Johnson had referenced and hopped onto his bed, cross-legged, with his laptop.

"Dev," Darion said, glancing at Devon's face in the corner of the mirror. He was about to head to work and was primping himself. "What's up wit' you?"

Devon stared at the laptop screen in utter shock before he started reading out loud:

Mr. Devon Woods, thank you for your time and cooperation in the investigation of the allegation regarding Ms. Monica Angela Jones. Our findings rule in your favor, and you are cleared of this matter in its entirety. We wish you the best in your future endeavors...

Devon blinked. After wreaking havoc in his life, falsely accusing him of something he didn't do, getting him fired, and creating a crazy upheaval in regard to his future, all the school administration offered were a few sentences? No apology. No, sorry, we were wrong, and you were right, and you didn't do anything wrong?

When he finished reading out loud, Darion said, "Man. The system is crazy. How they gon just be out like that? Like they doing *you* a favor!"

His brother mimicked Devon's thoughts, and Devon could only shake his head. "Well, it gives God the glory even more, I guess." Devon shrugged. "If it wasn't for Him putting Mr. Johnson in place, then we already know what the ruling would have been."

"Facts. You right. It really shows God's goodness," Darion said thoughtfully, and Devon's heart smiled. "So, you think you gon go back to your job as a TA?"

Devon licked his lips. "Honestly, even if Marx wanted me back, I don't think I would go. He let Clark run all over me and didn't even respond when I asked him to be a reference for me. He's a straight coward, and I got no holler for him."

Darion said, "Yeah. Plus, you got the gig at Java's, which is dope."

Devon said, "Yeah. And Java's feels more like home. I'd rather finish out my time there with Frank the rest of the school year."

Just as Devon was about to click out of his emails, another one rolled through. This one was from Professor Clark. Intrigue mounted as he started reading.

Devon. It's been a few days since I found out that the ruling for the sexual allegation for Monica Jones was decided in your favor; however, I was told that you wouldn't receive an official notice until today. So, I've scheduled this email to be sent at that time. Hopefully, I'm not premature in contacting you!

I first want to say I'm sorry. After our conversation in the office with Marx, I had some things to consider. Your statements about Black men being falsely accused and incarcerated stayed with me, and I decided to get educated. In my findings, I discovered numerous stories of inmates being released after decades of serving time for crimes they didn't commit. Some of these crimes were due to false witnesses, tainted evidence (such as blood or DNA samples), and often the false ID of someone who resembled the real perpetrator (in skin tone and gender only). Sadly, I admit, though I've been a

staunch supporter of women's rights issues and consider myself an advocate for injustice, my view has been limited. Thank you for helping to expand it.

Devon sat back on his bed, clutching his laptop. He couldn't believe what he was reading. He continued.

After finding thorough research indicating that, yes, Black men have been frequently falsely accused, I decided to follow up with Monica. When I did, I let her know the weight of her actions. I told her that you may not graduate due to her allegation. She was shocked and started tearing up again. She came clean, saying that she had actually come on to you. She disclosed that her boyfriend had just dumped her the day prior, and she was exceptionally emotional. She felt like a fool after you also rejected her and was feeling sorry for herself in the bathroom. When I approached her that day, she said the first thing that came out of her mouth. In our follow-up, she admitted that her hurt had more to do with her ex than it did with you. I was horrified. I let her know this matter would not be taken lightly. I wrote a letter to the board detailing my conversation with Monica and made sure the Title IX Coordinator was notified. I also wrote a recommendation letter to vouch for your character.

"Oh my God." Devon murmured.

Darion asked, "Wuz up, bro?"

Devon said, "Bro, you are *not* going to believe this. Any of this!" He sat up in his bed and started re-reading the email out loud to Darion until he reached the part where he had stopped.

"Damn. That's crazy!" Darion plopped down next to him, and Devon continued reading.

I'm not sure what the board will decide regarding Monica, but I know she will face academic consequences, more than likely be put on academic suspension. Devon, this is the first of a false allegation I've witnessed, but maybe it's just the first that was discovered. I want to thank you again for helping me broaden my understanding

of equality. Going forward I'll make a greater effort to use my own privilege to support those who are less privileged. You've always been a bright young man in my book, and I'm sorry I let my first instinct be swayed by my own blind spots. I'm sure you will thrive in whatever you have planned next, and feel free to reach out if you need a referral.

Wishing you all the best.
- Stephanie M. Clark, Ph.D.

The brothers sat in awed silence for a moment. Devon couldn't believe how much God had moved! He was already blessed to know that Johnson was his advocate, but to learn that Clark was too? It was almost too much.

"Dude. Miracles do happen," Darion said, stunned.

"Dude. I was thinking the same thing!" Devon responded. "I guess a raging white feminist *can* be woke!" The brothers cackled.

"Dawg. I wonder what they gon do to ol' girl?" Darion asked, hopping back up and throwing on his jacket.

"Right. Whatever it is, I know they better come for her with the same energy they came at me wit'!"

"Word. I gotta head to class. I'll see you tonight at Antonio's vigil."

Devon started scrolling through his other emails, but the smile wouldn't leave his face. "See you there."

It turns out Antonio had attended several of the campus ministry meetings that Devon and Darion had visited. The group kept a record of each attendee and had him listed. When the school was notified of his death, they announced it to all campus organizations. When the ministry got wind of it, they notified everyone in their network that they would be hosting a vigil in his honor.

Devon just kept on being amazed at how God had a plan for his friend, and even how his own pushing him away had pushed Antonio towards God. That knowledge had helped lessen his guilt, even though his heart still ached every day from the loss.

Mr. Johnson would be in attendance that evening, along with Jasmine and their other friends. Devon had texted her after he got back to campus, and they arranged a meetup after the vigil. They were in desperate need of a one-on-one. So much had happened between them in such a short time.

Just two months ago, Devon had been ready to spend the rest of his life with this woman. Now, he felt certain, she was not the one. After experiencing what he had with Lena, the characteristics she exuded, her faith in God, her quiet, gentle spirit, God seemed to be showing him traits that his wife would carry. Even if Lena wasn't his wife. But his feelings for Jasmine were still there, and it would take time for them to go away. The engagement ring he had purchased lurked inside the top drawer of his desk, gently reminding him of his emotional attachment. That's why he was grateful graduation was in just three weeks. Being off campus would give him the physical distance he needed from Jasmine to really move on.

Lord, help me to make it these three weeks! Devon cried out in prayer when he was preparing to return to school. He had witnessed firsthand how weak the flesh was. This time, when he cried out, God answered quickly.

You need to fast.

Huh? Fast? That was a new concept. Devon hurried to search the Bible his mother had gotten him after typing, "fasting in the Bible" in his phone. He landed on a scripture that seemed to apply:

Matthew 6:16-18

> *"When you fast, do not look somber as the hypocrites do, for*
> *they disfigure their faces to show others they are fasting.*
> *Truly, I tell you, they have received their reward in full.*
> *But when you fast, put oil on your head and wash your*
> *face, so that it will not be obvious to others that you are*
> *fasting, but only to your Father, who is unseen; and your*
> *Father, who sees what is done in secret, will reward you."*

When Devon talked to Mrs. Woods, she explained the importance of fasting secretly and not outwardly, so that he wasn't being boastful about it. She said that fasting helped to kill fleshly desires that would lead him away from God. She also recommended that Devon read about Jesus fasting in the wilderness.

"You can even fast from other things and not just food," she added.

That's when Devon decided he would do a three-day fast with just fruits and vegetables *and* from social media. Then, he felt an even stronger urge.

Coffee, came the prompting in his spirit.

He cringed. *Oh, Lord. Don't take away my coffee!*

There was no question about it. Coffee would be his greatest sacrifice. So, for three whole days, the longest period Devon had *ever* gone since he had started drinking the stuff, he did not have coffee. Darion said he was pretty cranky, and Devon agreed, but other than that and the consistent rumbling of his stomach, he felt stronger than ever. He especially felt strong enough to meet Jasmine that evening after the vigil without giving in to temptation.

Even while working at Java's for those three days, Devon had this supernatural strength that allowed him to be around the very thing he loved most without succumbing. He hoped it was an indication of how things would go when he was around Jasmine. Fasting was a wild experience, and he could never have thought he could feel so empowered when his body was so empty.

That's when Devon learned the power of fasting.

————

THAT EVENING, the students each held lit candles, flickering in the warm spring breeze. Mid-May brought jacket weather, easing temperatures into a comfortable low 60s. Mr. Johnson had brought the blown-up picture of Antonio used at the funeral. His son's ashes were safely in his study on the mantel in a platinum urn next to his brother's. The group had the photo featured near the front of the chapel on a large easel, just outside the front steps. After lighting their candles, most of the attendees mingled on the grassy knoll before things got started.

Devon was in the front, bookended by Johnson and Darion. When Jasmine, Kimberly, and Sheila arrived, he didn't get a chance to greet them. He was too busy reviewing the notes on his phone. Devon was slated to speak at the vigil. This time, when Mr. Johnson asked, there was no way he could refuse.

One of the leaders, a plump, kind girl with freckles, said a few nice words about meeting Antonio and about his thirst to understand the scriptures. She was grateful for the short time they had been acquainted and glad that their ministry could provide him with a safe place to learn about God. That's when she locked eyes with Devon, and he took her place to face the group. About 30 were in attendance, many who he wasn't familiar with, but that didn't matter. They were all united by love, and Devon was touched that he was chosen to represent his friend.

After his eyes briefly caught Johnson's, who gave him a tearful smile, Devon cleared his throat.

"Antonio was the friend I never knew I needed," he began. "He blew into my life just as quickly, it seems, as he blew out of it. But with his presence and exit, there were lessons he taught. He taught me not to take life so seriously. He taught me the importance of seizing the moment and living in it. He taught me brotherly love. But the hardest lesson I had to learn was the importance of forgiveness."

The audience was silent. Only the soft chirping of crickets in the distance resounded with the shuffle of late evening students strolling by. It was getting darker later, and so, the warm glow of the setting sun shadowed each one's face.

Devon swallowed the lump in his throat all the way down to his beige-colored Vans. He quietly shoved his phone into his back pocket, foregoing his notes, and continued from his heart.

"I had to learn the hard way that life is short. We don't always get time to say, 'I'm sorry'." He paused. "Or to say, 'I forgive you'. But that's also when God shows up. When we're fallen and weak, He uses our weaknesses to reveal His strength. I believe Antonio is with Him because I didn't get to say, 'I forgive you'. And if nothing else good came from my weakness, well, that's enough for me."

Devon looked around, meeting each one's gaze in the dimness of the evening. "That is the grace of God. But I encourage you, don't learn the hard way. If you have an offense you're harboring against some-one, don't wait to forgive them. You may not get a chance."

He then glanced at the large picture of Antonio, smiling widely, holding a basketball and clad in his favorite jersey. Devon smiled at the image, thinking of their first time playing together. He truly sucked.

"I also learned a mean jump shot from him," he added, and the crowd chuckled.

"Antonio was the best player in my life, and one day I look forward to playing with him again."

When Devon finished, the crowd softly clapped. He returned to his spot so that a few of the leaders could lead them all in song. They sang, "How Great is Our God," by Chris Tomlin, in perfect harmony. The song floated across the campus as the wind stroked Devon's face. Suddenly, he distinctly sensed a presence so strong hugging him that it caused his eyes to flutter open. Even though there was no one there, he smiled.

"I'll see you soon," he whispered, knowing that he was heard.

———

AFTER THE SERVICE ENDED, Mr. Johnson murmured to Devon, "Thank you." He enfolded him in a hug.

Catching a whiff of alcohol on the man's breath, Devon thought, *I need to pray for him more.* He stroked Johnson's quarterback-wide build as they embraced.

The crowd slowly dispersed, and Devon shook hands and hugged those who came to pay their condolences. Finally, Jasmine was before him. Her eyes wide, hands awkwardly clasped in front of her, body angled, slightly leaning onto one hip.

"You did good," she offered, trying for a smile.

"Thanks." Devon tried, too, but the complications between them prevented the smile from reaching his eyes.

"Can we...can we go somewhere and talk?" she asked. Her eyes roamed around the area. Most of the folks had left, but some were still chatting, his brother and her friends among them. Darion was still going strong with Kimberly and had an arm possessively around her waist.

"Oh. Yeah. How about we go inside? The chapel is open," Devon suggested, so Jasmine followed him in.

The short walk to the sanctuary was quiet as Devon was entangled in a cobweb of emotions and thoughts. He assumed Jasmine was as well. Only the soft clicking of her heels accompanied their journey.

When he took a seat in the back row, she did the same. She breathed deeply. The chapel was a tomb. No one else was there. Aside from a yellow light buzzing near the front, they were almost bathed in darkness; the stained-glass windows with angels painted on were a poor source of light after the sun set.

"I-I have something I need to talk to you about," Jasmine began while running a hand over her neck. She was still so beautiful, and Devon was grateful he was fasting. He could feel desire starting to grow fangs while being in her presence.

Devon said, "Yeah. A lot has been going on." He inched back a little. Maybe if they weren't so close together, she wouldn't be having this effect on him. Even with the increased distance, the familiar scent of her perfume played with his nostrils. He shook it off. He started to tell her how he knew she wasn't the one, and that they needed to *really* end things, but Jasmine had also started to say something, so he stopped.

"Uhh, you go first," he offered.

"Well, ok. Umm. So… I have some news," she began again. He looked at her.

"Okay," Devon said slowly. Waiting.

Jasmine rubbed her palms a few times on her dark, ripped skinny jeans, then finally spoke.

"I'm pregnant."

What? Devon stiffened. The low buzzing of the light emitting in the front of the sanctuary grew louder, as did the faint chatter from outside. All of his senses suddenly seemed heightened. The floor started moving. The ceiling caved. What was happening?

"Devon?" Jasmine asked, eyeing him wearily.

Oh. She was expecting him to say something. He hadn't realized he hadn't said anything.

"Umm. Ok. I mean. *What*?"

Jasmine nodded, her eyes starting to moisten. "I know. It's—it's *crazy*." She looked away as a tear slowly climbed down her cheek.

Words were stuck in his throat. Mindlessly, Devon reached for the tear. Stroking the back of his finger over her face, he said, "How, how do you know?"

"I took a test a couple of weeks ago. My period was late. My breasts were sore. I-I *knew*. My body had never felt this way." She sniffled, her trembling hand wiping the spot on her cheek he had touched. "I've never been pregnant before," she added. Both eyes lowered to the holes in her jeans.

Oh my God, was all Devon could think. *Oh my God. Oh my God. Oh my God.*

His breathing started coming rapidly. "What. What are you gonna do?" he managed.

Remembering how liberal Jasmine was and the fact that she had a whole year of school left, Devon needed to ask. He couldn't make any assumptions. He didn't even really know what *he* wanted, only that it was her choice. He was still trying to wrap his brain around the news.

Pregnant?!

Jasmine replied in a firm tone, "I'm keeping it."

She looked at him with fear, but the first thing Devon felt was relief. He honestly didn't know why. A baby with a woman who, just two seconds ago, he was about to dismiss from his life forever, was a huge inconvenience. Yet something inside of him valued this child's life even more than he could comprehend. Then his mind started rewinding to every single sexual encounter they had had.

"Weren't—weren't we careful?" he asked, his eyes squinting at the memories. "I thought. I thought we used protection. I-I thought we always did."

Jasmine had been such a stickler about it, even more than he was. There were times, especially when he thought they were getting married, that Devon was willing to throw caution to the wind. That he was down for whatever. But she was adamant. *She wanted to finish school,* had always been her go-to response. Even just a couple of weeks ago, when he was caught in her web of seduction, they were protected.

Did the condom break? he thought incredulously.

Devon looked around the sanctuary, the weirdest place to be having thoughts about his sex life. Then he thought, *Well, God invented sex.*

"This is the thing." Jasmine shifted uncomfortably beneath his flabbergasted expression. She licked her lips then started picking at one of those holes in her jeans. "I-I don't know if it's yours."

Devon gaped at her. *"What?"* How out there had she been? He suddenly felt like he didn't know her at all. Had she been cheating on him the whole time?

"See, the day I found out I was pregnant, I had actually scheduled an abortion."

Jasmine paused and looked around the chapel, no doubt thinking of how crazy it was to be admitting that information inside a church.

"I was gonna go and everything. But the very day of, only hours before, actually...I found out...I found out about Antonio."

Silence filled the space between them. Devon was in shock. He had forgotten about Antonio. He had somehow forgotten that his girlfriend had cheated on him with his best friend.

"And then this wild thought came to me. What if it's *his*? What if it's his and this is his legacy?" Jasmine looked back up at Devon, her eyes pleading for him to understand. "What if this is the only thing left of him?" she whispered.

Devon let out a deep breath. He nodded slowly, trying to let his brain catch up to the words being slung at him. His ex-girlfriend/fiancée was pregnant, and the baby could possibly belong to him, or it could possibly belong to his best friend, who had just died.

"There's only one way we'll know for sure," Devon finally decided after a long pause.

Jasmine bobbed her head.

"I'll get a paternity test." The words tasted like a foreign language on his tongue, and it was the last thing on earth Devon could have fathomed that he would be doing three weeks before graduation. But there was no doubt that it had to be done.

TWENTY-TWO
JASMINE

YOU'RE NOT MARRIED YET

WHEN DEVON PROPOSED, JASMINE WAS SCARED TO SAY YES, BUT SHE WAS more scared to say no. *I don't want to lose him,* she thought, peering down into his hopeful brown eyes as he knelt on the white sandy beach in Cancun. Hands down, Devon was one of the best men Jasmine had ever met and definitely the best man she had ever dated. She had learned a long time ago, men were like untrained puppies. They had to be kept on a leash, or they would bite the mess out of you and then run away. Her very first experience with a guy taught her that. Ever since that bite, she had learned to keep her man on a leash.

Growing up in a family of womanizers, players, and whoremongers, Jasmine had an up-close view of the effects of women who got sprung on men. Her mother included. It was never pretty.

Her father was the father of at least five other siblings that she knew of, none of whom she had any real relationships with. They were all boys. Her mother had three more kids by two other men; they, too, were the offspring of players. Everywhere Jasmine looked, men treated women like trash.

When she hit puberty and discovered the power of her hips, butt, and chest size, she vowed to use them to her best ability. At a young age, Jasmine had already discarded the notion of happily ever after. While her friends were watching Disney fairy tales, dreaming of a Prince Charming, Jasmine was watching too, only she was thinking about how to create the illusion of one. She already knew that real love didn't exist, but fell in love with the power of storytelling to make others believe that it did.

That's when she discovered her dream to become a filmmaker. Her number one goal was to go to college, get her degree, and get to L.A. She guarded her goal fiercely, and nothing and no one was coming in between. Every man she was with was second, and there really had never been anyone who could threaten the idea that her life wouldn't turn out exactly the way that she planned: become a major film producer, create spaces for female leads in cinema, curate Black stories, and take over the world. *Period*. Then, just months after meeting Devon, she felt something new. Something different. Something that was both wildly exciting and scary as hell. Jasmine had never opened her heart up to anyone. She had a one-track mind. It allowed men for sex, attention, and a free meal, but that was about it. Even when they tried to entrap her into their false promises for the future and make her their baby mama, her rule was set in stone. No glove, no love.

When she was first sexually active, Jasmine had tried birth control, but she learned quickly that the hormones it released into her bloodstream left her with a bad case of acne and 20 pounds of extra weight. No thank you! Her looks were too much of an asset to get in the way of what she wanted. It would be condoms from this point on.

So, for 21 years, Jasmine was on a mission, until her feelings for Devon began to grow. That's when she did the unthinkable and said yes to love. She had never known love really existed, and yet suddenly it was staring her in the face, with beautiful, caring brown eyes. Yet after the high of the proposal settled, the fear of entrapment gripped her. When Devon went home to tend to his dad, she tried to calm herself with rum. Then Antonio kept giving her the vape. Ok, so she kept asking for it. Either way, her old ways of flirting and using men for pleasure began surfacing as her go-to coping mechanisms.

Antonio was someone Jasmine knew wanted her. He practically

salivated every time she entered the freaking room. She suspected he was even jealous of Devon for locking her in. Her Devon would never see that because he was just too good of a guy.

As the liquor flowed in Cancun and the weed took hold, all of Jasmine's fears were whisked higher than the stars in the sky. Her thoughts started turning dark.

What would it be like to screw Antonio?

She had never had him, even though they had that one close call some years back. She didn't even know if he remembered it because they had both been drunk at the time. Even when she resurfaced in his life as Devon's girlfriend, he never gave any hint of recognition. Well, neither had she. Jasmine was built to hide her feelings, just like Antonio. In a lot of ways, they were cut from the same cloth, though they fought like cats and dogs. Antonio would have easily run in the pack with her brothers, uncles, and father, and so Jasmine never really paid him any mind. She knew how to handle *those* types—with an emotional ten-foot pole. Then, with the warm air rubbing her skin, the euphoric feeling of the smoke in her lungs, and the numbness of alcohol plunging and bursting into a visceral moisture between her thighs, she kept having this one thought:

You're not married yet.

The statement repeated itself even as she felt her legs carrying her forward on the beach beside Antonio. The duo walked along the shore, searching for a safe place to go skinny dipping.

You're not married yet.

You're not married yet.

Over and over, it was like a chant that Jasmine finally responded to.

Yea. You're right. I'm not *married yet.*

Throwing caution to the wind, Jasmine gave in to the overbearing ecstasy that enwrapped her in the waves as Antonio thrusted inside of her. He was on a mission, and she was left very satisfied. Until the next morning, when she felt horrible as the chain of events from the night before slammed into her psyche. Coupled with it was the fierce hangover from all the crap she had inhaled and drunk.

Oh God. What have I done?

Then Kimberly was at the door, telling her they had to get ready to go.

I can't see him!

At just the thought of facing Antonio, agony gripped her with long, bony fingers. It was going to be hard enough being around Darion. Lucky for her, Antonio had it worse than she did, and he was glued to the toilet. Apparently, he was going to catch a later flight. Relief swept through Jasmine as she popped two gel Advil, downed a bottle of Gatorade, and started packing.

At least I won't have to sit next to him on the damn plane.

But the overwhelming issue wasn't Antonio. It was Devon.

What have I done?

A million and one scenarios ran through Jasmine's mind, and they all ended with Devon leaving her. Why *wouldn't* he leave? She had done the unthinkable. She had slept with his best friend. And for what? For the life of her, Jasmine didn't know why. She just knew she was sorry and that it would never ever happen again. Ever. This simply could not be their end.

Devon was the first man Jasmine had actually felt love for. There was no way she could let that go. So, she did what she always did. She set out to get what she wanted. When he blocked her, she showed up at his job. She showed up at Darion's work. She begged Kimberly for intel. She showed up at his interview for the investigation with the Title IX Coordinator. Then, she did her big one. She showed up at his door, half-naked in a trench. And just like that, she had him back. Jasmine knew he couldn't resist her. Devon was hers, and no one was going to make her lose him again. Then, he cut her off again. He pushed her away, and she didn't know why. She had never not had a hold over a man, and Devon had definitely been under her sway. Even as Jasmine wrestled with confusion over his rejection, her body began to feel different. Her breasts were suddenly tender. Once in a while, that happened on her cycle, but not often. On top of that, she was drowsy *all the time*. Jasmine had always been high-energy and doing a million and one things, but the demands of all her leadership roles and schoolwork started taking their toll. How is it that she kept oversleeping for her damn 8 am?! She had never been this tired in her life. Then her stomach dropped. She felt queasy.

When was my last period? The thought nervously tugged at the edges of her mind. Bracing herself, while alone in her dorm room (her roommate was at class) she opened her phone. Her eyes scanned the chart until they fell on her last entered cycle date *from almost two months ago.* With a sickening feeling, she gulped.

How did I miss this? How the hell did I miss that I haven't had a period in almost two damn months!

Well, she knew how. She had been so focused on getting Devon back and juggling all of her extracurriculars, she hadn't been paying attention. Still, *how*?

How could this be happening?

How can I be pregnant?! Jasmine practically screamed in her mind. She collapsed on the floor, in the middle of the room, crossed her legs, and strangled her phone. Staring at the screen, she channeled it with all her might to change the information. Then she realized she needed a test. She couldn't just go off an app. Maybe it was wrong. It *was* technology. It *could* be wrong.

Quickly, she dialed Sheila.

"I need a pregnancy test," was the first thing out of her mouth.

"I got you, friend." Sheila didn't blink an eye. She was at Jasmine's dorm in less than 30 minutes.

Jasmine said, "Thanks," grabbed the test in a brown paper bag, and peered at Sheila with grateful eyes.

Both girls walked side by side to the nearest bathroom, and Sheila stood outside the stall while Jasmine peed on a stick.

In less than five minutes, a bright pink plus sign shimmered in the little rectangle near Jasmine's trembling hand.

"Oh my God!" she cried and fell into Sheila's arms.

"It's ok, love. It's ok. We'll make you an appointment."

Sheila walked her back to her room, where they fell on the bed, and Jasmine caved in sobs. She simply couldn't believe it.

This can't be happening!

All of her plans. Everything she had been working for. 21 years of hustle and unrelenting focus and escaping all the fools who had tried to knock her up. She was finishing up her junior year for God's sake!

How could this be happening *now*?

Jasmine sobbed as Sheila held her. Then Sheila's words from the bathroom reminded her.

"Oh. I can make an appointment?" Jasmine asked in a childlike voice. Her eyes were wide, and Sheila nodded.

"Yeah. I had to make one last month myself."

Jasmine sat up a little in her friend's arms, surprised. "What? How-How come you didn't tell me?" In the midst of her turmoil, she couldn't help but feel put off that her best friend didn't confide in her about something so major.

Sheila shrugged. "It wasn't my first one. And honestly, I don't feel like it's that big of a deal."

Jasmine sniffed. "Wow." Then it dawned on her. "Is that why you couldn't make Cancun? Is that why you were sick?"

Slowly, Sheila agreed. "Yeah. That was it. I didn't know I was pregnant until a few days after y'all left and I took a test."

"Wow." Jasmine peered at her friend in awe. "I wish you would have told me. I would have been there for you."

Sheila smiled sweetly. "I appreciate that, Jas. But honestly, I got through it. And you'll get through it too." She held out her hand to cover Jasmine's, and gratitude flooded her.

"Thanks. I-I'll call tomorrow," Jasmine decided.

The next day, she made the appointment at the nearest clinic, certain that that was the best decision. Jasmine had always been pro-choice, but now life was asking her if she was really pro-choice. She had been on the sidelines, staunchly ranting and raving for female rights and unleashing her battle cry. But now she was in the game. It was one thing to be a cheerleader, yet another entirely to be called on to play.

As she tossed and turned that night in bed, mulling over her situation, Jasmine struggled with her own self-view. She had always prided herself on being a woman's advocate. How dare anyone tell a woman what she should do with her own body! Especially how dare any *man*!

It was her right to exercise her agency to utilize her free will to make a choice.

You can always use your agency to make a different choice, came the still small voice.

Huh? Jasmine's eyes popped open and blinked into the darkness of the dorm room. The faint outline of her roommate hovered nearby, but no one else was in the room. Still, there was this presence that seemed to be prodding her to a new idea. Didn't being pro-choice not just mean the choice to abort a fetus, but to also raise a child? Whoa. That was a new way of seeing things. Jasmine teased her lip with her tongue and tried to bury the thought. Still, even as she fidgeted in her bed, attempting to go back to sleep, it clung to the back of her mind. She was scheduled for 3:30 pm at the clinic the next day. Sheila had already volunteered to come with her. Finally, after tossing and turning for hours, Jasmine dozed off.

The next morning, her stomach flopped as she tried to finish her communications class speech. It was hard to concentrate. She was still in shock about the pregnancy. The other thing that was tripping her out was how careful she had always been. Every time a guy tried to go raw, Jasmine shut it down. Even with Devon, *she* was the one to make sure they were always protected.

But there was that one time…

The memory of Cancun hit Jasmine with a vengeance.

You can't use a condom in the water…

She shuttered.

The thought spun around her mind as images of her encounter with Antonio flashed before her. Jasmine hadn't even thought about it too much after they got back to campus. She had been so focused on Devon. Devon was the one she loved. Out of anyone, Devon is whose baby she would want to have! Even still, the stark realization that she hadn't used any protection with Antonio stared at her from the blank laptop screen.

Oh my God.

Antonio was *not* dad material! Out of all of her years of sexual activity, this *one time* Jasmine chooses *not* to be careful, it's with *this* fool! The brotha who thinks *Michael Davis* should be The U.S. F-ing President!

"Ugh!" Jasmine screamed out loud, grimacing at the blinking cursor. She rolled her eyes. It was laughable, really. How in the world did she manage to get pregnant by one of the biggest chauvinists on the planet when everything she stood for was anti-chauvinism? This had to be the Universe's greatest trick if there ever was one. Then there was Devon. Devon, who was the sweetest man alive.

Her stomach sank. Even more of a reason to go through with the procedure. She could still have something with Devon. They could still get married.

Within the hour of all these thoughts tormenting Jasmine and swimming around the half-filled page of her Word document, Mr. Johnson called. At first, she was startled, seeing Antonio's name. *Did he know?* Of course not. That would be *crazy*. Then she wondered whether he was relaying information about Devon, so she answered. Devon had been avoiding her, and she was greedy for any sort of intel. Surprise engulfed her when Mr. Johnson spoke. Then, Jasmine really had the wind knocked out of her. Antonio had an accident. Antonio had died upon impact. Antonio was dead.

Antonio was *dead*?

One solid tear rolled down Jasmine's cheek. She sank to the floor, the bed against her back, her phone in her hand. After uttering a few sentences of condolences to Mr. Johnson, she hung up. She stared at the name in her recent call history: Antonio. Mindlessly, she looked at Antonio's last text:

> Jas. We messed up, I know. I take the blame. I should have said no. I knew I should have. Just know I'm sorry. I take full responsibility.

Antonio had sent Jasmine that message maybe a couple of weeks ago. It had held a different tone than anything he had ever sent. Even through text, she could tell something was different. *He* was different. She hadn't responded just because she didn't know what to say. Sitting there, grasping the phone in the face of the news of his passing, one crazy notion gripped Jasmine.

What if this baby is the only thing left of Antonio?
Then she thought, *What if I'm carrying his legacy?*

TWENTY-THREE

DEVON'S CAFE

For four long days, Devon was stalking his phone. Every time there was any kind of notification, whether social media, his email account, or somebody randomly texting, he was on it. Every time, it was a false alarm. There was absolutely nothing from the lab where he had the paternity test done. While sweeping up at Java's, he checked his phone for the one millionth time. Frank had gotten so comfortable with him that when Devon came in at 2 pm, he let Devon close the store all by himself, taking a much-needed break.

"Thanks, Devon, for everything," the kind older man said before he left earlier that day.

Devon was touched. "No. Thank you. It's working here that's illuminated some things for me," he revealed.

Frank asked, "Oh? How so?" with warm green eyes.

Devon then shared with Frank how much he had been struggling with his purpose and the bold decision to leave Jack & Jill. How he had been floundering with his next steps, especially with things being so topsy-turvy with Jasmine.

"But you know how you said running the cafe wasn't difficult because it's like, your purpose?"

Frank smiled at the memory. "Yep. It's definitely gotten me through some tough times, knowing that I can help others in some small way get through theirs."

Devon smiled back. "Exactly. That's exactly how I've been feeling. Like being in this space, doing what I'm doing at Java's, is somehow— tied to my purpose."

Frank said, "Wow. Well, I'm glad I could be a part of you discovering that, Devon. Keep me posted on your next steps after graduation, would ya? I'd love to hear how things turn out for you!" He winked, and Devon agreed.

Frank had been a godsend, and the sudden opportunity to work at the cafe amid the false sexual harassment allegation was one of the few bright spots in the semester. Especially when things went left with Jasmine. Then Antonio. Both thoughts prompted Devon to check his phone once again. Nothing. The lab said they would email his results, but an automated text would also be sent. It was supposed to take three to five business days. Since it was now Friday, and day four, he feared he would have to wait until Monday. That meant a long weekend boxing anxiety. As Devon started mopping, his stomach somersaulted.

Jesus. Please be with me!

Since Jasmine had told him she was pregnant, Devon had been all over the map with his emotions.

How could she cheat and put us in this situation of not knowing the father? Maybe I should marry her. How can I raise a child that isn't mine?

What if it is *mine?*

Devon had run through every possible scenario, and it was that last one: What if it *is* mine? that really caused him alarm. He wasn't ready to be a father. He didn't even have a job! Regardless of whether he was ready or not, life was coming fast. During Devon's prayer time, he had been on his knees, crying out for guidance. The last couple of months, Lena had been a great shoulder to lean on with his myriad of life obstacles, but there was no *way* he could come to her about this. Besides, she was gearing up for Uganda and would be leaving right after he graduated. His mom was a great prayer partner, but could she handle a potential grandchild on the way? Or the hopes of one, to only have it dashed? Devon wasn't really sure how this new version of his mother would respond.

He did, of course, mention things to Darion after the vigil, who said, "Dawg. That's wild. I can't even imagine what you thinking right now," and sat with Devon the rest of the night in shock.

Classes were pretty much coasting at this point. Only two more weeks until graduation. Now that he was out of the clear from the sexual allegation, Devon's attention returned to figuring out life after college. The vision he had during prayer in his bedroom kept recurring in his mind. The part that stood out was the little girl. She did resemble him. Not dead on, but he could tell they were related.

Was it our child? Devon wondered, mopping the floor at Java's.

He flashed back to the little girl on the airplane. Beautiful, sweet, and chocolate. He had yearned for a daughter with Jasmine as he looked at her. *But things are so different now.* Devon's stomach switched from somersaults to back flips. When his phone buzzed in his pants pocket, it nearly scared the mess out of him. He dropped the mop and dove for it.

Jasmine:

> You wanna hang tonight? I don't want to be alone.

Wrestling with her invitation, Devon hesitated. Then he figured he didn't want to be alone either and really had no other plans. Darion had invited him to go bowling with him and Kimberly, but their budding love caused a tender spot. Devon was still nursing his own heartbreak. He graciously declined the invite. Insted, he typed to Jasmine:

> Ok.

Finishing up cleaning, Devon made sure to lock the door, then tucked the key in his back pocket for safekeeping. Within the hour, he was at Jasmine's.

Her roommate had gone to a party, Jasmine explained. It was then that Devon wondered if he'd made the right move by being alone with her. Seeing her slumped on the floor against her bed, sullen and fearful, he decided that he had.

She needs a friend.

Sinking into her desk chair, he stretched his legs. "It looks like we'll have to wait until Monday," Devon said, stating the obvious.

Jasmine's head bobbed glumly, her eyes not reaching his. Instead, she stared at her roommate's computer, buzzing on the desk across from her. This was probably the first time Devon had ever seen Jasmine this down. She had on yoga pants. Her hair was in an unruly poof, and her eyes were red from crying.

"I-I'm sorry," she whispered, finally looking up. "I'm sorry for putting you through all of this. For everything." She peered at him, regret staining her pretty brown eyes. Those were the same eyes that had swept Devon off his feet when they first met at the Meet N' Greet.

That feels like forever ago.

Devon swallowed, thinking of all they had been through in such a short time. Then he answered sincerely in a thick, husky tone, "I forgive you, Jasmine."

The confession sat between them in the intimate space, surprising them both. As Devon pondered all the pain she had caused him (he still had the engagement ring in his desk drawer) he realized that even as they awaited the verdict on whose child she was carrying, the underlying issue was the state of his heart. If his heart was full of malice and hurt, then regardless of whether or not this child was his, his own soul would be scarred. Then, if he was in this child's life to whatever capacity, that malice towards their mother would be passed on.

What was pressing on Devon most after he fell to his knees, begging God for guidance, was the need to forgive. It was the need to make sure that his own heart was clean.

Jasmine stared at Devon in wonder at his proclamation. Her eyes enlarged as she gnawed on her lip. "But. But I don't deserve your forgiveness. I-" her head fell, and her chin met her chest. "I put you through so much," she whispered, shame filling each word.

Devon's heart ached. For the first time ever, he saw Jasmine's vulnerability. She was like a child.

She is My child, Devon heard God say. The statement surprised him.

Of course Jasmine was God's child. Of course God had a plan for her. Devon kicked himself for not seeing her before as God's child. Even his own dealings with her had been purely selfish. He wanted her because she was beautiful. He wanted her because she was fun, confident, and exciting. She was all the things he wasn't. But he wanted her for himself. Never once had he asked God for her hand. If God was her Father, then he should have asked God for her hand in marriage first.

The revelation shocked him, and he stared back at Jasmine.

"Jas," Devon started softly, rubbing his face with a hand. "None of us deserves God's forgiveness. But He still sent His Son to die on the cross for us anyway."

Jasmine looked at him, a tear freely streaming down her face. "I-I don't know if I believe in God," she mumbled. Her shoulders trembled, and Devon felt a rush of wind around him. It felt like angels were in the room.

"But He believes in you," he said in a voice so tender that it had to be the Holy Spirit.

Jasmine looked up. "I-I didn't want this child," she admitted. "The only reason I'm keeping it is because I found out Antonio died. I don't even know how I'm gonna take care of a child and still graduate." Her voice was wavering, and the tears were rushing down her face now.

Devon spoke what was on his heart. "God is going to provide for you. And no matter what the paternity test says, He is going to father this child. Just like Hagar in the Bible, God will provide."

Jasmine swallowed, then in a raw, humble voice, she asked. "W-Who's Hagar?"

Devon smiled softly. He pulled out his Bible app on his phone, then sat next to her, crossing his legs. He read the scriptures to her, the story of Hagar, Sarah, and Abraham. He shared with her the gospel. He answered her questions about God to the best of his ability. And that's what they did the rest of the evening. Devon taught Jasmine the gospel of Jesus Christ.

———

MONDAY MORNING, Devon's eyes drank in the paternity test results in the email link. There was a 99.9% chance that he was not the father. Relief flooded him.

"Thank You, *God!*" he cried alone in his dorm room, falling to his knees in the morning light streaming through the window. His head bowed as he thanked God profusely.

"My God!" Devon yelled, thinking about how much he had been afraid of being tied to Jasmine forever. He would always care for her, but a child would tie him to her *forever*. He was simply not ready to be a father!

"Thank you for a new beginning!" Devon said again and again.

The overwhelming gratitude at being freed from her that washed over his soul was in stark contrast to his initial euphoria at wanting Jasmine forever. For months, Devon couldn't see his life without this woman, even being willing to alter his future plans for her. He thought Jasmine was his purpose. Now Devon understood that his true purpose was to serve God.

After entering into a powerful praise session in his dorm room, other feelings surfaced. How would Jasmine provide for this child? How would she make it? Devon, once again, bowed his head but this time it was in prayer for his ex. A vision of Mr. Johnson flashed through his mind.

Oh my God, Devon thought. *Mr. Johnson has a grandchild!*

It was now obvious that Antonio's father had been slipping into depression. Devon could tell from their last conversation. There had been a trial for the bus driver who had hit Antonio. It was ruled an accident, but Mr. Johnson confessed he struggled with the ruling. Being a judge, he wanted some type of justice. How is it that no one was at fault for what had happened to his son? How is it that nothing good came from his death? That there was no justice. He confessed all of these woes, and Devon's heart broke. He had no answers at the time. Now he did.

Devon dialed Jasmine, and she answered. She, too, had seen the paternity test results, though she sounded like she wasn't surprised.

"Do you mind if I tell Mr. Johnson? I-I think he needs this news," Devon asked.

Jasmine replied ok, saying she hadn't spoken to Mr. Johnson much since he called to tell her about Antonio and really didn't know the man. She was trusting Devon's judgment. She shared that she was dreading the prospect of telling her mother, who inevitably would go on and on about having another mouth to feed. Jasmine still had two younger brothers at home.

Immediately, Devon hung up to make the call. It wasn't even 9 am, and he didn't know the man's schedule, but Johnson picked up on the second ring. He sounded happy to hear from him.

"Mr. Johnson, I-I'm sorry to be calling so early," Devon started, plopping into his desk chair.

"Son, you can call anytime you want. I'm always happy to hear from you."

"Thank you. Well, I-I have some news."

Devon disclosed everything to Johnson. How he and Antonio fell out because he slept with Jasmine. How Jasmine found out she was pregnant. How she was going to abort the child, but got the call from Johnson.

"She-she kept the baby because it could be Antonio's." That's when Devon paused, wonder bursting in his heart. "It's his," he stated, feeling emotional and not really sure why. He told Johnson about the paternity test.

At first, there was silence on the other end. Mr. Johnson sniffed. Then his raspy voice kissed Devon's ear. "You mean. You mean I'm going to be a *grandfather*?"

Devon said, "Yes," his voice cracking. The joy of the Lord enshrouded his being the same way that it had when he was on the basement floor of North Star. It was always an occasion to rejoice when a child was born. No matter the circumstances.

"Oh my God," Mr. Johnson uttered. "Oh my God." Then he said, "I'm going to be a grandfather!"

Devon laughed, repeating the phrase. "Yes! You're going to be a grandfather!"

After that, Devon initiated a three-way video call with Johnson and Jasmine. Jasmine looked fearful and weary, but Mr. Johnson's beaming face began to erase her concerns. He was adamant that he would help her in any way possible. He would pay the remaining tuition she owed, arrange her childcare, and cover her medical bills. "Anything for you to finish school," he said adamantly.

"I'm going to be a grandfather!" Johnson kept raving, and for the first time since she found out she was pregnant, Jasmine looked hopeful.

"Thank you so much, Mr. Johnson," she said with a watery smile.

"No, Jasmine. Thank you! You're giving me one of the best gifts in the world. And now I can finally see that something good has come from this."

Devon was silent as the two made their plans. He marveled at the hand of God. Even how God has used him to be the vessel to connect them.

It was your clean heart, the Lord said.

Devon realized it was true. If he hadn't chosen to forgive Jasmine and even Antonio, he couldn't be used to this capacity. Still, his heart ached at his own loss. In less than two months, he lost his first love, a brotherhood, and then his best friend died, all on top of being falsely accused of sexual harassment, putting his academic future in jeopardy. Not to mention getting fired as a TA and losing the respect of his favorite professors. It was bananas! That's when he remembered the story of Job.

Wow. I really had a Job season.

When they ended the call, Devon sat on his bed. He thought about how God had led him to North Star that night to hear about the book of Job. How Lena had been given to him to walk it out. How the relationship he had with God took off just before all hell broke loose. Finally, Devon remembered his dream.

"These were the storms," he whispered, putting two and two together. He finally realized that the storms in his dream were the ones he had endured over the last few months. His girlfriend cheating on him with his best friend. His best friend dying. His being accused of sexual harassment. His girlfriend getting pregnant by his best friend.

"My God." Devon fell on his knees again, thanking God. "You kept me!"

In response, the peace of God drowned his heart.

———

A well-deserved graduation day finally came, surrounding Devon with love. He donned his best suit and took all the pictures they wanted with his family members. Debra, his parents, Darion, Kimberly. Even Jasmine and Mr. Johnson were there. After the ceremony, they went out to eat to celebrate at a local Italian restaurant not too far from campus.

"I'm so proud of you, son!" Mr. Johnson said, handing Devon a thick card that no doubt held a wad of cash.

Devon smiled and graciously took the gift. "Thank you, Mr. Johnson!"

His own father had made similar remarks, which helped Devon to forgive him. Devon realized he had needed to forgive his dad's lack of gratefulness for him sacrificing Cancun to run Jack & Jill.

"You know I love you," Mr. Woods stated, and Devon took that as his apology.

The Woods chatted with Devon and Darion's friends, as Devon sat at the wide circular table with a grateful smile. His future, was once again, bright. It wasn't what he had thought it would be just months before (taking over Jack & Jill and marrying Jasmine), but it was God's plan. That gave him assurance that even though he didn't know how everything was going to come about, it for sure would work out for the good. Even more than likely, have a few twists and turns along the way!

"Honey, your father said it's ok for you to help at the restaurant this summer," his mother's voice broke into Devon wading in the love around him.

"Hmm? Oh ok. Yeah, I figured as much," he responded. He took a hefty bite of his chicken alfredo.

"And take your time in figuring out what happens after that," she added, sweetly patting him on the shoulder.

Before responding, Devon slurped up a few noodles and chewed. He then said, "Oh. I know what happens after that."

The chatter at the table faded as his mother's brows lifted. She looked at him with a blend of intrigue and surprise.

"Oh? And what's that?"

Devon wiped his face with the white cloth napkin and grinned. "I'm going to open a cafe," he said with more certainty than he ever had in his life. More certainty than he even had about getting married.

His mother eyed him, weighing his words as the corners of her lips turned slightly downward in a thoughtful way. "Hmm…is that so?" Moments later, she seemed to reach some decision and then nodded. "Yeah. That sounds about right."

Devon chuckled. "Yep. I'm gonna call it, Devon's. Devon's Cafe."

AS LONG AS IT TAKES
EPILOGUE

7 MONTHS LATER

Antonio Derrick Johnson Jr. was born at 7:08 pm, 8 lbs., 22 inches, with a head full of hair like his momma. Jasmine sat with a dazed smile squeezing her lips, cradling him. Devon was in awe. The child was a good blend of both parents, so it was difficult to see who he favored. One thing that was immediately evident was the splotchy dark birthmark on his chin. Just like his dad's. He was a few shades darker than Antonio, so it wasn't as prominent, but to know his friend was to know that this specific trait had been passed down.

Wow! Devon thought as the group ooh'd and ahh'd over the new little guy.

Mr. Johnson, Sheila, Kimberly, Devon, Jasmine's mom, and one of her brothers were all bunched in the room. Even though Jasmine's hair stood in patches of wild, poofy curls all over her head and her eyes were barely open from exhaustion, to Devon, she had never looked better. She had that motherhood glow.

"You wanna hold him, Uncle Devon?" Mr. Johnson asked, as AJ (as they were already calling him) was being passed around gently to different loved ones. Devon grinned.

"Definitely."

Carefully, he took the small bundle into his arms and peered down at his little frame. Antonio Jr. was cooing and gurgling the way that babies do, but it felt like he was already using his charismatic powers to sway all in his presence. Just like his father, he held them in his tiny palm.

Devon handed AJ over to the next eager attendee and caught eyes with Jasmine. She gave him a worn smile. After graduation, Devon returned to his parents' home and started back at Jack & Jill. He had been sending her a few bucks here and there, **"For whatever the baby needs,"** he had texted. It had been on Devon's heart to let Jasmine know that she wasn't alone. She had support. She had a village. Too often, the pro-lifers didn't think about what it took to raise that life. They could be so bent on saving a child from abortion, but not offering support to raise the child once it was saved. He was also reminded of Antonio's voicemail about David and Jonathan. It spoke to him about his own role in the child's life. Maybe Devon wouldn't be the father, but he would look after the father's heir. Jasmine had even named Devon godfather. All of that was just the grace of God. Given the heartbreak and betrayal his ex and best friend's actions had caused, Devon couldn't say it was humanly possible to demonstrate such character. It was simply God's supernatural grace.

After leaving the crew at the hospital, he met with his mother at the Woods's. "How is he?" she asked, eagerly, her eyes twinkling.

"He's perfect!" Devon gushed, excitedly displaying the pictures on his phone. "Great health, two eyes, ten fingers, and ten toes. Mr. Johnson filled the room, of course, with all kinds of stuffed animals and toys he's too young to play with."

"Ohhh, I bet he did! Did you give her our package?" Mrs. Woods peered closer at Devon's phone as they stood in the living room.

"Yep. She said, 'Thanks'. She was worn out, though."

"I'm sure she was. Having a baby is no joke, son," his mother said with knowing eyes.

"I'm sure. I'm just glad I have time to find out," Devon said.

His mother gave him a look and said, "Yeah. Me too."

She had never shared her thoughts on Jasmine being pregnant with

Antonio's child. She only responded in support of her keeping the baby. Still, Devon suspected she was glad things didn't go further with him and Jasmine. More than likely, she thought that the baby was a blessing in more ways than one, since that was one of the reasons Jasmine and Devon didn't work out.

As his mother continued drifting through pictures, he noticed the time on his phone. Devon asked, "You ready?"

"Yep. Let's go."

The two caught a rideshare from Brooklyn Heights to Harlem. As the city cruised by, Devon breathed in the sights and sounds flooding in through the window.

I can't believe I was going to give this up, he thought, once again.

There was no way Devon could see himself living outside of NYC. The fact that he was willing to do so for the sake of Jasmine just showed how much he was under her spell.

Lord, thank You again for deliverance!

Just a few months ago, Devon had been smitten by love. Or what he thought was love. Now that he was more sober-minded and could see the situation more clearly, he realized it was more like the heartbreak book had said. It was more like misguided love.

As Devon grew in his faith, he understood that he had made Jasmine an idol. He had put her not just before God but before his own purpose. He was even willing to conform to her purpose over his own. He knew she wanted to be a film producer more than anything, and so he was willing to compromise his personal vision to make that happen. The thing was, his insecurity had caused him to elevate her, and, in the process, take him off track. Then, God had him walk away from Jack & Jill. Taking that step had solidified his identity more in God and less in his father. It was like what God had told him during his first time at North Star. With God's lead, Devon was learning who he really was and what *his* dreams were. He was learning his true identity, which was different than what he had thought prior to God's intervention. Even with all these major shifts in his life, he was still walking by faith and his purpose was still unfolding. It was clear his calling wasn't to run his dad's restaurant. But what was it?

"Here," the driver announced as they stopped in front of an old storefront. It stood between a few broken-down homes and a battered apartment unit.

"Umm, you sure this is it?" Mrs. Woods looked concerned as they got out and peered around. It wasn't the prestigious upscale environment they had just come from. In fact, just a few feet over, Devon caught one young brotha making a clearly illicit pharmaceutical transaction with a beatdown-looking client. Still, that didn't deter him. He set his eyes on his prize.

"Yep," Devon said, then texted the realtor. They were a few minutes early, so Devon let him know they had made it.

During their ten-minute wait, Mrs. Woods clutched her pearls and choked her handbag. Devon moved closer to her for extra protection. Every time anybody suspect walked by, which was pretty much everybody, she nervously swayed her hips.

Still, Devon knew, *This is it*! and felt the leading of the Holy Spirit.

Gary White arrived in a grey suit and red tie, apologizing for his tardiness. "Let's get you folks in here!" he said, swinging his suitcase in the direction of the store.

"You say you lookin' to make this into a, what now?" he asked, opening the front door and turning on lights.

Stepping inside the musky ambiance, dust sprayed Devon's nostrils. The wide-open space was bare. The floors were lifting. The ceiling was cracked. Whoever was selling the place had forgotten the importance of sprucing it up.

No wonder it's been on the market for two years.

Before answering Mr. White, Devon took long, thoughtful strides around the circumference of the room.

"A cafe," he finally replied. "I'm going to make it into a cafe." His eyes scanned the interior. "There's another door there?" When Devon pointed at the door, Gary nodded.

"Yep. A large storage space is there." Gary started toward the door. "Follow me," he said, unlocking it.

Devon and Mrs. Woods peered behind him. Mrs. Woods only said, "Hmph," as they stared into the large space. Yet what Devon saw, he was sure his companions could not. Instead of another room, he saw the wall being knocked down, a hall being laid, other rooms being installed. Even in the main room, he could see the mahogany bar counter at the bar, charming bar stools, a grand stage in the front. He could see it all.

"A cafe, huh?" Gary scratched his stubby chin as they drifted back into the main area. "You gon have to do a loooot a work to make this thing into a coffee spot." His light brown eyes looked doubtful.

Devon kept swiveling his head around, eyeing the room. "It would take a lot of work for sure," he admitted out loud. He put his hands on his waist. "It would probably take a couple of years even to get it ready."

Mrs. Woods stood next to him. "And what about the clients, Devon?" she asked, in her usual practical way. "I don't think there are too many coffee drinkers around here."

Devon respected his mother's business experience. His father was working, but even if he could see the spot, he probably would have echoed her sentiments. Even still, Devon couldn't shake the prodding in his gut. They had looked at a few other spaces, and even though others were more ideal for location, or in better shape, this one seemed to be beckoning him.

"It's this one," Devon said definitively. He looked at the realtor.

Gary nodded in submission. Devon had received some money from his parents and Mr. Johnson. He had finally returned the engagement ring and had been stacking his funds for the last six months, working at Jack & Jill. The Woods agreed to cosign a loan, and that gave him a nice bundle to put down. Still, the extra work and funds it was going to take to get this place into shape were something he hadn't considered.

Trust Me, that still small voice said. So, Devon shook Gary's hand and said he would sign the paperwork as soon as it was emailed over, given that everything checked out. Of course, Mr. Right and his parents would look it over first.

"Well, honey. You did it!" Mrs. Woods, ever his cheerleader, said, stuffing down her own inhibitions.

Devon breathed. "Yeah. It's gonna be work, and it's going to take time, but I keep thinking of that dream I told you about. You know the one where I'm in the house and everything is a wreck, but then God remodels it after the storm?"

When Devon reminded his mother, her eyes glimmered with recognition. "Oh. Yea. I do remember that dream."

"That's what this place reminds me of. Like, me and God are gon get it together and then it's gon look brand new."

His mother's grey-brown eyes lightened. "Ahhh. Now I see! Ok. Well, you know your brother and uncle will help. And your father, whenever he's free," she added as they walked back outside. "And I'll be helping in prayer that God raises up coffee drinkers in this community. Honestly, honey, they look like they prefer something a little stronger."

Devon cracked up and squeezed her waist one-handed as he opened his phone to grab the ride share. It was then that he saw Lena's email. When she had returned from her missionary trip, they had hooked up a couple of times to play chess. Then she was off to seminary school in Boston. Since then, they had been emailing each other once in a while, kind of like pen pals. It was a nice, comfortable friendship. Devon tried to be content with that.

I'll email her when I get home, he thought as their rideshare pulled up.

"Honey, how's Lena doing? Have you heard from her?" Mrs. Woods asked. They hopped inside the black Nissan.

"I actually just got an email, so I'll have to see." Devon marveled at his mother's gift. *How does this woman do it?* He eyed her from his peripheral.

"Well, you tell her I said hello," she said. Then she really surprised him. "It's a shame the two of you didn't work out."

"Ma. How did you even know that was a possibility?" Devon chuckled.

"Boy, I have eyes. I saw how y'all was boo'd up at that bake off!"

"Oh my God, Ma. You're too much sometimes." Still, a tinge of sadness surfaced. Devon was still healing from his breakup, though he finally understood that he had been looking for all the wrong things with Jasmine. After meeting Lena, he felt like he had a better understanding of what to look for.

If only I had another chance, he thought.

"But I do think Lena's a little ahead of you in some ways," Mrs. Woods stated simply.

Devon tried not to be offended. "Ma, how you gon play me like that?"

She shrugged. "I'm not saying you're behind. I'm just saying y'all are in two different life stages. I think whoever you end up with won't be leading you, but you'll be leading them."

Devon thought about his mother's statements. He had to be honest with himself. As much as he was growing spiritually and probably had a crash course in many foundational spiritual practices this past year, the calling on Lena's life as a pastor required that she be partnered with someone spiritually mature. Devon wasn't sure he was there yet. Then, when they finally arrived back home, he settled on his bed and popped open her email on his phone. It became clear as day that his mother's words were true.

Devon,

It's been a while since we last connected. A lot has happened. First off, I want to thank you for being a great friend and brother. You've been a safe place to vent and help me navigate a pretty lonely season. I didn't share this with you before because, well, you had a lot going on. It probably wouldn't have been appropriate. But I was dealing with a lot of loneliness during the initial stage of our friendship. After my divorce, I was so traumatized I didn't date for two years. Then, when I did start dating, I learned why they say the dating pool is polluted!

Devon had to stop and laugh at that one.

I say all that to say, God brought you into my life to offer companionship, amongst other things. I needed it. I know you got a lot out of our friendship, but I wanted you to know that it was valued on my end, too. I didn't know if I would ever meet someone, and then connecting with you showed me that good men still exist. I knew you weren't available emotionally, and it would take time for

anything to happen if it were to happen between us, so I gave it to God. I'm sharing all of this so that you know how much I value you and do care. And that you were an actual contender. At least, on my end, LOL.

Devon smiled, thinking of how he had felt the same, then kept reading.

I say all that to say, I did meet someone not long after I started school. I've been seeing him for the last few months. I didn't mention it because I've been really cautious about getting too excited. I made such a mess of things last time. But God has given so much confirmation, and he is nothing like my ex. In fact, in some ways, he reminds me of you.

Devon's heart dipped a little. Lena had met someone? She's been dating?

And that is why I feel completely confident in saying yes to his proposal. He proposed last night! We're engaged! We haven't publicly announced it, but you'll be seeing pictures soon on social media. I hope you find the happiness you deserve, Devon, and thank you for being a part of my journey in me finding mine. I look forward to hearing updates from you, too. TTYS.

-Lena

Devon sighed. Wow. Lena was engaged. Two minutes ago, he didn't even know she was dating! It was a lot to take in. He rolled on his back and held up the phone, re-reading her email. Nope. The message didn't change. He thought about their connection and compatibility. How Lena's kindness and selflessness had been just as beautiful as her outward appearance.

"Lord, did I miss it? Did I miss this opportunity?" he asked out loud.

For some reason, in the aftermath of his breakup with Jasmine, it had never occurred to Devon to ask about God's plan for his love life. He had just been trying to recover from everything, get settled at home, and focus on his new business. This email and the conversation with his mother stirred up that desire for love again. He may not have been ready for marriage now, but he did want it. Did God have that for him?

Devon put down his phone, fell on his knees, and decided to pray. Immediately, the loving connection and intimate warmth swarmed his heart. When he finished praying, the answer was very clearly there. God *did* have marriage for him, and to his relief, it wasn't Lena, so there was no missed opportunity. Yet there was a caveat to this promise that God was giving, and only one word echoed in Devon's heart.

Wait.

God had promised Devon marriage, but he would have to wait for it. Thinking of the mess he had made when he tried to do things his own way, and the poor choice in the type of woman he chose, Devon had no problem being in agreement.

He nodded his head, his hands still folded, and said, "Ok, God. I'll wait. I'll for as long as it takes."